SHARK
BEACH

Also by Chris Jameson

SHARK ISLAND
DEVIL SHARKS

SHARK BEACH

CHRIS JAMESON

St. Martin's Paperbacks

This is a work of fiction. All of the characters, organizations, and events portrayed in this novel are either products of the author's imagination or are used fictitiously.

SHARK BEACH

Copyright © 2019 by Daring Greatly Corporation.

All rights reserved.

For information address St. Martin's Press, 175 Fifth Avenue, New York, NY 10010.

ISBN: 978-1-250-29616-0

Printed in the United States of America

St. Martin's Paperbacks edition / June 2019

St. Martin's Paperbacks are published by St. Martin's Press, 175 Fifth Avenue, New York, NY 10010.

10 9 8 7 6 5 4 3 2 1

CHAPTER 1

Corinne Scully lay on the beach, gazed out at the vivid blue water of the Gulf of Mexico, and tried to imagine the crashing waves the hurricane might bring. They were calling the storm Juliet, which had launched a thousand bad Shakespeare-related headlines, but there was nothing romantic about the news coverage. The storm had already blasted a path of destruction through the Caribbean, and now it had begun its journey through the Gulf. The only remaining question was where it would make landfall.

She heard the familiar *hiss-pop* of a beer bottle being opened and glanced up as her husband, Rick, handed her a Corona and began fishing inside their cooler for the small plastic container in which they'd placed a sliced-up lime.

"I'm okay, thanks," Corinne said, shielding her eyes a bit so she could see his face.

His brow furrowed. "You sure? I thought you wanted another."

"Maybe in a little while. I'm feeling a little queasy."

"The sun," Rick replied. "You should hydrate."

"With beer?"

Rick smiled. "You don't want that?"

"Water would be better. You're right about hydration."

He retrieved the beer and traded it for a plastic bottle of water. If Rick had taken offense at her rejection of the Corona, he gave no sign, and Corinne took notice. There had been growing tension between them over the past couple of years and she had been dubious about this vacation as a result, particularly since they were sharing the beach house with friends. Jenn and Matti Hautala and their son, Jesse, were more like family. The couples were together so often their kids had grown up squabbling like siblings.

Before marriage, it had never occurred to Corinne how difficult it would be to find another couple whose company both she and Rick would treasure, but Jenn and Matti were that couple. Which meant the four of them knew one another's secrets, and that Jenn had begun to sense the turmoil brewing in the Scullys' marriage before Corinne herself had consciously become aware of it.

On his beach towel, Matti reached out a hand without even opening his eyes. "My psychic gift tells me there is an unwanted beer floating in the ether. Come to me, lost soul, and we shall be one."

Corinne laughed. Rick nodded in satisfaction and

slapped the dripping bottle of Corona into Matti's hand. With a grunt, Matti sat up and stared at the bottle as if it had magically manifested in his grasp, then looked up to the sky and mouthed "thank you" toward the heavens before tipping the bottle to his lips. When he lay back down, the bottle nestled into the sand by his head, Jenn reached over from her towel and laid a dark arm across his pink-tinged back in the quiet, contented way they always seemed to manage so easily.

We used to be like that, Corinne thought. Or at least she believed they had. But she and Rick both worked so much that they were often apart, and the less time they spent together, the harder it was for her to remember that she loved her husband, and the easier it was to see the traits she found irritating about him. She could tell that Rick felt the same, that their frequent sparring and the many nights they went to bed with a chilly space between them had taken a toll.

So they had returned to paradise.

The Scullys had been to Captiva, Florida, many times. It always seemed to clear their heads and give them time to breathe and take stock of their lives. Over the years there had often been talk of the Hautalas joining them, and now it had finally happened.

Captiva Island was connected by a small bridge to Sanibel, which was itself connected to the mainland by a miles-long causeway, but out here at the end of the tiny island they might as well have been a thousand miles from their working lives, what Corinne thought of as their office selves. Normally, that distance from the so-called real world was enough to let them exhale, and to ease any tension between them. But this trip felt different to Corinne. It seemed as if Rick found it impossible to relax. If anything, thanks to Hurricane Juliet, Rick had been getting more wound up by the hour.

He opened a new beer for himself and sat on the edge of his beach towel, watching her.

Corinne squinted at him. "You want to go for a swim? I'm sure Kelsey would love it."

Kelsey, their nine-year-old, was still Daddy's buddy. Emma, who had turned fourteen in April, had grown too serious to let her father toss her around in the waves. The girls had set up their own beach camp a little ways down the sand with the Hautalas' son, Jesse. The kids wanted their own space, their own vacation, and although it made Corinne sad, she couldn't blame them.

Rick did not respond. He sipped his beer.

"Babe?"

He took another sip. "You really think it's safe to stay?"

She knew he hated when she rolled her eyes, but she couldn't help it. "We've been through this," she said.

"I still think—"

"We *know* what you think," Corinne said, her voice low, glancing over at Jenn and Matti, who were studiously ignoring the conversation. "But the odds of Juliet hitting us are slim, and you know it."

"Slim, and growing. And if they're so slim, why evacuate?"

She took a deep breath. He wasn't wrong, but she

was sick of talking about it and knew the Hautalas were equally tired of the topic. The storm had been headed for East Texas, and then for the Louisiana coast. Its track kept wobbling, and so every national meteorologist had started to cover their ass by posting a variety of possible paths for Hurricane Juliet, including several models that showed it striking Lee County, Florida, passing over the islands. It had gone from a Category 4 down to a 1, then back up to a 2, its strength just as much a variable as its landfall location. The governor of Florida had ordered the islands and the coastal area on this stretch of the Gulf shoreline to begin voluntary evacuation, but Corinne, Jenn, and Matti all agreed it was too soon to panic.

"We paid a lot of money for this house," she reminded Rick for at least the tenth time. "Let's give it another day, see what the forecast says. If they make the evacuation mandatory, we'll go."

Rick took a long draught of beer. At forty-one, his hair remained dark and his handsome features sharp, but he had worry lines around his eyes and dark circles beneath them. He looked tired, and they had already been in paradise for two nights.

He turned those tired eyes on her. "And if we're putting the kids in danger?"

Anger rippled through her. She pressed her lips together, fighting the urge to tell him off. How dare he accuse her of risking her daughters' safety? But snapping at him would only make things worse, so instead she stood and turned toward the Hautalas.

"Who wants to go for a swim?"

* * *

Floating in the waves helped cool her down in more ways than one. Corinne lay on her back in the water, rising and falling with each swell. She knew the surf on Captiva could be calm, the waves minimal, but with the storm wreaking havoc out in the Gulf, the beach had begun to take a pounding. When she set foot in the water, she had felt the undertow and had been tossed by the power of the waves. She had to swim out farther to be able to just float. For now, it seemed safe enough. The authorities hadn't closed it off to swimming yet, but she had no doubt they would if the surf got any worse.

The sun baked her face, and she dunked under the water and came up again, shaking out her hair. She had floated out farther than she would have liked, and the current had begun to sweep her northward, so she began to swim back, watching the beach. One of the things that made Captiva so special was the lack of parking. The beach might be public, but unless you were staying at one of the few hotels or had rented a house, it was nearly impossible to find a place to put your car, which kept the beach from being too heavily populated.

It was a quiet island, only a few miles long, situated between the Gulf of Mexico to the west and Pine Island Sound to the east. For most of that length, Captiva was only wide enough for a house, the road, and another house. In its midsection, Andy Rosse Lane ran from west to east, with restaurants and colorful rental homes on the Gulf end and kayak rentals on the sound. Music filled the air on that street, from acoustic guitars to steel drums, Jimmy Buffet to calypso. Somehow the island had been mostly undiscovered by the college spring-breakers who descended on many Florida beaches and turned them into raging parties.

But it couldn't remain undiscovered forever.

The Scullys and the Hautalas had sprung for one of the most expensive rentals in Sunset Captiva, an aging development whose sprawl of two-story, stilted beach homes ran along Andy Rosse Lane. They had taken one of the few rentals that sat right on the Gulf, shaded by towering palm trees. The house was so close to the water that Corinne had felt comfortable with the idea of the kids walking back and forth on their own. The only downside was the group that had rented the house next door.

Corinne spotted their neighbors splashing in the water, not far from where she and her group had made their camp on the sand. This squad of college kids had somehow decided to avoid the massive weeklong raves their peers would be throwing in Daytona Beach and Cabo San Lucas this week, and planted themselves in quiet Captiva instead.

The spring-breakers' parties had gone late into the night. The first evening, Matti had asked them to keep the music down. Jesse Hautala might be sixteen, and her own Emma fourteen, but Kelsey was only nine, and blaring hip-hop loses its charm when the clock starts ticking toward midnight. To their credit, the spring-breakers had kept things fairly under control and seemed like an amiable enough bunch.

Maybe I'm just jealous, Corinne thought now, watching the tallest of the boys, a muscular guy she'd heard the others call Rashad. He picked up one of the girls and hoisted her onto his shoulders, and then the six of them were playing chicken, those on top trying to knock the others into the water. They were half-drunk—and if the smell wafting from their house each night was any indication, probably high more often than not—and they hooted and laughed like they were having the time of their lives.

"He *is* delicious, isn't he?" a voice said.

Corinne whipped around in the water, startled to find that Jenn had swum up to her while she was lost in thought.

"Jesus! You scared me half to death!"

Jenn laughed. "You were a little distracted."

Corinne splashed her. "Don't be evil. They just look like they're having fun."

"They do at that." Jenn bobbed in the water as a wave rolled beneath them. "You can't deny it, though. The boy is attractive. And I can promise you, Rick and Matti have been watching those girls out of the corners of their eyes like mountain lions stalking prey."

"That's nasty."

Jenn swam a few feet nearer to shore. "They're men. Men are nasty."

Facts were facts. Besides, Corinne would have had to be blind not to notice how attractive the younger women were. None of the three was perfect in the stereotypical beach bunny way, but they radiated youth and energy and freedom in a way that was impossible to ignore. One of them was a curvy Latina, and Corinne knew her husband well enough to know that Rick would have stolen second and third glances at her. The idea did not trouble Corinne. The problems growing between herself and her husband had nothing to do with him sneaking looks at women in bikinis, nor would shaming him for it make the relationship any better.

Not to mention I'd have to stop looking at Rashad, she thought.

"Woman, you need a night out," Jenn said. "Tomorrow night we should leave the husbands with the kids and go listen to music and drink far too many brightly colored fruit-and-booze concoctions."

Corinne paddled in the water, smiling at Jenn. "That sounds fantastic. You think they'll go for it?"

"I'm not asking them, I'm telling them."

"What about the storm?"

Jenn smiled wistfully. "Then we'll drink Hurricanes and bring our umbrellas."

Corinne made a noise in her throat. It really did sound like what she needed. She swam a few feet away from Jenn, floated for a while with her face toward the sun, and then glanced again at the beach, easily spotting the huge yellow umbrella they had rented from GulfDaze, an all-purpose beach-fun place on Andy Rosse Lane. The girls had taken the umbrella for themselves and Corinne squinted, catching a glance of her daughters.

Fourteen-year-old Emma lay on her belly on a bamboo beach mat, half-asleep, her hair tied into a bun while she tried to get a tan. Corinne and Rick had argued about the girl's bikini. Rick thought the cut too daring for a girl Emma's age, but if he had seen some of the suits she had tried on, Corinne thought he might have had a heart attack. Nine-year-old Kelsey sat under the umbrella reading one of her sister's discarded paperbacks, a spooky story aimed at kids at least a few years older than she was. The girls had reading in common, but otherwise could not have been more different.

Emma had always been shy and unsure, but with high school looming so near, she had begun to come out of her shell. Corinne was of two minds about this, happy that Emma seemed ready to engage more with the world but concerned that her daughter had begun to use social media, and to become more worried than ever about her appearance. Thin and fit, she worried about the curve of her belly and the space between her thighs. Smart, offbeat Emma loved ghost stories and alien-invasion movies, but those interests had faded of late, and Corinne feared her daughter was erasing her own uniqueness, making herself more generic in order to fit some social media concept of normal. The idea made her sick.

Corinne did not think her daughters' anxieties had dug their claws in too deeply yet, but she found herself on alert where Emma was concerned.

Kelsey, on the other hand, never gave a damn what anyone thought. At least not yet. Adorably wide-eyed at nine, she shared her sister's intelligence but had sharper edges, louder and sillier and with a cutting wit that had manifested in the second grade. Kelsey seemed unfazed by concerns that haunted her older sister.

Corinne's girls made her proud, but worry gnawed at her. She recalled her mother once saying that the fears of a parent never went away, they only evolved, and she had begun to see how true that statement was.

She heard Jenn call to her and began to turn just as a massive wave crashed over her. It knocked her backward, pushed her down, and she came up sputtering and wiping at her eyes just as a second wave hit. Corinne hurled herself toward shore, letting the wave carry her, almost bodysurfing instead of being pushed under, and this time when she put her feet down they touched bottom. She stood, still shoulder deep, and turned around to face the next wave. It almost disappointed her to find the size of the waves had diminished, but then she felt the undertow dragging at her legs, the sand whipping past her ankles underwater. Shells bumped across her feet. Thirty feet away, the spring-breakers were all recovering from the big waves, their game of chicken momentarily interrupted.

"You okay?" Jenn called, swimming toward her.

Corinne gave her a thumbs-up, but her thoughts were awhirl. Maybe evacuating was premature until they knew the storm was definitely coming this way, but she decided to keep Kelsey from going into the water alone. The riptide was too powerful.

Jenn called her name. Corinne wiped at her eyes

again, blinking salt away. Another wave rolled around her, lifting her briefly off her feet, and Corinne felt herself brush against something big. Something tough and smooth that slid past her, gliding against her thigh.

When she turned and saw the fin jutting up from the water, she let out a stream of barely conscious profanity as she dove toward shore, swimming hard, legs kicking and arms pulling. Hip deep, she stood and rushed for the seashell-strewn sand, adrenaline shooting through her. Panic blotted out rational thought, shut down all of her senses, focused only on that fin and the inescapable feeling of vulnerability at her back. She could feel the shark closing in, knew her legs and thighs were still in the water. Corinne thought of the girls, of all she had yet to give or teach them, and her heart broke a little.

She glanced over her shoulder, knowing what had to happen next.

Only it didn't. The fin had vanished. Up to her knees in water, she scanned the waves and saw the fin pop up again, farther away, and saw the now-familiar curve of the marine mammal's back and the blowhole there. Fear kept her flushed, heart thundering, but embarrassment began to creep in even before her other senses kicked in and she heard Kelsey laughing at her from shore.

Corinne turned to see her nine-year-old standing in the surf with one hand over her mouth and the other propped on her hip.

"Mom," she said, giggling. "It's a dolphin!"

Beyond Kelsey, Emma sat on her blanket, rolling

her eyes. Jesse waved amiably from the water, wearing a huge grin. Farther up the sand, Rick and sunburnt Matti sat facing each other, drinking their beers and deep in conversation. They hadn't even noticed.

"Well," Jenn said, wading up beside her. "That was a close one."

Corinne shot her a withering glance. "I thought it was a shark."

"I'm glad to hear it. If you'd had that reaction to a dolphin, I'd force you to seek therapy."

Not the worst idea in the world, Corinne thought. Still embarrassed, she decided she wanted to dry off and get herself a beer. Leaving Jenn in the waves, she waded over to the sand and glanced up to find Rashad swimming about a dozen feet away. When he spotted her, he stood and let the water sluice off the smooth lines of his toned body. Jenn had not been wrong about him. He might only be twenty-one or so, but there was no harm in admiration.

"Your husband didn't seem too concerned about you being eaten alive," Rashad said, smiling mischievously.

"It was a dolphin."

Rashad shrugged. "He didn't know that. Don't worry, though. I'd have come to your rescue."

As flirtation went, the line was pretty lame, but the delivery felt sincere and that went a long way.

She raised an eyebrow and smiled. "Yeah. And who's going to rescue you?"

Rashad laughed softly, and she saw a bit of shyness in him. She had surprised him, and it gave her a pleasant little tremor. He was a college kid, and Corinne had no intention of cheating on her husband, but she did feel flattered, considering she was nearly twice his age.

"Careful what you fish for, kid," she said. "You never know what you'll reel in."

His face went blank, totally startled, and Corinne grinned as she started up the beach toward her husband and Matti. She walked past the little camp of mats and towels and the umbrella that Emma, Kelsey, and Jesse had set up. Kelsey had begun making a sandcastle, adorning it with various seashells. Emma said something quietly to Jesse, but Corinne ignored them.

As she approached, Rick got up from his chair, his expression turning dark. He gestured toward Rashad with his beer bottle. "What the hell was that about?"

Corinne shrugged. "Oh, nothing. He wants me, that's all."

"He's like ten years old," Rick said, brows knitted.

She smirked at him. "What about the girls with him? Are they ten years old, too?"

From his beach towel, Matti hooted. "Better stay on your toes, old man."

It should have been nothing but a joke, something to lighten the moment. Instead, Rick shot Matti a hard look and marched back the way Corinne had just come, making a beeline toward Rashad.

"Rick!" Corinne called. "What are you—"

"Oh, shit," Matti muttered, pushing himself up off the towel.

Together, Corinne and Matti hurried after Rick, but not before Rashad had seen him coming. A couple of the other spring-breakers started calling out warnings and taunts, and Rashad seemed confused by Rick's angry expression at first.

"Can I help you with something?" Rashad asked, straightening up, visibly defensive.

"Yeah. You can keep your fucking dick in your pants and your hands to yourself."

"Rick!" Corinne yelled, glancing over her shoulder, hoping desperately that Kelsey hadn't heard her father's words.

Rashad raised his hands as if to ward off the craziness. "My hands are pretty much always kept to myself. Maybe you'd better ease up on the afternoon beer parade."

Rick stormed into the surf and shoved Rashad. The guy stumbled and nearly fell, but managed to stay upright. Corinne knew that would only make Rick more frustrated, and she snapped at him again, following him into the water.

"You don't want to do this," Rashad said. "You're embarrassing your family."

Corinne winced. She saw the moment Rashad realized that his calm, reasoning voice had only made things worse. Then Rick reached out to grab him, fist cocked back for a real fight. Rashad slapped his hand away, mostly deflecting the blow, though Rick's fist struck him in the shoulder. Stepping after him, Rashad gave Rick a shove in return, and Rick went down on his ass in the rippling surf.

The spring-breakers started to laugh, and Corinne couldn't deny how foolish Rick looked. Humiliated, he would be angrier than ever. But when Rick climbed to his feet, Matti grabbed Rick around the chest and drove against him, maneuvering him toward the sand.

"Little prick," Rick snarled at Rashad. "Nobody talks to my wife like that."

Matti hugged Rick close. Corinne heard the rasped words between them.

"He's not wrong, brother," Matti said. "You're embarrassing everyone."

It was me, Corinne wanted to say. *I flirted with him.* But she knew that in this case the truth would only make things worse. She would tell him later, when they were alone and this had quieted down.

"Hey, asshole," Rashad called, as a parting shot. "You ever think maybe if you weren't a guy who behaved like this, you wouldn't need to worry so much about her flirting with other people?"

The other spring-breakers hooted again, applauding this line. Rick turned to stare at him, but by then he had noticed the horrific embarrassment on his daughters' faces, and he deflated in front of them. He went to the cooler, retrieved a fresh beer, and then stalked back to the path that led to their rental house without bothering to carry his chair or even grab the T-shirt he'd worn to the beach.

"What the hell?" Jenn asked, walking over to join Corinne and Matti.

Neither of them had an answer.

It was going to be a long week.

* * *

A few hours later, Rashad had mostly forgotten the incident on the beach. Rick Scully might be a hothead asshole, but he was really his wife's problem more than anyone else's, and Rashad had bigger concerns. He knew he and his friends were being stupid about the evacuation, but he didn't have the freedom to argue with them. His mother had called three times today and sent a dozen texts, very worried about the fact that they weren't already off the island. He had explained that the evacuation was voluntary, that the hurricane might not even hit here, that historically forecasts had been wrong more than they'd been right about where storms would make landfall once they'd entered the Gulf of Mexico.

Really, though, if it had been up to him, he would already have left. There had to be places on the mainland where people could take shelter if the hotels were full or if—like Rashad—they couldn't afford a hotel after having already paid their share of the spring break rental. Simone and Marianna were in the same boat, but Nadia had money, and Tyler and his boyfriend Kevin never seemed concerned about the cost of dinner, or anything else for that matter. The trouble was that Marianna was the only one who seemed to agree with Rashad, and neither of them wanted to rock the boat and piss everyone else off.

As he stepped off the beach and onto Andy Rosse Lane, he glanced over his shoulder. They had just watched the sun set over the Gulf, along with about a hundred other people who had applauded when the last burning edge slipped into the water, as if it had been a show performed just for them. The horizon still glowed with the last remnant of sunset, but that glow had a strange hue, a dark and angry purple. There were few clouds in the sky, but those few were ominous, and the air hung dense with moisture. Humidity bothered the others more than it did Rashad—he had never sweated much, unlike poor Tyler—but he felt as if it had become harder to draw a breath. The thickness of the air could be suffocating.

A breeze kicked up, stronger than before, and that made it better. He found himself simultaneously hoping the breeze would grow and that it would vanish, but the latter was wishful thinking. Even if the hurricane didn't hit Captiva, they were still going to get a hell of a storm.

Marianna linked her arm with his. "Snap out of it." She bumped her shoulder against his.

He grinned, so happy she had come along. Nadia and Simone had gotten into some kind of drama with her just three weeks before the trip and had tried to figure out some way to get her to pull out without telling her they hoped she would pull out. They had ghosted her for about a week until Rashad and Tyler had stepped in. Whatever the issue had been, it had apparently blown over, because the girls were all in synch again, or they seemed to be.

Whatever it had been, Rashad figured the information was need-to-know, and he neither wanted nor needed to know.

"I'm good," he promised her.

"You're on island time, remember." She beamed at him, bright smile framed by springy coils of natural hair.

Rashad couldn't help but beam back. "Island time. I need music!"

They picked up their pace, moving past the others. They had already passed The Mucky Duck, a beachfront restaurant with indoor and outdoor dining, where a white guy in a peach linen shirt played guitar on the patio and sang raspy-voiced songs perfect for white guys in peach linen shirts. Rashad had been born and raised in Philadelphia. His parents were from Pakistan. But down at Keylime Bistro, maybe a hundred yards up the street from The Mucky Duck, a trio of musicians played Caribbean music on steel drums and a fat-bellied guitar, and though Rashad didn't know shit about Caribbean music, he knew it lifted his heart. It wasn't the food that drew him to pick up his pace, it was the music.

"What are we drinking tonight?" Marianna asked.

"Something cheap," Rashad replied. "So we can drink a lot of it."

"That is an excellent plan."

The wind kicked up, a hot gust swathing them in a thick blanket of humidity. Rashad glanced back, but they were too far along the road to see the waves. He had a feeling he knew what he would see, however—had a feeling that the tide would be rising, that the surf would be pummeling the sand. His friends could say whatever they wanted, they could ignore the evacuation order because it was still voluntary, but Rashad could not ignore the tingle of dread in his heart or the chill that ran up the back of his neck.

A storm approached. The only questions remaining were how long before it arrived, and whether they would be smart enough to get off Captiva before it was too late.

CHAPTER 2

—

Most people on Sanibel had no idea the Institute existed, and those who did—the fishermen who knew better than to enter its tiny inlet harbor, or the lifelong islanders who could remember the days when it had been built—paid very little attention. In order to run across it, you would have to go to the end of Seaspray Lane, where a narrow gravel road was barred by a low metal gate. A small sign read NO UNAUTHORIZED ADMITTANCE, beneath which was a logo and, in half-inch letters, SANIBEL ISLAND MARITIME RESEARCH INSTITUTE.

The gravel road beyond the gate was overgrown, the foliage creating a canopy overhead. The curved path meant that none of the Institute's buildings could be seen from the end of Sea Spray Lane. The neighbors weren't often interrupted by trucks or even cars, as most of the visitors came by sea. This was no Woods

Hole. The public was not welcome. An electrified perimeter fence a hundred yards into the trees made that clear to the unhealthily curious.

From the Gulf, boats could enter through a small, rocky inlet and disembark on the private pier, but a boom lay across the inlet to prevent unauthorized entry. On the beach, signs warned that this section of the island was private. In amongst the palm trees and underbrush, amidst the lizards and insects, were camouflaged guardhouses.

Maurice Broaddus had been a security guard at the Institute for sixteen months. He had spent the first seven of those months in one of those guardhouses, getting bitten by bugs and bored out of his mind. In all that time, there had been only six attempts at unauthorized entry, and all of them had been drunk vacationers wandering along the beach and then deciding to investigate the mysterious inlet despite all of its signs warning them to stay away. For certain kinds of people, particularly when drunk, a No Trespassing sign was better than an engraved invitation.

Broaddus descended the south stairwell, watching the shadowed corners. The lights were on night mode, three quarters of them turned off and those remaining switched to a dimmer setting. Even on an ordinary day the place felt spooky after hours, but this was no ordinary day.

He used his key card to buzz himself through a security lock hardly anyone on staff could open, then made sure the door shut tightly behind him. He glanced left, into the low-light gloom, and then turned right, walking along a corridor that ended in a junction. To the right was the hallway that led to the Selachii research lab and the vast structure known only as "the pools," where all of the sharks in residence at the Institute were kept. There were nearly a hundred of them now, and they had all been tampered with in some way or another. Broaddus had no special love for sharks. These were apex predators, always hungry and determined to sate that hunger—nothing like the dolphins or seals found in other buildings on the property. But the more he had seen of their treatment, the more it had begun to get under his skin.

I need a new job, he thought. But even if he left here, found a security gig somewhere else, he knew what he had seen here would linger in the back of his mind. Broaddus had a pit bull named Sugar—short for Sugar Ray, named after a boxer he'd admired as a kid. He had rescued Sugar from a shelter, saved the dog's life, and heard an endless stream of worry and ignorance from friends, relatives, and strangers about the risk involved in having such a vicious animal in his house. None of them had seen the sadness in Sugar, or felt the love radiating from the dog. The gratitude and sweetness and relief. Sugar was a good boy who liked squeaky toys and barked happily when Broaddus sang in the shower. He slept at the foot of his master's bed at night, alert for the sound of any intruder, protecting his own home as much as he protected its human owner.

Not that Broaddus thought a shark wanted to cuddle. He was an intelligent man and knew better than that. Maybe he didn't have the scientific background of the Institute's staff, but he had done his own research, in his own time. Sharks did not attack humans on purpose, despite what popular myth had established. They were wild creatures, smart and cold and incredibly efficient. Broaddus had worked security for animal research labs before, but no matter how much his heart had broken for the monkeys and the mice, he had always been able to tell himself medical breakthroughs would be worth it, that saving human lives was more important than what the researchers did to their animal charges.

Sanibel felt different.

He turned left, went down a small flight of stairs, and then used his key card to swipe through an additional security door. Very few people had access to these doors, but Broaddus did. If the place could not trust its own security guards, then what would be the point of having security at all?

Broaddus smiled to himself as he walked toward the Recovery Tank. An inner door separated him from the interior of that chamber, but the walls were mostly glass, so he could see the large, cylindrical aquarium within. There were all sorts of fish inside the Recovery Tank, but only one Great White shark. It swam listlessly, moving just enough to keep from drifting to the bottom. In the darkened tank, the shark's body moved back and forth, tail propelling it forward. As it slid by the glass, Broaddus caught sight of the metal glinting on its head, the strange lens over one of its black eyes. The slowness with which it moved, little more than floating in the water as it healed from surgery, reminded Broaddus of a gun still in its holster—not dangerous until it is put to work.

Cutting into their damn brains, he thought. *This is just wrong.*

A plan had begun to formulate in his head. The question would be whether or not he had the courage and the wits to pull it off.

A rattling of metal came from behind him, and Broaddus turned and began walking back the way he had come just as Arthur Tremblay came marching into the place. His expression was troubled, and when he spotted Broaddus it became more so.

"I've been looking for you, Maurice."

"What can I do for you, Dr. Tremblay?"

The scientist frowned, glancing back and forth between Broaddus and the Recovery Tank. "Hang on. Why are you down here?"

Broaddus shrugged. "Doing my rounds. At least three times a shift I conduct a walk-through of the building."

"This is a secure wing."

"Isn't that the point? The places in need of the best security are the places you don't want anyone else to see. I was told that when I hired on for my first security job, and I've always believed it. But if you want me to—"

"No, no, it's fine." He seemed distracted now. "I came to let you know the board has instructed us to send all non-vital staff home. You're encouraged to evacuate."

Broaddus hesitated, thoughts awhirl.

"Maurice?" Dr. Tremblay said. "You feeling all right?"

"Just thinking. Non-vital staff implies there are members of the staff who are vital. Someone to look after the tanks and pools, make sure nothing goes wrong. But if there are going to be people here—and even if there aren't—there ought to be security."

Tremblay nodded. "You're right. I wasn't thinking. Are you saying you don't mind? I could ask one of the younger guards . . ."

Broaddus put on a fake smile and placed his hands on his hips. "Hell, doc, now you're just being insulting. I'm fifty-six, not eighty."

Dr. Tremblay exhaled in apparent relief. "I know. But if you're anything like me, some days you feel a thousand years old. This is great, Maurice, truly. It's a weight off my mind to know the staff who are staying behind will have you as a resource if there's any issue with trespass or a power disruption."

Broaddus gestured for the Institute's director to walk beside him, and they went out through the door, leaving the secure area.

"Happy to do it. I'm sure it'll be fine. Are you not sticking around, doc?"

Tremblay grimaced. "I wanted to, but my wife decided we were evacuating whether I liked it or not."

Broaddus tapped a finger at his temple. "Smart man. The wife always knows best."

The two men shared a knowing look, a kind of easy camaraderie, but then Dr. Tremblay headed through a metal door and up a narrow staircase, leaving Broaddus to continue his patrol of the building.

He glanced back the way they'd come, thinking about rescuing Sugar. Thinking about the sharks, and the oncoming storm, and how few people were going to be staffing the Institute in the next couple of days. An idea formed, and Broaddus couldn't deny that even in his own head, it seemed crazy.

But it felt like a good kind of crazy.

Deputy Agnes Hayes stood on the side of the road and watched a minivan roll up Captiva Drive in her direction. She had parked her cruiser in the lot beside the Manatee Grill and her flashing blue lights strobed across the minivan as it slowed to a halt. The window shushed down and the driver—a thirtyish woman with her hair in a thick braid—poked her head out.

"Excuse me, Officer?"

Once Agnes would have corrected her, explained that she was a sheriff's deputy, but travelers seemed only to become confused by the distinction. "Officer" was fine.

"What can I do for you, ma'am?"

"This whole evacuation. . . . How long do you think it will be before the governor knows if it's necessary?"

Kids started fighting in the back of the van, their voices floating out through the window. In the passenger seat, another woman turned and snapped at them to be silent.

"Are you asking when we'll know the storm's path for certain?" Deputy Hayes said. "When you can come back?"

The woman's forehead crinkled, as if the deputy's tone irritated her. "Well, if the storm doesn't make landfall here—"

"Go somewhere and settle in, ma'am," Deputy Hayes said. "The governor and his staff are watching the reports the same as you and I are. As soon as he's sure it is safe for you to come back onto the island, he will make that announcement."

The woman in the passenger seat began to mutter angrily, rude words sprinkled into her monologue despite the presence of the children. The driver cast Deputy Hayes a regretful glance as she began to drive away, leaving the street empty for a moment. The deputy looked up and down the street and what she saw worried her deeply. Even though they should know better, even though the whole world had seen coverage of one extreme weather event after another, people just assumed everything would be fine.

Headlights swept around the corner to her left—a car coming the opposite direction. Someone returning to Captiva, maybe from a restaurant on Sanibel. Deputy Hayes sighed. What she wanted to do was stop the car, ask the passengers how stupid they must be to stay when rational thought suggested getting the fuck off the island would be the right move. Instead, she stood where she was. The sheriff had posted her out here to facilitate with the evacuation, but it was after ten p.m.

and the flow of traffic had trickled down to almost nothing. The people who were going to leave tonight had already gone.

"Excuse me, Deputy?"

She spun around, boots crunching on the gravel in the Manatee Grill's parking lot. Unconsciously, she shifted her hand so that she could quickly draw her gun if she needed to, but she relaxed when she recognized Charlie Wellman, the restaurant's owner. Wellman shambled toward her, six-foot-six and pushing three-hundred-and-fifty pounds. He'd played pro football for many years, finishing his career with the Miami Dolphins. Though he'd racked up some impressive statistics, commentators had noticed the Florida native's weight and what they perceived to be his slowness, and they'd nicknamed him the Manatee. With his thick gray mustache he looked more like a walrus, but the name had stuck. His local friends usually just called him Tee for short.

"Evening, Mr. Wellman."

The man smoothed his mustache. "Anything I can get for you? Something to eat? A coffee?"

Deputy Hayes softened. "Kind of you, but I'm okay. Just another hour out here, I think, unless the voluntary order becomes mandatory overnight."

Wellman stiffened. "You anticipate that happening?"

"I don't know what to anticipate."

"I hate this 'voluntary' bullshit," Wellman said. "It's such a cop-out. Either evacuate or don't. If there's not enough danger to force an evacuation, what's the point of fucking up people's vacations—not to mention my profits—by scaring them away?"

She almost gave an honest reply, because she agreed. People weren't frightened enough by something the authorities told them might never happen at all. They had come seeking paradise and they would not abandon it voluntarily. But there was another side to that argument.

"You ever been in the middle of an evacuation from Captiva or Sanibel?"

"By boat," Wellman replied. "From here to the mainland." He shrugged. "But I know the traffic is a nightmare."

"Nightmare doesn't even cover it."

Most of the streets on Captiva and Sanibel were two-lane roads—one in each direction. The governor had put the voluntary order in place in hopes that more than a trickle of people would take the wise course and get out early. If the order became mandatory, the scene would become very ugly. There were not enough Lee County deputies and Sanibel police officers to keep it all running smoothly, but they would do their best, as always.

Wellman started into some farewell pleasantries, but Deputy Hayes's radio squawked and she turned her back on him, even as she waved for a slowing car to speed up. Every vehicle leaving the island was one more she wouldn't have to deal with later.

"Hayes," she said.

"Agnes, it's Heidi. We got a call from Sunset Captiva earlier. Some kind of scuffle on the beach today.

I've put the guy off twice but he insists he wants to file charges, so the sheriff wants you to go out and take statements."

Beautiful. This was all she needed.

"I'm on it," she told the dispatcher. "Anything's better than standing on the side of the road and waiting for the wind to blow."

Emma Scully barely heard the doorbell. She lay sprawled on the loveseat in the beach house's living room, legs dangling over the side as she scanned through Instagram posts. Her father hated her being on Instagram, said it encouraged a shallow mindset for young people to need so much psychological reinforcement when it came to everything from their bodies to the food on their plates. Emma had bitten her lip so many times to avoid telling him she had to get her positive reinforcement somewhere, but she knew how that conversation would go, so she kept her mouth shut. She loved her father, but sometimes he seemed so old.

When the doorbell rang again, she frowned, wondering where the noise had come from. Only when Kelsey jumped up from where she'd been lying on the floor with a coloring book did Emma realize what she'd heard.

"Someone's at the door!" Kelsey called toward the back of the house, where the four adults sat on the screen porch, drinking and making sightseeing plans for later in the week.

"Hey, kid, wait up," Jesse said, rising from the couch.

He'd been reading a book—some historical thing—but now he cast a disapproving look at Emma and followed Kelsey toward the door.

"I didn't hear it," Emma said, squirming a bit.

"No worries. I got it," Jesse replied.

But it bothered her, the quiet implication that as the big sister, she ought to have gotten up right away, not allowed her nine-year-old sister to answer the door in a strange place, long after dark. Mostly, it bothered her because she couldn't stand Jesse disapproving of her. They fought like siblings sometimes, and they'd spent enough time together growing up that when they were little it had sometimes felt like they were, but they weren't little anymore and Jesse had grown quieter. Quieter and way, way better looking.

She stayed on the loveseat, trying to pretend nothing mattered to her.

"Can I help you?" she heard Jesse say.

"I'm looking for Richard Scully. Is he in?"

The sound of scurrying feet whipped through the living room, and Emma sat up to watch as a wide-eyed Kelsey raced through the kitchen to the sliding glass door that led to the screen porch. As her little sister hauled the slider open, Emma turned to see Jesse leading a uniformed police officer into the house. She stiffened, throat going dry, wondering what the hell was going on.

Emma's parents came in from the porch, leaving the Hautalas out there alone.

"I'm Rick Scully," she heard her dad say. "This is my wife, Corinne."

"Deputy Agnes Hayes, Lee County Sheriff's Department," the woman replied. "I'm told you had an altercation on the beach today."

"I called three times, Deputy," her father continued. "I didn't think anyone was going to show up."

Emma rolled her eyes, flushed with embarrassment. She'd had no idea her father had called the police, and she could tell from her mother's expression that she wasn't the only one.

"We're shorthanded with storm preparation, Mr. Scully. Is there somewhere we can sit, so I can take your statement about the incident?"

"Em, I'd like you to take Kelsey for a walk on the beach," her mother said.

Normally Emma would have argued, but she could see the stress on her mother, and she really didn't want to be here for this anyway.

Mr. Hautala poked his head in from the screen porch. "Jesse, go with the girls."

Jesse didn't argue either. He looked from the deputy to Emma's father and then nudged Kelsey with his foot. "Come on, kid. Put your flip-flops on. We'll see if we can spot any good shells in the moonlight."

Kelsey agreed happily, as she always did when Jesse asked her to do something. Even when he called her "kid" she didn't mind, but whenever Emma tried it, Kelsey was furious. Her little sister might only be nine, but Emma figured Kelsey had her own sort of little kid crush on Jesse.

"Deputy, let's talk on the porch," Corinne said.

The adults started moving toward the screen porch. Rick offered the deputy a drink, which seemed monumentally stupid to Emma, but by then she and Jesse and Kelsey were headed for the front door. Emma went out first, let the door hang open behind her, then hurried down the steps. Tiny lizards scurried out of her way. Big curled leaves that looked like something out of *Jurassic World* skittered on the round stone tiles of the front walkway.

"Emma, what's your hurry?" Kelsey said, irritation tightening her voice.

"Just eager to get away from them," Emma said. "It's so embarrassing."

Jesse came up beside her, matching her pace. "Let them worry about it. You have nothing to be embarrassed about."

Emma glanced over her shoulder at Kelsey, who struggled to keep up with them. "It wasn't *your* father punching some college kid."

"He didn't punch the guy, dummy," Kelsey said. "All he did was push him a little."

"Does that make it okay?" Emma asked, slowing down, studying her little sister.

"Of course not. But he's just 'Dad,' y'know? He's not even really jealous. He's just angry and he doesn't even know who he's angry at—which is himself, as usual—so he's trying to find someone to blame."

Emma and Jesse both stopped in their tracks and stared at her.

Kelsey scowled and twisted up her body like she could make herself disappear. "Why are you guys looking at me like that? You're so weird!"

"And you're, like, ridiculously smart," Emma replied.

"Perceptive," Jesse said. "And wise."

Kelsey squirmed again. Emma could see how much she liked the compliments, just as she could see how much her sister didn't want to show it.

"Beach," Jesse said.

With a tacit agreement to change the subject, they fell into silence as they walked along the path to the wooden boardwalk, which led out onto the beach. The boardwalk had been put in maybe a decade before and the wood was in excellent shape, beautifully maintained by the property managers of Sunset Captiva. Emma loved the thirty feet of thin tree cover that separated the houses from the beach. Kelsey went wild for all of the animals they could see around the island, including dolphins, sea otters, and manatee, but Emma always found herself staring at the trees and their underbrush. She counted what appeared to be at least four varieties of palm tree, not to mention many other trees, including a mango. At night, with the wind picking up and the menacing whisper of wind through the branches and leaves, she loved the strange layers of shadow they provided.

When they reached the end of the boardwalk and stepped out onto the sand, Emma hoped to see the moon over the water. Instead, clouds had moved in and the waves on the Gulf seemed angry as they crashed on the shore. The night they had arrived, the moonlight had been beautiful, the sky clear, the waters gently beckoning, and she had laughed as she'd taken her sister's hand and they had run into the ocean together, still in their shorts and shirts.

Not tonight. Looking at the Gulf of Mexico now, with the low clouds lit from within by dim, diffused, almost suffocated moonlight, Emma did not trust the water.

Laughter erupted off to her left. She glanced that way and saw that there were others who did not share her feeling of unease. Two of the spring-break girls were sitting on the sand, bottles of beer in their hands. Emma had been watching the group for the past couple of days, sometimes eavesdropping while she lay on her beach mat. The girl with the flawless skin and massive brown eyes was Nadia, while her shorter, louder friend was Simone. Nadia might be beautiful, but Simone had the sculpted muscles and powerful legs of a gymnast. The way she walked—back straight, light but confident on her feet—Emma guessed that had to be it. Dancer, possibly, but gymnast seemed much more likely.

As the two college girls gossiped about their friends, sipping their beers, Emma walked within thirty feet of them. Kelsey had begun regaling Jesse with dramatic complaints about the teachers and principal at her school, with Jesse offering meaningless grunts and faux interested replies. Emma glanced over and immediately understood the reason—he shot a furtive glance at the spring-break girls, then a second look, this one lingering a moment on Nadia.

"Jeez," she muttered to him. "Stare a little longer."

Jesse glanced away guiltily, then fixed Emma with a withering look. "I wasn't staring."

"She's just jealous," Kelsey said, in a high, squeaky voice. She smirked with such satisfaction that Emma silently vowed to murder her later.

"You were definitely staring," Emma countered quietly, as they reached the crashing waves. "The way tigers watch mothers push baby carriages past their enclosures at the zoo? That was the look you just gave her. Even worse, your taste in women sucks." She glanced over her shoulder. "You want the girl who tosses her hair and laughs at your jokes instead of the one who won't take the back seat to anyone."

Jesse faced her. The sky over the Gulf rumbled with distant thunder. "What do you know about what I want?"

A wave crashed onto the shore. Kelsey laughed and raced away from it, but neither Emma nor Jesse moved an inch as the water rushed around their legs.

"Why do you even care?" Jesse said.

"I don't." Emma felt the surf dragging at her calves as the wave receded.

"I wasn't staring."

"Fine."

"I—"

Kelsey shouted something. Emma turned toward her, tried to rewind in her brain to figure out what her sister had said, but even in the split second she did that, she saw the look on Kelsey's face, the way her sister's gaze shifted oceanward, and Emma turned to see the wave coming at her. She reached out for Jesse, but then the wave hit. It came up to her chest. If she'd braced herself she might have stayed on her feet, but the wave crashed into her, carried her with it, drove her under and then began dragging her backward. She felt the undertow grip her, felt the power and hunger in it. As she choked on salt water, panic seized her and she flailed, unable to tell up from down, rolling in the undertow.

Something struck her in the water. A fresh jolt of panic surged through her, but then arms wrapped around her and she felt herself hauled bodily from the waves. Drenched, coughing, she grabbed hold of her rescuer, knowing it had to be Jesse, the only person close enough to have reached her.

He set her down where the water still came up to her knees. A fresh wave of fear washed over her and she rushed from the surf, coughing up a lungful of salt water. She dropped to her knees and drew long, ragged breaths, with fits of coughing in between. Someone knelt by her, and for a moment she thought it was Kelsey, but then she heard her little sister crying. Emma looked up to see Simone beside her. Kelsey stood with the other college girl, Nadia, the two of them staring.

"You're okay," Simone said, her eyes narrowed with concern. "Just breathe."

"That was terrifying," Jesse said, his voice coming from somewhere above and behind Emma. She wasn't sure if he had been speaking to her or to the spring-break girls.

Nadia swore, unconcerned about Kelsey's age. "Totally fucked up. They need to put up signs warning people not to swim until after this storm has passed."

Emma coughed again, or she would have laughed. "They want people to evacuate. They're probably not thinking about swimming."

As Emma stood, Kelsey hugged her.

"You weren't even swimming," Simone said, studying Emma's face as if to make certain she hadn't suffered any real damage. Then she glanced at Nadia. "We need to tell the others, or someone's going to go for a drunk skinny dip and we'll never see them again."

"Oh, can it be Marianna? Please?" Nadia said.

"You're such a bitch," Simone said. But she laughed.

The moment when they had all been one group, five people together, seemed to have passed. The two spring-breakers moved together again. Kelsey hugged her sister, something Emma realized she hadn't done in a long time.

"You okay?" Jesse asked, shifting closer to the Scully sisters.

Emma nodded. "Yeah. That was pretty scary, though."

Nadia and Simone started back toward the beers they had left jutting from the sand.

"Good thing you had your own personal lifeguard," Nadia said, flipping her hair and smiling at Jesse as if bestowing a blessing on him. Simone bumped her,

Nadia stumbled, and then the two of them plucked their beers from the sand and started walking back toward the footpath to their rented house.

"Yeah," Emma said, looking at Jesse. "Good thing."

Kelsey took Jesse's hand. "Thanks, Jess. You saved her life."

"I don't know about that," Jesse said. "But I definitely saved her from swallowing a lot more water."

"Well, if I drowned," Emma said, "at least Mom and Dad would have to stop being assholes to each other for a few hours."

They all turned to look back through the trees, but they could see only the outline of their rental house and the glow of lights from within. With the sheriff's deputy showing up at the house, and the tension between her parents, Emma worried far more about what was happening on dry land than she did about what happened in the ocean.

But then she remembered the panic she'd felt when the wave had dragged her under, the terror as she'd swallowed water, the certainty that she would drown. And then Jesse's arms around her, hoisting her out of the Gulf.

Emma glanced up at him, touched his arm, and thanked him quietly. Jesse looked faintly embarrassed, but he managed a muted "You're welcome." Kelsey watched, smiling thinly, but this time she didn't tease Emma about her crush.

The storm might be coming, but it wasn't here yet.

"Let's keep walking," Emma said, gesturing further along the beach.

"But no swimming," Kelsey replied.

Emma gave a nervous laugh, but she wasn't afraid anymore. They were in paradise, after all, and nobody dies in paradise.

CHAPTER 3

Simone stood at the kitchen island in the beach house, slicing limes to squeeze into the bottles of some of the local beers they'd bought at the Island Market. The others were scattered around her—Nadia, Marianna, and Rashad at the kitchen table, Tyler and Kevin perched on the edge of the sofa. The TV in the living room had been muted, but nobody was looking at it anyway.

Everyone's attention was on the fucking cop.

Not that Simone had any particular hatred for cops. Sure, way too many of them were either violent, racist bastards or totally fine with other cops being violent, racist bastards, but she had encountered her share of folks in blue who seemed to be genuinely interested in doing their jobs and wanted to improve their communities. And this particular woman did not seem to have any issue with Rashad being Pakistani American, or with any of the other brown people in the room. But she was still here, fucking up their night.

Marianna was the first one to get fed up enough to say something. She pushed her chair back from the kitchen table and stared at the deputy. "You know this is ridiculous, right?"

Deputy Hayes cocked her head, lasering in on Marianna. "Sorry?"

Rashad shifted uncomfortably. "Be cool, guys."

"*Guys*?" Nadia said. "As in more than one of us? Nobody but Marianna has done anything but answer questions."

Simone sliced one last piece of lime, put down the knife, and picked up a beer. When Nadia seemed irritated, there was always the possibility of fireworks. Marianna shot Nadia a dark look, apparently hoping she wouldn't start trouble.

"Folks, I'm not sure what you're getting upset about," Deputy Hayes said. "If your friend Rashad was the one assaulted—"

"*If*?" Marianna echoed.

Kevin tutted the way Kevin always tutted. It normally irritated Simone, because Tyler had brought Kevin into this group. Tyler was the only one they'd all agreed could bring a significant other on this vacation, mainly because the rest of them only had insignificant others. But it still felt like presumption anytime Kevin acted like he had some intimate knowledge of them.

"It's pretty straightforward, Officer," Tyler said, holding Kevin's hand on the sofa, both of them very serious. "Rashad was nice to this man's family, including his wife. The guy seemed to get angry."

"Jealous," Kevin put in.

"Jealous," Tyler agreed. "Words were exchanged and the guy—"

"Scully," Simone said, finally speaking up as she twisted a lime wedge into the neck of her beer bottle and then took a sip. "His name's Rick Scully."

Tyler shrugged. "Whoever he is, he shoved Rashad pretty hard. Like, slammed him in the chest. Rashad didn't fall down and that seemed to make this Scully guy angrier. When he tried a second time, Rashad knocked his hands away and shoved him back. Scully fell on his ass. I admit we laughed, and I'm sure he was embarrassed in front of his family and friends, but whose fault is that? He started it. He assaulted Rashad. The push back was self-defense."

Deputy Hayes glanced around at them all. "Everyone agree with that version of events?"

"Jesus." Marianna sighed. "It's not a fucking *version*. It's what happened."

Rashad threw up his hands. "Look, Deputy, we're right here. Nobody's going anywhere unless you make us. I don't deny I was kind of flirting with the lady, but it was all in good fun until Mr. Scully decided he needed to prove his manhood. I know you have a job to do and I respect that, and I know it's harder to believe us than it is to believe them—"

"Not necessarily," the deputy said. "His wife and the other adults over there didn't exactly contradict him, but they didn't back up his version, either."

That was enough for Simone. She set her beer bottle down hard on the kitchen island counter. "Then what the fuck are you doing here?"

"Simone," Rashad warned.

"No," Nadia said, touching his shoulder. "Let her alone."

Simone knew that was Nadia just enjoying her flaring temper, but she didn't care. She stayed where she was because she didn't want the deputy to get nervous and accidentally shoot her in the kitchen, but she didn't hide her frustration.

"Seriously, Deputy," Simone said, staring at the uniformed woman. "I know we're younger, and college students on spring break have a reputation, and yes we're drinking, and yes there was a scuffle, but we told you what happened and the guy's own wife won't back his play, so why are you still here? With everything else going on, don't you have something better to do?"

The deputy's weary politeness cracked. She inhaled sharply and straightened her spine, looked as if she might be trying to decide how much trouble she would get into if she smashed Simone's head into the kitchen island.

"I don't get to decide which calls I respond to and which I don't," she said. "But you're right. Here I am giving you kids the benefit of the doubt, when I could certainly be doing something much better with my time."

Simone felt her throat go dry. "I wasn't . . . I didn't mean . . ."

Deputy Hayes fixed her with icy blue eyes. "You should stop talking now."

Rashad sighed. "Good idea. Thanks for suggesting it."

The deputy looked at him. "I believe you, Rashad. I don't think Mr. Scully is a bad guy, but I think he's embarrassed and taking it out on you. For everyone's sake, I hope he decides not to press charges. Less trouble for everyone involved."

Deputy Hayes glanced at Kevin and Tyler on the couch. "I'll see myself out."

She walked toward the door. Simone followed her, trying to find the words to apologize. The woman had come in with an open mind, trying to do her job, and Simone and Marianna had made it difficult for her.

"Deputy . . ."

Hayes drew open the door. The wind howled past them both. "Keep an eye on the forecast. If it hasn't changed for the positive by morning, get your asses out of here."

Then she was gone, tugging the door closed behind her.

Simone shook her head as she locked the door. Unlike a lot of her friends, she tended not to drink herself into oblivion for amusement or to escape her troubles, but tonight felt like a good night for beer. A lot of beer.

"Well!" Tyler said, clapping his hands as Simone walked back through the house. "We won't forget *this* vacation!"

Nadia shoved Rashad playfully. "That's for fucking sure."

Simone retrieved her beer from the counter, grabbed a second one and two more lime wedges, then opened the sliding glass door and went out onto the screen porch at the back of the house.

"Anyone wants to join me out here, I'll be drinking in silence and wondering if we've made a terrible decision by staying here."

Rashad was the first to join her. Nadia and Marianna followed, and Kevin and Tyler went upstairs to have sex. While the four of them didn't drink in silence, Simone got the feeling they were all wondering what tomorrow would bring.

The leaves on the palm trees behind the house bent with the gusting winds and they could hear the crashing of the surf even from this distance. A light rain began to fall, whipping sideways, spattering through the screen and forcing them all to shift their chairs backward to keep from getting wet. In the sky, thunder rolled, muffled and far off, but promising more.

"So much for paradise," Nadia said, after her third or fourth beer.

"It is what it is," Rashad said, slumping in his chair with a nodding wisdom. "Even Eden had a snake in it."

Jim Lennox had lived on Sanibel Island for twenty-three years, and in that time it had gone from feeling like heaven to feeling like a prison. His marriage hadn't fared much better. Once upon a time he had viewed

Kris as his guardian angel, and now he called her his warden, often to her face. They had been together a quarter century, starting off across the bar at Dunphy's Upstairs Lounge, a century-old drinking hole in Philadelphia frequented by a lot of the players in the city's advertising and marketing fields. Lennox had been in there twice a week with clients—big man, rolling high, paying the tab—and the gorgeous Caribbean princess tending bar had caught his eye the very first time. He'd been performing for her ever since, like he was DiCaprio in some Martin Scorsese movie instead of director of client services at an ad agency. He wasn't even a creative. What the fuck did he have to be proud of, except his expense account?

Two months later, she'd finally broken it off with a loser boyfriend who had been selling drugs on the side—and banging his female customers who would do anything for a discount—and Lennox had taken her home.

Her home, of course. Lennox couldn't take Kris to his own house because back in those days, his family had been living in it. First wife, Noreen. Two sons who had been toddlers at the time. A lot of guys had women on the side, especially in his business. Some of those fuckers even took the women away with them on business trips, traveling with colleagues, acting like everyone should just ignore it. Maybe those wives missed the signs or maybe they looked the other way, but not Noreen. She *smelled* Kris on him, more than once. Told him he smelled like a strip club, and that once might be a hug from a client or an actual night at a strip club, twice was suspicious, and a third time was pussy on the side—and she wouldn't stand for that.

Noreen was as good as her word.

His wife tossing him out of the house, dumping his clothes on the driveway, smashing his old acoustic guitar, had a curious effect on him. Lennox could have taken the path so many guys he knew had followed, moved into some apartment, taken whatever custody deal a judge would allow, worked his ass off to maintain an income that bled out to the ex and the kids but left him no money to spoil the women who'd been worth it all—but fuck that.

Lennox had grown up fishing the Delaware River, and at the Jersey shore in summertime. All through college, fishing had been the only thing that really made him happy. Noreen had claimed she understood, but he had always seen the truth behind her eyes, that she begrudged him that time, and the second she gave birth to Timmy, their first, his fishing days had been over. After fucking in the back of his Audi one night, he had told Kris his real dream was just to buy a little fishing boat, move to Florida, and do charter trips and dolphin tours; spend his life at sea, in the sun, and never put on a goddamn suit again, not even for his own funeral. Kris had looked at him with those green eyes, little golden sparkles in them, and told him that sounded like Heaven.

They'd done it. At first, he had seen his sons a couple times a year, but by the time the younger one hit high school, he had stopped trying. The boys were even less interested in him than he was in them, and there seemed no point in pretending. Last he'd heard—about six years back—Timmy had joined the Marines. What had become of the younger one, Drew, he had no idea. If they wanted to find him, they were grown men now. Their mother knew where he lived.

Heaven. Sanibel hadn't turned into Hell for him, but yeah, prison was a good word for it. Kris had wanted children, but Lennox had convinced her that was a bad idea, been so persuasive that she had believed it herself for a long time. Now the resentment had piled up. Once she had been a free spirit, came out on fishing charters with him, entertained the tourists, but then she had gotten a job in a real estate management company and her sense of humor—of fun—had withered on that particular fucking vine. She came home tired, and he had learned not to ask her how she could possibly be more tired than he was after a day hauling fish out of the Gulf and babysitting tourists who sucked at fishing and thought they knew every damn thing about boating.

Fifty-three years old, and Lennox wanted to run again, take off on yet another wife. He had been thinking about it for the past couple of years and had decided on Seattle, for a change of pace. Trouble was, what little money he had was invested in the business and his boat, and Kris had always kept their finances separate. Maybe because she'd seen the way he'd vanished on his first family and always suspected he had it in him to become a ghost again.

Which meant he needed money.

All of his trips had canceled. He had deposits from

the charter clients, and some of the tickets he'd sold for dolphin watches and shelling day trips were non-refundable, but this hurricane was sucking money out of his wallet already, and nobody even knew if it would make landfall in Florida. A lot of boat owners and fishermen had already started relocating their craft, moving them up the Caloosahatchee River toward Fort Myers, finding a mooring up there. Others figured that was premature and were rolling the dice for now. Most of those who were staying behind would keep an eye on the forecast and lift their boats out of the water if the storm came calling.

Lennox had other plans. He knew the old-timers on Sanibel and Captiva used to shelter in Braynerd Bayou over in Buck Key, or in the bayous in the Ding Darling National Wildlife Refuge. If the blow turned out to be anything less than catastrophic, his boat—the *Kristen*, naturally—ought to be safe there, and it meant he could take shelter at the last minute, which was good, because Lennox had some errands to do on Captiva if the storm really started to kick up.

All of those houses on the Pine Island side were owned by rich fuckers. Some were rented to comfortably middle-class folks week to week—people on vacation—but not all. The ones that weren't rented, that were owner occupied all winter and empty much of the summer, would be full of the owners' precious possessions right now. Lennox knew which houses were which, and he had a pretty good idea about who had already left for the mainland during the voluntary evacuation. As the wind picked up, glass might shatter. Doors might blow open. Burglar alarms were certainly going to go off, but nobody would be coming out to check on them until after the storm passed, meaning a guy with a boat might tie off at one private dock after another, rob a few of those mini-palaces, and sail away as soon as the storm was over.

He doubted Kris would miss him. Seattle would be colder, and rainier, but after twenty-three summers in Florida, he was ready for it. Lennox had never robbed anyone before, but that hadn't been due to any moral hesitation. He had just never needed money badly enough to take the risk, never had an opportunity like this before.

If the storm really came knocking, she might just break him out of the prison his Heaven had become. Lennox figured he was the only one praying for rain, for waves, for winds that would scour the island clean.

Hurricane Juliet might just be his saving grace.

Maurice Broaddus had driven back to his little one-bedroom condo just long enough to take the dog out for a short walk and fill her food and water bowls. The air-conditioner sounded clanky and he knew he ought to take a look or shut it off until he could find the time, but the humidity outside was suffocating and he didn't want to leave Sugar to pant and sweat on his own until he could sneak home again.

"You'll be all right, pup," he said, crouching by the door. He held the dog's head in his hands, tugging on the loose skin of Sugar's face. "Gunther next door is going to come and check on you tomorrow, feed you if Daddy can't make it back. Maybe by the time I get home, I'll have done something you can really be proud of."

Sugar licked his face. He kissed the dog's snout and then slipped out the door, knowing Sugar would whine for a few minutes and then shuffle back to his favorite spot on the living room floor and conk out for a while before hunger dragged him into the kitchen. *Lazy dog*, he thought, a smile on his face.

When he stepped outside, whipped by the wind, his smile vanished.

Broaddus got into his car and started it up. When he flicked on the headlights, their beams illuminated the palm trees at the edge of the condo parking lot, and he could see the way the trees bent and swayed. A tremor of regret passed through him as he wondered whether he ought to have left the island already. Too late now, though. He'd promised Dr. Tremblay that he would stay and guard the Institute, and he would keep that promise, with one significant exception. No man could protect the world from himself.

It started to rain again as he pulled out of the parking lot and turned toward the Institute. The rain, strangely cold, had come in pockets thus far. It would drizzle for ten minutes and be dry for an hour, then it would pour for five minutes as if the apocalypse had come, and then dry up again.

Somehow, when the rain kicked up this time and he flicked on his windshield wipers, Broaddus did not think it would abate again. Not until the story of this storm had been written and the only question left was how much the cleanup would cost.

Of course, by then, Broaddus would have risked his job. He had been thinking all night about how to put his plan into action, and if there was a way to do it without anyone knowing he had been involved. If he could avoid being fired—more important, if he could avoid going to jail—he'd prefer that option.

The hurricane might provide some cover. If the island lost power, even with the Institute's generators, he thought he could figure out some lie that would explain it all, then just play stupid and hope the assumptions people like Dr. Tremblay made about people like him would make them less likely to suspect that it had been more than an accident.

Broaddus knew the layout of the Institute very well. He'd been in the lab, seen the work in progress. Some of the researchers were desperate to talk to people about their projects, and he had often shown enough interest that when something happened to excite them, they would share. The graduate students who spent semesters on Sanibel were the most likely to tell him things that were meant to be confidential. But he worked there, after all . . . and he was only a security guard.

Broaddus was kind to them all, never let on how much the shark research bothered him. All that pain for nothing, playing God, cutting living creatures open and messing about in their brains. . . . It horrified and haunted him.

The rain pounded his windshield, the wipers unable to keep up. He slowed down, watching the road in front of him. As he drove, the wind gusted hard enough to rock the car, but he didn't have far to go. Once he reached the Institute, he wouldn't be going home again until the storm had passed.

By then, the sharks would be free.

Matti lay in bed, staring at the swirl of the ceiling fan and listening to the creaking and moaning of the house. The wind gusted and subsided, gusted and subsided, and the whole structure seemed to sway with that rhythm. Most of the houses out here were built on stilts, so in the event of a tidal surge the water would flow in and flow out without damaging the homes above it, so it felt to him as if the whole thing might just topple over if the wind blew hard enough. Such thoughts were the price he paid for a vivid imagination.

The other price involved insomnia. Sleeplessness had plagued Matti since college. Unlike other insomniacs he knew, Matti never had trouble falling asleep, but he often woke during the night and found it virtually impossible to drift off again. Tonight, he had risen to relieve his bladder a little after three a.m., which had become a familiar time for him, his personal witching hour. Back in bed, he had tossed and turned a bit, trying to get comfortable, but eventually surrendered and just listened to the noises of the house. The air-conditioner clicked on and blew chilly air into the room. With the wind and the light rain falling, a look out the window might imply that AC was unnecessary, but the storm sat out in the Gulf, where the air hung hot and thick and the humidity could suffocate.

The beams creaked and the fan whirred and the rain pattered the glass. Matti glanced over at his wife and felt a surge of love and envy. The woman could sleep through anything, not to mention fall asleep just by closing her eyes. He leaned over, the soft, torturously uncomfortable bed creaking beneath him, and kissed her forehead. Then he climbed out of bed, snatched the mystery novel he'd been reading from the bedside table, and slipped out into the hallway. There had been hundreds of times in his life when he'd done this, padded quietly to some unoccupied space hours before dawn, clicked on a light, and read until he either nodded off or the sun came up. This would be no different, but it saddened him just the same.

This morning, he knew there would be no falling back to sleep. As he started down the carpeted stairs, he had already surrendered. The upside of this self-knowledge would be a very hot, very black cup of coffee. He could practically smell it already as he reached the living room. A small lamp on a corner table illuminated the peach-colored walls and the various island-and-maritime-themed wall decorations. So many shells, which made sense given Captiva was so well known for the volume and variety of seashells on its shores.

"I hope I didn't wake you."

Matti jumped a couple of feet, bumped the back of

the sofa, and clamped a hand to his chest as he stared at Corinne Scully. She sat at the kitchen table with one hand wrapped around a mug of tea and her cell phone in the other. The phone screen glowed—she'd been on social media or something—but she looked pale and drawn and rumpled, just as he knew he must look. In her Villanova T-shirt and a pair of thin pajama pants, she reminded him of his college days, and for a moment he envied the spring-breakers next door.

"You scared the shit out of me," he said quietly, his heart beginning to return to its regular rhythm. "What are you doing down here?"

"Same thing you're doing, I guess," she replied. "Couldn't sleep."

"Yeah, but that's the norm for me." The house around them groaned, probably just the wind but it reminded him that everyone else was still in slumberland. "I'm going to make a coffee. Want to go sit on the screen porch?"

Corinne frowned and stared out through the sliding glass door, looking at the rain spatter on the floor or the palms bending behind the house.

She shrugged. "Sure."

While she went outside and found a dry chair, far enough back from the screen, Matti made himself a quick Keurig coffee and joined her. He slid the door closed behind him.

"Now we won't wake anyone up," he said.

But when he sat in the chair beside her, Corinne remained silent. She gazed out at the darkness and so he did the same, just listening to the storm and watching the night. He sipped his coffee, enjoying the burn.

"I can go back inside, if you want," he said after a minute or two of quiet. "Or upstairs. I didn't mean to intrude."

She smiled and sipped her tea. "On my moping, you mean? My brooding session?"

"Call it soul-searching."

"We can call it whatever we like."

Matti studied her over the rim of his mug as he took another long sip. "You're worried about Rick?"

"It feels like he's unraveling," Corinne said quietly, even though nobody else was there to overhear.

"He lost his temper yesterday," Matti admitted. "He's unhappy with himself, I think, and doesn't know how to fix that. He was jealous."

"He was a prick."

Matti smiled and toasted her words with his mug. "True. He was that."

Corinne fixed him with a hard look. "It's not my job to make him happy, Matti. He has to find that for himself. Figure it out, because in the meantime, it's doing a lot of damage. It's not just him that's unraveling. The whole family's starting to fray. I think we're unraveling—Rick and I—and I just . . ."

She sighed and looked out at the dark again, maybe regretting what she'd said. How honest she'd been. Her mug quivered a bit when she lifted it to her lips.

"I was surprised he called the police," Matti admitted.

"For something he started."

Matti nodded. "You want me to talk to him?"

The question hung between them for a long while, and this time he didn't interrupt her silence. Instead he joined her in listening to the storm and watching the darkness as the rain continued to spritz through the screen. Maybe the hurricane wouldn't turn their way after all. The storm didn't seem to have gotten any worse over night, though the wind had picked up a little.

"We should enjoy ourselves," Corinne said at last. "This might be the last vacation we all take together."

Matti glanced down at his coffee. "Well, that's fucking depressing. Now I wish this was whiskey."

"We do have whiskey," Corinne replied with forced brightness.

"Too close to breakfast."

"I'm sorry this is all so awkward, because of all the tension between me and Rick."

Inside, Matti squirmed, but he didn't want Corinne to see his discomfort so he fell back on humor, as he so often had. "Hey, if you want to have sex with one of our college neighbors, I won't stop you. I want to be supportive of your needs."

Corinne pushed her hands through her short, unkempt hair. "Well, at least there's one man in this house interested in my needs."

Matti laughed, threw his hands up and leaned back in the chair. "Okay, now that *was* awkward."

She pushed back her chair, picking up her mug. "Which is my cue to go back upstairs. Maybe I can steal a couple more hours of sleep before morning . . . if morning ever comes, given the wonderful weather we're having."

"You've got to love the tropics."

Corinne arched an eyebrow, giving him a salacious look. "I know *you* love the tropics. You tease me about college boys, but I saw you checking out those girls."

"Purely concerned for their dermal health. There were exposed parts of them that needed sunscreen."

With a laugh, she rolled her eyes, opened the slider, and went back into the house, closing it behind her. Matti drank his coffee while he watched her head back upstairs to join her husband in bed, and he felt sadder than ever, thinking about the tension their room must hold, and more grateful than ever that he and Jenn were at peace with each other. It felt to him like an era was coming to an end, and he knew he would always mourn its passing.

He thought about heading back up to bed himself, but he knew there would be no point. Sometimes, in the middle of the night like this, he would have lit up a cigar out there on the porch, but tonight he could not muster the proper motivation. Instead he sat in the chair and stared out at the dark. The wind had really begun to kick up, even since he had come out to the porch. Now, as it blasted through the trees, it sounded almost as if it were screaming.

CHAPTER 4

Morning arrived under a blanket of silence. The wind managed a powerful gust here and there, but the rain had ceased for the moment and the clouds had thinned enough that columns of sunlight shone down as if Heaven itself were peeking through. The calm before the arrival of the real storm.

Rashad laced up his running shoes and hit the beach, desperate to clear his head. He'd had too much to drink the night before and his thoughts had cobwebs on them. The weird passive-aggressive dynamic amongst the girls had started to grind on him, and the visit from that sheriff's deputy had left a sour taste in his mouth.

When the storm passes, he told himself, *it'll all change*. With the sun out, the threat of a hurricane gone, he would persuade the others to go parasailing or biking—anything to get them off the beach and away from the jackass next door. The group in the neighboring house seemed very nice and relaxed, except for Rick Scully. All Rashad had done was make a couple of wiseass comments and give his wife a charming smile—a smile she'd returned—and the guy had gone off the rails.

How many days did they have left? Four, or was it three? Either way, he wanted to make the most of them.

Sand flew up behind him as he ran. Though the weather had momentarily subsided, the waves were still huge, crashing onto the shore. He had seen a few people out picking up shells, but only a few. So many had left the island the previous day that there were several massive conch shells on the sand, along with thousands and thousands of smaller shells, the majority of them shattered by the violent waves. He had seen a lot of sand dollars and been tempted to pick one up, but instead kept running.

Now, as he drew near the Mucky Duck restaurant—where the enormous plate glass windows had been boarded up in preparation—he saw the Scullys' daughters walking along the beach with a bucket, stooped over and sifting through broken seashells in search of keepers. When the older one glanced up, she froze on the sand. The younger one kept walking, and Rashad shifted to the left, farther up on the beach, planning to run right past them.

The younger sister lifted her head and spotted him. She smiled and gave him a wave, and as Rashad lifted his hand to return it, he found himself slowing down and walking toward them. The older sister glanced around, looking like she wanted to hide.

"Morning," he said. "Find any good ones?"

The younger sister held up an enormous, gleaming conch shell, maybe the biggest Rashad had ever seen outside of a shop.

"Nice, right?" the younger girl said.

"More than nice," he replied. "That's amazing. You could probably sell that for a ton of money."

"It's beautiful," the older sister said, frowning. "Why would we sell it?"

Rashad shifted uncomfortably. His left hamstring felt tight and he started to stretch it, glancing away from them.

"Listen," he said, focusing on the girls again. "I just wanted to say I'm sorry for what happened yesterday. I was just being nice, trying to be funny. I didn't mean to upset anyone."

The little girl was solemn. "We know. Our dad's just been in a crappy mood lately." She held out her hand to shake. "I'm Kelsey."

Surprised, he took her hand. "Rashad."

The older sister looked as if she wanted to crawl inside her own sweatshirt and hide forever. He reached to shake her hand as well.

"How about you?"

When she shook his hand, she blushed deeply, and Rashad tried not to smile. There were teenage girls in his neighborhood at home who reacted the same way when he was around. However old she was—fifteen, maybe?—she was still just a kid, and if she felt shy or had been crushing on him at all, he would not do anything to make her feel embarrassed.

"Emma," she said.

"Right. I remember now. I heard your parents saying your name."

Her smile burned away any shyness. "You mean yelling at me."

Rashad released her hand. "I'd have noticed anyway." She beamed, and he turned to continue his run. "I'll see you guys later. Be careful out here. I heard what happened with the waves last night. I'm sure the undertow is still a monster."

Kelsey made a tsking sound, glancing back and forth between them. "We're not stupid."

Emma whacked her gently on the arm, and the sisters started giving each other dirty looks. Kelsey shook her head in disgust and stooped to look for shells again.

Rashad started off down the beach, but when he heard a voice calling to the two girls he glanced over his shoulder. The other kid from their house, Jesse, came running off the boardwalk to Sunset Captiva and hustled toward the girls. Rashad would have kept running, but something about the kid's facial expression and the tone of his voice when he called for them made him pause.

Jesse reached them. He used his hands when he talked and he gestured back toward the house. Whatever was going on had obviously upset him, and Rashad wondered if something had happened, if maybe Rick Scully had lost his temper again.

He started back toward the kids, first just a few tentative steps; and then he saw the girls' faces, saw the fear there, and he picked up the pace.

"Hey," he called, hurrying back to them. "What's going on? Is everything okay?"

Jesse scowled at him. "Not even close."

"You need to go, Rashad," Emma said, pointing up toward the houses. "Get your friends packed up and get moving."

Confusion froze Rashad. Was this some more bullshit from the skirmish the day before, more cops on the way? But then Jesse took Kelsey's hand, and the three of them started hurrying toward their rental house.

Kelsey hung back, half-dragged by Jesse, to call out to Rashad.

"We're going, too. Everybody has to go."

A sick feeling settled into the pit of his stomach as he understood. The weather had improved this morning, but it wasn't going to last. Hurricane Juliet was headed their way, and the evacuation order had just been made mandatory. They had to go.

He swore under his breath as he broke into a run, wondering if his friends already knew, how long it would take them to pack up. It had all seemed so impossible, even with the wind during the night, but now he could envision these houses tumbling off their stilts as waves washed down Andy Rosse Lane.

He wondered how much time they had before the worst of the storm hit.

Suddenly the mainland felt very, very far away.

* * *

When the power went out, Jim Lennox was ready. He
had scouted the east side of Captiva early in the morning, before dawn, watching the most grotesquely expensive mansions on Pine Island Sound to see which
ones had lights on in the windows. As the sun came
up, he'd watched for activity, looked for any sign of vehicles in motion, people packing up. He knew the
wealthiest residents of the island had probably been the
earliest to leave. They could afford to have someone
else come and look after their property, could afford a
luxury hotel on the mainland, where they could ride
out the storm with the finest whiskeys and a fifty-dollar
porterhouse. He had seen a couple of families taking
their leave, so he knew for sure those homes were
empty.

All he'd had to do was wait.

He had taken some food, a case of water, and half
a case of beer, and steered the boat over to Buck Key
Preserve, at the heart of which the open span of
Braynerd Bayou offered a spot shielded from the worst
of the wind and storm surge to come. Several other
fishermen had the same idea and had already chosen
places to drop anchor where they would be far enough
away from the trees that their boats wouldn't be
crushed if one came down. It was a fucking risk, no
question, but for guys who sometimes lived on the ra-
zor edge of bankruptcy, there might not be a choice.

Lennox had cruised around the circumference of
the bayou, sorted out several spots where he thought

his boat would be safe, close enough to the thick clusters of mangrove trees that he figured he could swim to shore if the boat went down. Then he had steered her back out into Roosevelt Channel and watched as the sky got darker, waiting for his moment.

By the time the power went out, the wind had turned fierce. Lennox knew he didn't have much time—a matter of hours—but he intended to make the most of it. The first house he drew up to belonged to Jonas Alvart, a German film financier who had been wintering on the island for close to twenty years. Lennox had never heard of him until some googling had given him the name the night before. All he knew was the Alvart family had left Captiva.

He drew up to the dock, tied off, and said a prayer that the surf wouldn't be bad enough to smash the boat against the pilings before he got back. The day before, he had purchased two enormous wheeled duffel bags. Now he extended the handles and rolled them up the dock, kicked open the rear gate of the Alvart estate, and hurried past the huge backyard swimming pool. With the wind howling, even he had barely heard the clatter of the lock shattering on the gate, so when he reached the sliding glass door he made a decision—time was more important than subtlety. He found a decorative stone by the pool and tossed it through the glass, then stepped through, shards crunching under his boots, dragging the wheeled duffels behind him.

Rain swept in, swirling on the wind.

An alarm sounded—run by a backup generator—which made him move a bit faster. But the main road was clogged with evacuating vehicles, and Captiva didn't have its own police force. Even if that alarm signal somehow connected to a security firm, and even if they didn't just chalk it up to wind damage, it would take a long time for anyone to come and check it out. Lennox would be long gone by then.

With a grin on his face, he unzipped the first duffel and began his first-ever robbery.

He'd never felt happier.

Simone flung her suitcase into the back of her rented Honda. They were all moving fast now, with surprisingly little chatter. Knowing this group, she would have expected them to be doing nothing but talking about the hurricane, but it seemed fear had shut them up. Marianna had gone and dragged Kevin and Tyler out of bed, so the two of them were last out the door. Simone heard them come out onto the wooden landing overhead, thumping their rolling suitcases down the steps.

"Hey," Nadia said. "Who's riding with who?"

Simone resisted the urge to correct her grammar. She turned to look at the others, all of them standing in the rain, and she wiped water from her eyes. "Marianna should ride with me."

Nadia blinked in surprise, then nodded. "I'll ride with the lovers."

She dragged her suitcase over to the silver Audi Kevin had rented. "Come on, boys. I'm with you."

Marianna had watched this exchange with interest.

Another day she might have had questions, but nobody had time to do any deep thinking just then. She hoisted her too-large suitcase and slid it into the trunk beside Simone's. They both waited while Rashad did the same.

At the neighboring house, the door banged open, slammed into the wooden railing outside, and the two families began to emerge. They processed their fear differently, apparently, because they moved as if a tornado was on the way instead of a hurricane, parents urgently snapping at their kids, the kids ignoring them.

Their urgency amplified Simone's own fear. Mandatory evacuation felt so much different than the voluntary order. Some people would stay on the island, she knew, people who wanted to remain with their property, or who thought they were in no danger, that they were smarter or heartier than everyone else and could ride out the storm. The night before, Simone might have claimed to understand, but now that the evac order was mandatory, she thought those people were complete idiots.

"Come on," she said, climbing into the car. "Let's get out of here."

Rashad got into the back seat, Marianna taking shotgun. Simone fired up the engine, reversed out of the little driveway, waved to Kevin, Tyler, and Nadia, and then roared along the loose stone road, not pausing for the speed bumps, intent upon leaving Sunset Captiva behind.

She got as far as the exit from the development, where she needed to turn right onto Captiva Drive, before she had to stop and wait. The traffic from the northern part of the island was bumper to bumper, and by the time she slipped out onto Captiva Drive, Kevin's rented Audi was behind her, and the Scullys and the Hautalas were following him.

The traffic crawled. The windshield wipers swept back and forth. Hard gusts bent the trees and swirled the palm fronds that already littered the road.

Marianna had said nothing. Now she clicked on the radio and tuned it to a news channel whose commentators were doing a great job of scaring the shit out of anyone in the path of the hurricane. Simone changed the station, found some Latin music and left it there, the windshield wipers swishing. She glanced in the rearview mirror, where Rashad seemed to be trying to sleep.

It felt like it might be the longest day of her life.

"Marianna, listen," she said, glancing over at the passenger seat. "This is . . . maybe it's good that we have some time to talk."

"About you guys trying to ghost me, you mean?" Marianna asked, giving her a knowing look.

"That. And about why. I mean, there's no excuse. We were totally immature—"

"I won't argue that. But I know why. I get it, Simone, and it's one of the reasons I wanted to come with you guys. Whenever there's a group of friends, it always comes down to two girls—two women, 'cause we're women now, I guess—getting closer. Maybe I pissed you guys off, maybe there are times I'm irritating or a bitch, but we all are."

"We definitely all—"

"I'm not done," Marianna said in an icy tone. "My point is that women do this shit to each other all the time. You guys could have handled it better, but in general, we have to stop doing this, treating each other like the enemy, pairing up and shutting out the ones who don't seem to belong. Witches gathered in covens, in circles, and there's power in that. Do you think it's an accident that men are afraid of women gathering in groups and standing up for themselves? But we undermine our own needs by doing this horribly, bitchy thing where we have to have some outsider to mistreat in order to make ourselves feel better."

"You're saying you understand, and I guess you do, but you sound like you're still pretty pissed about it."

"I am. But I'm glad you wanted to talk about it. Step in the right direction."

Simone nodded in agreement and muttered, "Okay." It was a beginning, anyway. As much as she had just taken a verbal beating, it had been worth it just to get the conversation started.

The wind gusted hard enough that they felt it pushing against the car. Simone tightened her grip on the steering wheel. In the back seat, she heard a clinking of glass and glanced in the rearview mirror just in time to see Rashad using his opener to pop the cap off a bottle of beer.

"Are you kidding me? It's not even nine a.m."

Rashad grinned and held the bottle between the front seats, waiting for one of the girls to take it. "We're in dead-stop traffic. It's going to take us hours to get to the mainland. By then, these beers will be warm and we might be drowning."

Simone glanced at Marianna, who shrugged her shoulders and took the sweating beer bottle.

"The hell with it," Marianna said. "When you put it that way."

With a shiver, Simone looked into her mirror again. "Fine. Give me one. Hurricane Juliet can kiss my ass."

She cranked up the music loud enough that the whole car thumped with the bass. When Rashad handed her the beer, she took a long sip and then raised the bottle to toast the oncoming storm.

"Good morning, Florida!" she shouted over the music. "Fuck off and die!"

Matti drove, with Jenn in the passenger seat. Jesse lay sprawled in the back, center seat belt around his waist in spite of his prone position. He held his phone aloft, staring up at the screen, scanning for whatever information he could find on the hurricane.

"Anything?" Jenn asked.

"Anything not on the radio?" Matti amended.

"Barely any signal," Jesse replied. "But it's pretty clear we're not getting anywhere fast. We could binge a season of something on Netflix and still be stuck on this road."

Matti feared he might be right. He hadn't really considered how many of the people would be staying at South Seas Plantation on the northern tip of the island. The condo complex must have been much larger than he'd imagined. Too many people on Captiva, and on Sanibel, had waited for the evac order to become mandatory. They had all been stupid.

"You all right, honey?" Jenn asked.

Matti nodded, watching the cars ahead of them. An SUV waited a few seconds too long to inch forward and someone started honking a horn.

"I'm all right. No idea why anyone would beep. Nobody's getting off island any time soon. Only one road in, one road out."

"I'm sure by now they've stopped letting people drive onto the causeway," Jenn said. "They'll have opened the oncoming lane, so that's twice as many people who can leave at once."

Matti watched the Scullys' rented Toyota RAV4 creep ahead a few feet in front of them. "If so, it doesn't seem to be helping much."

Jenn took his right hand and squeezed. "Breathe, Matti. We're in the same boat as all of these other folks. Worrying about it won't make the cars move any quicker."

He lifted her hand and kissed her fingers. "I know, love. I'll breathe."

In the back seat, Jesse piped up. "Hey, at least we're not in the car with Rick and Corinne."

Matti laughed, but immediately felt badly about it. "They're doing their best."

"Are they?" Jenn asked.

"They're trying," Matti said.

Jesse let his hands flop down onto his chest, covering his phone like it was treasure. "Dad, you don't have to make excuses for them. Mrs. Scully seems like she's trying to keep it together, trying to keep Emma and Kelsey from dealing with a lot of it, but Mr. Scully has some serious issues. The guy needs therapy yesterday."

Matti couldn't argue with the truth. The families had been friends for a long time, and he had never seen Rick as on edge as he had seemed this week. Every relationship had its rocky periods, stretches of time when stress and anxiety and outside forces conspire to wind up one or both people so they grated on each other, fraying the connection they shared. Matti and Jenn had gone through a very bad patch when Jesse had been a toddler, and it had almost been the end of them. But they had made it through, and now he couldn't imagine life without her.

He squeezed his wife's hand. "I really hope they make it through this."

"Me too," Jenn replied. "But I swear, honey, I'm not holding my breath."

The traffic crawled forward a little, then stopped again. Matti breathed deeply and watched the back of the Scullys' rental, wondering where they would all sleep tonight. Not that it mattered, really. As long as Jenn and Jesse were safe and they were all together, he did not care where they ended up.

When Deputy Hayes noticed the boat zipping in toward Blind Pass, she spared it only a single, stray thought. *Coming in fast.* That was it, because why wouldn't it be coming in fast? If she had been out in the Gulf with the hurricane churning toward landfall—if she had been stupid enough to take a boat out on the water, as rough as the seas were getting, the way the waves were crashing and the wind pounding—well, she would have been full throttle toward safe harbor herself.

But she only noticed the boat for a second. The cars were a more immediate concern. There were only two lanes, one in either direction, but now both were filled with vehicles headed off the islands. Once upon a time, people would have evacuated the day before, when the governor had called it voluntary, but folks had either become more stubborn or stupider over time. As a cop, Deputy Hayes had come to believe it was that most people these days simply did not think the rules applied to them. They would rather ignore authority and wise counsel than let anyone tell them what to do . . . right up until they realized it might kill them.

Static flared on her radio, a crackling voice came on. "—got a problem over here. I could use some backup."

Deputy Hayes frowned, stood a bit taller, then walked a few yards onto the bridge at Blind Pass. With the rain slashing down and the gray sky, she could barely make out the tops of cars and the flashing lights of emergency vehicles on the other side. The bridge itself was not much to speak of, just a short span that crossed the narrow pass between Sanibel and Captiva. The tides rushed in and out below it, people fished from its railings, and there was a tiny beach parking lot on the Captiva side, but otherwise it was just a connector, maybe a hundred feet long.

Someone honked their horn, and Deputy Hayes spun to glare at the driver of a bright yellow Land Rover. The car in front had room to move but hadn't crept forward yet, and Mr. Land Rover had taken issue.

"You're not going anywhere!" she barked. "Three feet isn't going to make a difference!"

He glared back at her. Deputy Hayes yanked back the hood of her slicker to make sure he could see her face, see the disapproval written there. The rain soaked her, but she knew she would be soaked through for hours yet, so she did not care. Mr. Land Rover threw up his hands in exasperation, but he did not touch the horn again.

Deputy Hayes marched across the bridge, listening to the static and the voices on her radio. The Sanibel side was not her jurisdiction, but part of her job was to help other law enforcement personnel in need, anywhere in the county, so she approached a spot in the midst of traffic where Sanibel and state police officers had crowded in front of a dented Volkswagen. The VW sat in the parking lot of the little convenience market on the Sanibel side. The car's nose jutted from the parking lot, but it still took her a second to realize that the driver had come out of the little side street past the market and tried to get onto the bridge going the wrong way.

"—no vehicles allowed onto Captiva, sir," one of the Sanibel cops said, shouting to be heard over the storm. "You need to head off island. Get in line. If you stay—"

The driver of the car shouted something in return,

but the wind and rain and the crashing of the waves around the pilings of the bridge drowned him out. Deputy Hayes thought she caught something about his wife, and she picked up her pace. By the time she reached the car, the shouting match had turned fiery.

"You're not listening to me," said the driver, a good-looking bald guy with an accent she couldn't place. Somewhere they spoke Spanish was all Hayes could figure. "My wife is at South Seas Plantation. I have to get her—make sure she's safe!"

The Sanibel cops began making threats. Hayes didn't have time for this. What did they think would happen now? If they dragged him out of the car to arrest him, they didn't have anywhere to put him until the evacuation was complete. And the driver had even less brains—no way would he be able to drive all the way to the resort at the other end of Captiva with cars filling both lanes.

Behind her on the bridge, cars started to honk. Vehicles moved forward a few feet before stopping, then began to move slowly, making actual progress for ten or fifteen seconds before coming to a halt yet again. She could practically feel their frustration.

"Sir," she said, hurrying to join them. "I'm in contact with the folks at South Seas. If you know what unit your wife is in, I'll call them now and make sure they explain the situation to her and put her in a vehicle headed this way. I'm sure one of the employees or another guest would be happy to bring her this far. You can park here in the lot until she arrives. Fair enough?"

The man seemed about to argue, but the horns

blared again and the cars started to roll, and the guy seemed at last to really see how impossible a task he had set for himself.

"Yeah, yeah. That would be perfect. Thanks so much."

The Sanibel cops gave her grateful looks, even nodding. Gary Jensen rolled his eyes at her. Jensen was one of those cops who fetishized his authority and wanted civilians to obey him because of the uniform. He didn't care about logic or feelings, and he no doubt hated her reasonable solution to this problem, but Deputy Hayes didn't care. The problem had been solved.

People were shouting on the Captiva side of the bridge. Someone had snuck up on the dirt shoulder and tried to make a third row, hoping to cut the line to get over the bridge. Fucking assholes. There were always people who thought their needs were more important than the needs of others.

She started jogging back across the bridge. The rain and wind had swallowed the roar of the boat's engine, but now the whine pierced the storm. Halfway across the Blind Pass bridge, Deputy Hayes turned and saw that same boat. Instead of throttling down, if anything it seemed to be moving faster, bouncing atop the waves as it careened toward the bridge.

"What the hell?" she muttered to herself as she cut to her left, running for the railing.

Three guys in the thirty-footer, bearded twenty-something morons risking the storm just to go fishing and now realizing how stupid they'd been. The wind whipped across the bridge, gusting harder. The trees on either side of the pass bent and the rain came down sideways, and these fools had finally realized how fast they needed to get their asses somewhere safe. But at that speed, with the storm surge, the tide had risen so high that they were barely going to make it under the bridge.

When Deputy Hayes spotted the wave, she knew she could erase the *barely*.

"Hey!" she shouted, waving her arms back and forth, trying to get their attention. "Turn around! Slow down, goddammit! Slow down!"

One of them pointed to the gap beneath the bridge, and she knew they hadn't seen her and that the storm had stolen her words. They jetted through the pass and she realized time had run out. Swearing loudly, drowning in the noise of car horns and raging wind and crashing surf, she turned and ran for the Captiva side of the bridge just as the wave swept in behind the boat. The craft lifted, turned sideways, and crashed into the pilings beneath the bridge. Deputy Hayes bent into the wind, pumping her legs, but she heard the whoomp behind her as the boat's fuel tank blew.

The explosion hurled her forward and she struck pavement, rolling, smashing knees and elbows as she slammed into the front tire of some cookie-cutter SUV.

Groaning, swearing, her head throbbing, she stood and turned to stare at the fire that licked up over the side of the bridge. It flared high, the wind blew it across the road, cars rushed forward or jerked into reverse, smashing bumpers to avoid the flames. The fire died down in seconds, but people were climbing out of cars, rushing away from the spot just in case.

Deputy Hughes exhaled. A minivan had been badly scorched, but the family inside was piling out, some of the Sanibel cops rushing from the other side of the pass to escort them.

Then a section of the bridge gave way.

She stared as the southbound side, where the boat must have struck the pilings and the fire had blazed up, collapsed into the storm surge in the pass below. The scorched van and two other cars went with it, the van empty but the cars loaded with passengers whose screams could be heard only on a single gust of wind before the storm swept their voices away.

Behind Deputy Hayes, the driver of a little black convertible laid on his horn.

She turned and stared at him. "Are you kidding me?"

The convertible wasn't getting off Captiva Island before the hurricane hit.

Neither was anyone else.

CHAPTER 5

Broaddus was virtually alone in the Institute. A scientist named Natalia Rocco and her unshaven research assistant were in the overnight quarters, which puzzled Broaddus because the clock hadn't even rolled around to lunchtime. Dr. Rocco, whom everyone called Tali, had holed up in the overnight quarters from the moment they had arrived. Tali and Philip, the unshaven assistant, had volunteered to stay behind because at least one staff scientist had to stay, just in case something went horribly wrong. Broaddus had volunteered, but he was only a security guard, and in the midst of a hurricane there might not be any way to phone someone with the right answers.

He imagined Tali and Philip in the quarters watching television until the storm took out the cable signal and the Wi-Fi, then maybe playing board games. Maybe they would drink a few beers or make a meal.

His stomach rumbled at the thought, but Broaddus had plans that did not involve lunch.

It occurred to him that Tali and Philip might be involved with each other, though that kind of fraternization would be frowned upon amongst the staff. Of course they might have just been close. He knew he should not make such assumptions about people, but now that it had occurred to him, he remembered so many times he had seen the two of them laughing together, and the way Tali would touch Philip's arm, and the times they had stayed late together or arrived for work in tandem.

If they were intimate, that would make things easier for him. They would be that much more distracted if they weren't just hiding out from the hurricane. If they were having sex, riding out the hurricane in each other's arms, they were even less likely to wonder what the one security guard on duty might be up to.

His key card let him into the behavioral lab. The pad beeped and a light turned green and he heard the door unlock. With a deep breath, he pushed through the door and closed it quietly behind him. The lights flickered automatically to life as he moved quickly to the nearest computer terminal. There were a dozen desks in the lab, which looked much more like an office than a laboratory. All of the computer screens were dark, but this one flared to life the moment he tapped the mouse. A password field appeared, blinking, and Broaddus hesitated.

You're crazy, he told himself.

But even here in the lab, he could hear the distant

howl of the storm. He would never get an opportunity like this again, never be so alone in the Institute. Plus he had already swiped his key card to get into the behavioral lab. Someone would notice that and ask him why he had entered, and that line of inquiry might lead to him losing this job.

"Fuck it," he whispered, and he tapped in the override password that only the director of security used. Only the sirector of security was supposed to know it, but Broaddus had seen him use it to access the system seven months ago and knew he kept it written on the back of a takeout menu from the Hungry Heron, stuffed into the bottom drawer in his desk.

The system blinked to life.

His heart tightened in his chest, but he began clicking around immediately, searching for the files he needed. One of them opened a live-feed camera that showed him the shark tank. The sharks were swimming in languid circles, almost floating like manatees, without the sharp air of sinister purpose that other sharks seemed to carry with them. Just the sight saddened him.

"Jesus," he said. "What have these assholes done to you?"

But the question felt empty. Broaddus might not know the nitty-gritty details, but he knew what the Institute had been doing to sharks and he knew why. He had overheard enough, asked enough questions of researchers eager to discuss their work, and dug up enough information in his online research. He knew what they were up to.

Various governments, including Israel, Russia, and the United States, had been using trained dolphins for surveillance and espionage since the 1960s. The Department of Defense, through its Defense Advanced Research Projects Agency, had been doing research into controlling sharks' brains for years. Though the Institute would never admit their government connection or the percentage of their research financed by tax dollars, they had started over a decade before, implanting electrodes into a shark's brain to cause certain neurons to fire at certain times, attempting to elicit certain behavior on command. It should have been ridiculous, the kind of Cold War lunacy that had been left behind in the twentieth century. When Broaddus had gotten one of the researchers to explain it to him, she had asked him to imagine what would happen if they could make a shark's brain think it had smelled blood from a certain direction, when no blood was present. They could make the shark swim in that direction. If they could trigger certain responses, they could make the shark do virtually anything, from following a boat with a camera attached to its body to attacking a small vessel or anyone in the water to killing until the shark itself exploded from eating all it had killed. Broaddus had felt sick, listening to that description. Sick, then furious.

For many years, the Institute had been trying to perfect the process, finding new and better ways to program the firing of those neurons. As far as Broaddus could gather, they had done precisely that with a combination of stem-cell therapy to overgrow the areas of the brain that influenced preferred behavior and a liquid vanadium battery developed by the army at Fort Devens up in Massachusetts.

An old Soviet-era program had once used dolphins to plant explosives on the outside of ships. The Institute's behavioral lab had made sharks that would do that and so much more. They had made sharks that were weapons.

Broaddus hated them for it.

He watched the lethargic sharks drifting in the tank on-screen. The lights flickered—the effects of the hurricane—but he wasn't worried. The Institute's generators would kick in if the power went out.

With the computer's mouse, he clicked around to find the master behavioral control. This was far from the first time he had used the director of security's override password to access these files. He had read most of them, familiarized himself with the program, watched the researchers every moment he could, and eavesdropped, and it had been easy. As much as he liked many of the scientists, in spite of the work they did, to a woman or man they all thought he was stupid.

Maurice Broaddus was anything but stupid.

He checked the aggression levels on the master control. So low. Like a mental hospital keeping its patients drugged and complacent, the Institute kept the sharks calm this way. It was unnatural, hideous, shameful behavior. and it broke his heart.

With a click and drag of the mouse, Broaddus woke the sharks from their stupor, brought them up to their natural aggression levels.

Then he brought up the program that would allow him to open the shark tank. A flooded passage led from the tank to the vast outdoor saltwater pool, which itself was separated from the Gulf by a high seawall. Broaddus had always felt it was cruel to let them swim so close to freedom, but never set them free.

When the door slid open inside the tank, the sharks swam into the passage with startling speed and ferocity, fighting one another to get through and out into the pool.

They were awake now, and angry.

For Rick, the worst part of sitting in the traffic on Captiva Drive came from knowing his boiling frustration would do nothing to speed them along. All of that anxiety, all the fury he was bottling up with every minute they sat unmoving, or even when they rolled forward a few feet, had nowhere to go. He tried to be mindful, like he'd read about in a book Corinne had not-so-subtly given him on her own birthday, but the tension would not leave his body. His hands were tight on the wheel, his shoulder muscles rigid. In the back of his mind, in this calm and rational chamber of his brain, he knew that he and Corinne and their girls were in this together, but his nerves felt so frayed that he was on edge, ready to snap at them with any provocation.

He took a deep breath then let it out.

"You okay?" Corinne asked.

Rick smiled through his teeth. "Not even close. Trying to practice patience, but I'm no expert."

"That's the truth," Emma said, from the back seat.

Kelsey giggled, and the sound made Rick exhale. His smile relaxed, turned genuine, and for a moment he was able to let the tension bleed out.

"I hate to say it," Corinne observed, "but does it seem slower to you? I'm not sure we've moved more than fifty feet in the last ten minutes."

Rick nodded. "I didn't want to mention it."

"You think there's an accident or something?" Kelsey piped up.

"Almost inevitable in a situation like this," Rick told his daughter. "And with a road this narrow, there's hardly any room for emergency vehicles. If someone broke down or had a bad accident, we could be here till Christmas."

Corinne sighed. The girls settled in their seats. Kelsey started humming to herself while Emma tapped away at her cell phone, texting or posting or whatever she did with her friends. Rick glanced at his wife out of the corner of his eye.

"I know," he said. "You don't have to say it."

She frowned. "Say what? I wasn't going to say anything."

"That if we had left yesterday like you wanted, we wouldn't be in this situation."

Corinne gave a small shrug. "Maybe we would have. It doesn't matter now."

He tsked at her, clucking his tongue. "Those words are coming out of your mouth. But I know you."

"Maybe not as well as you think," she replied.

Rick glared at her. "What is that supposed to mean?"

"Just what I said. Look, all we need to do is be patient. The evacuation is mandatory. Everyone's going the same direction and the local authorities are on this. We'll be fine," she said.

He glanced in the rearview mirror. His daughters were quiet, but they were watching and listening. If he had learned anything as a father, it was that children heard everything, so though he wanted to point out that they would not be at all fine if they were still in the car when the hurricane made landfall, he forced himself to stay quiet. Rick had embarrassed himself on the beach yesterday, and he knew the girls must have been mortified. He felt as if he had done nothing but screw up again and again for a while now, and he figured the rest of his family must be as sick of it as he was. He did not have a lot of practice keeping his thoughts to himself, but he wanted to learn.

"Driving game?" he asked. "To pass the time?"

"Yeah. Ask me movie trivia," Emma said. "But it has to be something I've seen."

"Me too!" Kelsey chimed in.

"You've barely seen any movies," her sister argued. "You're too little."

That set off a chain reaction argument that made Rick roll his eyes. He glanced at Corinne, who smiled knowingly and patted him on the leg.

"A valiant effort, though," she said.

For a moment, he exhaled and all was well between them. Even the traffic did not seem to matter in those few seconds.

Then he saw the first car headed the opposite direction, back the way they'd come.

"What the hell? They're going back."

"Maybe it's an emergency," Corinne said. "It must be. They forgot medication, or maybe a family member who needed to get out. Something—"

"Or maybe they've just decided that it would be smarter to be back at the house prepping the place for the hurricane than sitting on the road waiting for the storm surge to sweep us all into the Gulf."

As if in answer to his words, another car went by, followed by a minivan. He craned his neck and saw another vehicle following.

"They don't all have emergencies," he said. His fingers opened and closed on the steering wheel as he weighed his options. After a moment, he put his turn signal on and began to pull out of traffic.

"What are you doing?" Corinne asked. "Don't be crazy. We're not starting at the back of the line."

"Dad?" Emma said, in that teenage girl tone that suggested he was out of his mind.

The car in front of them and the one behind them— the Hautalas' rental—were too close for him to pull a U-turn, so he waited, watching the oncoming lane and glancing ahead and behind. He mentally urged the car ahead of him to creep forward to give him space. He figured the Hautalas could decide for themselves what to do next.

"Rick, I'm serious," Corinne said. "Do not turn around."

That command triggered something in him. He glanced at her sharply, and when he spoke, he had no love in his voice and even less humor. "Don't tell me what to do. Are you blind? Can you not see we're not making any progress? We're better off going back to the house. If it's this bad here, it's probably this bad all the way through Sanibel and over the causeway. We'll end up running out of gas, because you know the gas stations will run out. No trucks will be delivering."

Corinne stared at him with a coldness that equaled his own. "And if it's just an accident? If some truck crashed and is blocking the road?"

"Then all of this would go much faster, but how likely is that, Corinne? They'd have a lane moving around it. Just sitting here is not making our girls any safer!"

"Neither is staying on an island a few inches above sea level during a hurricane!" she screamed. "Don't you turn this car around!"

"Goddammit, Corinne—"

Behind him, Kelsey began kicking the back of his seat. She screamed at them. "Stop it, stop it, stop it!"

When Rick glanced in the rearview mirror, he saw that both of his girls were crying. Emma had taken Kelsey's hand.

"You guys," Emma said quietly, "you're scaring her. You're scaring me, too. Just make a decision and we'll do the best we can."

The car ahead of them rolled forward five feet, but Rick could see that this was no real development, probably just a consequence of those cars leaving the evacuation line. He exhaled but it did not help relieve the tension that ratcheted through him.

"Dad?" Kelsey asked gently, as if afraid he would shout at her, too. It broke his heart the way she said his name.

"We're okay," he said, a pang of guilt in his heart. He glanced at Corinne. "We're okay."

Silence descended amongst them, so overwhelming that the hip-hop thumping from a car several vehicles behind them became loud enough to induce headaches.

"So . . ." he began.

Then he saw another car pass by going in the opposite direction, driven by a familiar face. "Did you see that? The car that just went by—that Simone girl was driving. Our neighbors have turned around and are going back."

"They're college kids," Corinne said. "They may be smart, but nobody ever claimed college kids had a good sense of self-preservation."

The rain pelted the roof and the wind rocked the car. Up ahead, people started laying on their horns, more aggravated than ever now that the creeping traffic had essentially come to a standstill. Rick glanced in the rearview mirror and could barely make out the silhouette of Matti Hautala at the wheel of the car behind him.

Rick clicked on his turn signal again. He glanced into the oncoming lane and saw headlights cutting through the rain, but still a distance away. When the car ahead of him rolled forward a foot or two, he pulled out of line and did a U-turn.

Corinne muttered some bit of profanity. In the back seat, Kelsey whispered that she was scared, but Rick could comfort her later. He rolled down his window and saw that Matti already had his down.

"Man, what are you doing?" Matti called to him, his voice almost swallowed by the wind.

"Going back to the house," Rick said. "Something's gone wrong up there. You want to park here and wait to drown, be my guest."

He rolled up his window and hit the gas, glad to just be moving for the first time in hours.

"You really are an asshole," Corinne said quietly.

Rick shot her a dark look. "The girls," he reminded her.

Corinne looked out at the rain. "Oh, the girls already know."

He glanced into the back seat again, but his daughters—like their mother—were watching the rain.

The beach felt otherworldly. Rashad moved quickly across the sand, glad for the raincoat that Nadia had loaned him. The wind had gained so much strength that an umbrella's life would have been marked in minutes out there on the Gulf. The sky had turned a mélange of deep orange, bruise purple, and charcoal gray that grew blacker and blacker out to sea. Enormous waves crashed on the shore, gobbling up chunks of beach that high tide alone could not have touched.

And this is just the beginning, Rashad thought uneasily.

There on this strange, alien landscape in the driving rain, he began to second-guess turning around. But that was the point of this lunatic, soaking wet stroll, after all. To see if they had made the right call, and to find out what the hell was going on. Rashad figured there would be some kind of emergency personnel on the road, someone with answers.

"Slow down!" a voice called.

Rashad looked back to see Tyler and Kevin, hand in hand, hurrying to catch up. Kevin could be arrogant and Tyler never managed to be as funny as he thought he was, but Rashad enjoyed being with the two of them when they were together. They soothed each other, smoothing their edges, and it was sweet to see.

"Me slow down?" he called through the wind and rain. "You guys hurry up!"

They did, running after him, laughing as if there was no hurricane bearing down on them and all of this would blow over.

Blow over, he thought. That was the problem, wasn't it? Looking at the trees bending in the wind, feeling the way each gust seemed to want to pick him up by his flapping rain coat and carry him off like Piglet in that Winnie the Pooh cartoon, he worried that every house and tree might just blow over.

"You sure you have a cell signal?" Kevin asked, as he and Tyler came right up behind Rashad. "I've got nothing. I don't want to walk all the way down to Blind Pass if we can't even call them to tell them what happened."

"Me either," Rashad said. "But yes, I have a signal."

Tyler laughed, turning his face up to the rain. "This is crazy. We should have just gotten out of the cars and walked. We were halfway there already."

Rashad didn't argue. He was right. They should have walked when they were closer, but they had not come up with the idea until they had already arrived back at their rented house in Sunset Captiva.

"We should at least walk on the road," he said. "Otherwise it'll take forever."

"This is like a dream, though, isn't it?" Tyler said.

"You're a romantic, Ty," Kevin replied, "but save it for after the storm."

With Tyler's reluctant acquiescence, the three of them cut over to the road not far from the Tween Waters Inn. The line of cars seemed to have stopped cold. Some people had even turned their engines off, conserving gas for when they could drive again. More and more cars were headed the other direction. Rashad flagged down a BMW and tried to ask the woman behind the wheel what was going on, but she said she didn't know in a tone so dismissive he actually flinched.

The rain kept falling and the wind picked up. Branches fell. A coconut thumped to the ground on the roadside. A few people called them crazy, taking the time to roll down their windows just to share that thought, but they kept walking. Rashad could be stubborn like that, and he knew it, but eventually they made it all the way to Blind Pass, where cars were jammed into the little beach parking lot and a single police car—a Lee County sheriff's vehicle—sat amongst them, emergency lights flashing. With the rain and the gloom, the sky had grown so dark it might as well have been night, so it was only when they were at the edge of the Blind Pass bridge and a sheriff's deputy—the same one who had come to the house the night before—shouted and started to wave them off, that Rashad realized that part of the bridge had broken away.

"Holy shit," he muttered.

Kevin wasn't so quiet. "What the fuck is this?" he shouted at the deputy. "What are you doing?"

The woman—Deputy Hayes, Rashad remembered—looked at him as if he were crazy. "Trying to keep people alive. What are *you* doing, coming out here on foot? Get back in your car or go down to the beach and wait for the fishermen to ferry you across."

Rashad frowned, wiping rain from his eyes. The sound of the wind whipping the hood of Nadia's raincoat around his head seemed to grow louder as he tried to make sense of what the deputy had said.

"We came from the house we rented," Tyler explained to her. "We walked."

Rashad dropped out of the conversation. He walked back toward the line of cars, then to the edge of the road. To his right, people were massing in the parking lot, in amongst the cars that were jammed there. They were going over the edge of the lot, down the incline to the beach, almost lost to view in the storm. Rashad glanced back across the bridge and saw the police cars and an ambulance there, saw the line of people stringing up from the seawall, and abruptly he understood.

The waves were massive, crushing things that

smashed through Blind Pass every ten seconds, but there were two fishing boats in the water and their crews were risking their lives and livelihood to help people get off Captiva. The inlet gap might have been only a hundred feet, but as Rashad watched, it seemed an impossible distance. The captains of those boats were taking turns blasting their vessels into the oncoming waves, unloading passengers on the Sanibel side, and then coming back to load up again. People were hanging on for dear life. Water crashed over the sides and onto the decks. Those who were fleeing had to hold ropes and jump into the shallows while waves battered them and people on shore helped drag them to land.

Rashad turned and strode back to Deputy Hayes. "This is insane. You'll never get everyone off the island."

"You think they don't know that?" she called, raising her voice against the wind.

"It's so dangerous," Rashad said. "Someone's going to drown any minute now. You've got to stop them."

Deputy Hayes glared at him. "I've been out here all day, kid. Accident took out part of the bridge maybe an hour ago and the fishermen started in on this immediately. They know the risk. No helicopter is going to fly in this and there's no other way off the island."

Tyler had gotten a look at the ferrying operation now, and he turned to her as well. "How long can they keep this up?"

"I've been telling them to call it off since ten minutes after they started," Hayes said. "But the people keep coming, abandoning their cars on the road."

Rashad thought about calling the others. His cell phone felt suddenly much heavier in his pocket.

Kevin came up beside him. "Even if we got across," he said, "we'd have no car and no luggage. Where would we go?"

Hayes overheard. "You'd be shuttled to a hotel on the mainland. The traffic on Sanibel's bumper to bumper, too, but the causeway isn't collapsing any time soon, so you'd still get off."

Rashad took out his phone. Even as he did, he glanced back down into Blind Pass and watched one of the fishing boats nearly capsize. It crested the wave and made it across, but only barely. Some of the people in the parking lot cried out in alarm and then there was much nervous chatter before some of them turned and went the other way, down onto the beach or back to the road, where they started a trek in the direction of whatever accommodations they'd had the night before.

He glanced at his phone. One bar. He might get through or he might not, but how long would it take the others to get here? Would the fishermen still be running ferry service by then? He thought not.

Most of the houses on Captiva had been built on stilts for just this situation. With luck, the structures on the island would survive. A lot of trees would come down. The water might cover a lot of the land, but their rental house would still be standing when it was over. He hoped.

"Tyler, Kevin, let's go," he said. "We're gonna ride it out."

Deputy Hayes started trying to talk them out of it. "You should get out of here while you still can."

Rashad looked at her. "So should you."

Neither of them had anything more to say. Rashad watched as Kevin reached out to take Tyler's hand again, and then the three of them started back along the street, picking up their pace, not speaking about the danger of the hurricane closing in.

Closing in? Rashad thought, as the rain pelted him and the wind tried to push him into a car. *It's already here.*

Corinne Scully had always loved folklore and legends from around the world. She loved all the monsters and gods of mythology, but some lingered in her mind more than others. Of late her thoughts had returned again and again to the story of Perseus attempting to slay the Gorgon Medusa, she with the nest of snakes where her hair ought to have been. The snakes were so spectacular that they seemed all most people focused on when it came to Medusa, and Corinne agreed it was a great visual. But it caused people to skirt over the other major element of Medusa's myth— that she could turn a man to stone with nothing but a glance.

My kind of woman, Corinne thought, not for the first time.

She stood just inside the sliding glass door that led

out to the second-floor balcony at the back of their rented house. Rick had popped the lock on the maintenance closet downstairs and found a fat roll of duct tape, and she'd been crisscrossing the windows with it ever since. The phone had rung shortly after they had returned to the house, a call from the property management company that looked after the place. The woman on the line had seemed surprised to find them at home, said they were calling to encourage any stragglers to depart, that the property management team had been trying to get to all of the houses to board up the Gulf-facing windows but that they had only finished half of the Sunset Captiva homes before the bridge over Blind Pass had gone out, cutting them off from a resupply truck. The staff was taking shelter at their Captiva office—yes, on the second floor, the woman had said.

Corinne had asked the woman if she thought they would be safe in the house.

Depends on the storm, doesn't it? the woman had replied.

The words haunted her now, and Corinne stood at the slider with the roll of duct tape in her hand and stared out through the curtain of rain. Several trees were already down. One lay diagonally across the screen porch of the house next door, and she hoped the spring-breakers were okay. They were irritating, those college kids, but they seemed decent enough in spite of it. She had zero interest in turning any of them to stone.

Her husband, on the other hand . . .

She loved Rick, but he had been making it progressively more difficult for a long time. Corinne had always believed that a marriage was the place you came home to, the place you laid bare your soul and shared your troubles, lightening the burdens of the world. Once, she had thought her husband believed the same, but little by little he had shut her out. Her theory was that Rick wanted to insulate her and the girls, to protect them from his anxieties and fears, but although she had tried to disabuse him of the notion, somehow he still failed to see the damage his philosophy had done. Was doing. The more he shut her out, the more frayed his nerves became, and the less interested she was in soothing them.

He's a prick, she thought. *Don't make him a victim.*

The urge to write him off had been growing in her for a while, but though her bruised ego and wounded heart wanted to keep it simple, she knew it was anything but. The man she had married had never been the sort to alienate his wife and children. He needed therapy, probably medication, and he sure as hell needed an attitude adjustment. The only real question that remained for her was whether or not she would still be married to him by the time he realized just how badly he had fucked it all up.

"Hey," Rick said, stepping into the bedroom, rapping softly on the door.

Corinne wanted to turn around, but she couldn't. Her hand gripped the roll of duct tape—she hadn't taped off the sliding glass door in their room yet and it needed to be done. The door shook, the glass seemed to flex, as if it might explode inward at any second. The wind howled outside. The whole house shook, bending away from the wind.

She thought about Perseus and Medusa. How many men had Medusa turned to stone with her gaze? Surely hundreds, at the very least. But then Perseus had come along with his shield and used it to reflect her own gaze back at her, and then it was Medusa who turned to stone, frozen forever.

Corinne had been a proud woman, strong and confident. She had dealt with the same abhorrent behavior by men that most other women encountered. Creepy colleagues, roaming hands, inappropriate comments, veiled threats, microaggressions. For most of her life, she had turned those men to stone with a glance, and she'd done it to her own husband many times. But out in the car today, the way Rick had behaved, she had felt as if Perseus had reflected her gaze back at her, and she had been the one frozen, turned to stone.

"You shouldn't be so close to the glass," Rick said, with an apology in his voice that she'd heard so many times. Not the words, just the tone.

Corinne remained stone. Though only late afternoon, it had gone dark as night outside. The rain swept across the sliding glass door, and as she stared at her reflection in that dark glass, she could see Rick behind her, standing just inside the bedroom, barely over the threshold. The weight of their argument remained, as if their marriage had been holding its breath ever since.

"Honey," he said. "You okay?"

She smiled at the audacity. "No," she said, proving a stone statue could speak. "Of course I'm not okay."

Her own voice seemed to reverse Medusa's curse, and she picked up the roll of tape and began to drag it across the glass, laying down a diagonal strip that sliced across the top half of the door. She completed the X, then started to make another one on the bottom half of the glass.

"Corinne."

On one knee, she turned to look at him. Wondering who he was. Who they had become, these two married people with their beautiful daughters, who didn't deserve any of this.

"I know you're angry," he said.

She wrinkled her brow, calling out the idiocy of the statement without saying a word.

Rick held up both hands. "Okay. I know. You have every right to be. I've got a lot of shit to work out. I feel like my thoughts are all tangled up, like crossed wires. Fucking power lines, on the ground, exposed, ready to electrocute me with the wrong step."

She refused to smile, just kept her face blank. "Were you always such a drama queen?"

"Pretty much."

"Look, now's not the time," Corinne said.

"I know. That's what I'm saying. I'm sorry, and I'm going to make my apologies to the girls, too. But right now they're afraid—"

"*I'm* afraid."

Rick nodded. "Me too. We'll be okay—I believe

that—but it's a scary scenario. We're all watching the news downstairs and it's a category three right now but they're thinking just before it really hits, it could die down to a category two, maybe even one. That's just a couple of hours from now. But . . ."

Corinne stared out at the storm, the sky so dark that she couldn't even see the raging Gulf beyond the trees. "Jesus," she whispered.

Rick came up behind her. He rested a hand on her hip, familiar but not intimate, connected to her as he always would be.

"I was just hoping we could call a truce for now, and work this out after the storm."

She looked at him in the glass, despite the slash of silver duct tape across the reflection of his face. "We *will* work it out."

"Absolutely."

I still want to turn you to stone, she thought, but it seemed like a less-than-productive thing to say out loud.

With a soft pop, the lights went out. Downstairs, where the girls were gathered at the television with the Hautalas, voices lifted in alarm and protest.

"Shit," Corinne said. "So much for watching the weatherman. Or anything else."

"We have our phones until the batteries die," Rick replied. "But this is probably for the best. It's time to choose the safest room and batten down the hatches."

He offered his hand. Corinne stared at it for a moment before accepting it, and they clasped fingers. Rick gave her half a hug and a kiss on the corner of her mouth, and that was all right. At the moment, it was the only thing she wanted from him.

When the storm had passed, she would decide what came next.

CHAPTER 6

———

Lennox knew he had waited too long. His boat bobbed beside the dock, tied to the pilings and smashing against the weighted rubber fenders that dangled both from his boat and from the dock itself. Too long, yes, but as he hurried down the dock, he could not muster up any regret. He dragged a rolling duffel behind him, but the real prize from this house—the third one he'd hit—was in a gym bag over his shoulder. Inside the bag, wrapped in two of the softest, most luxurious towels he had ever touched, was a vase that a quick Google search on his phone suggested might be worth about ten thousand dollars. Googling the thing on his phone had perhaps not been his smartest hour, but it would hurt him only if the police knew to question him in the first place.

The vase wasn't the only thing. The jewelry from

this third house had been a breathtaking haul. The
Marchand family hailed from France, and he figured
they had to have descended from nobility or something—or at least corporate nobility—because Mrs.
Marchand's jewelry box had yielded diamond ear-
rings, bracelets, and more, along with other items that
added up to tens of thousands of dollars. One ruby
necklace—discovered inside a safe that had been absurdly easy to pry open—had to be worth at least twice
as much as the vase.

Three houses. Once the power had gone out, it had
been so simple. The most difficult part of his life of
crime thus far had been selecting the homes to rob.
The movie memorabilia from the German director's
house would be hard to hock without getting caught,
but maybe he would just hang onto Alvart's collection.
Once he sold the jewelry and other valuables he had
gathered at the three homes, he wouldn't have to work
for a couple of years, at least. Of course he would have
to stay away from Captiva for a while, but there were
a thousand tropical places where he might hole up on
his ill-gotten gains. Saint Lucia would be beautiful any
time of year, and he could vanish there.

Lennox ignored the rain, but the wind gave him no
option. As he walked down the dock, he bent against
its power, leaning into it. A gust struck him so hard
that he tumbled sideways, the shoulder bag swinging,
the rolling duffel tugged from his grasp.

He shouted in panic as he fell, slipping, and managed to grab hold of one of the pilings. A soaking wet
rope tied around the post gave him some traction, and

he managed to stay on the dock as he watched the rolling duffel blow right off into the sound, sinking instantly into the waves that crashed against the dock.

"Son of a bitch!" he shouted, squinting against the rain.

A stream of profanity followed, but with the wind stealing his breath and the rain pelting him, his fury ran out of steam quickly. The things he'd stolen from the Alvart place and the home of a New York investor were worth enough, and the items in the overnight bag across his shoulder were the most valuable he'd found in the Marchand house.

"Don't get greedy," he told himself through gritted teeth, and then he laughed. His life had gone to shit. The people he had just stolen from were greedy. All he had been doing was taking crumbs from their table, getting a little justice from a world that wouldn't dole it out willingly.

He held onto the post and glanced at his boat. Waves were crashing against it, splashing onto the deck, high enough to swamp a lesser seaman. If the sea was this rough over here, with the island blocking the worst of the storm, he could only imagine how bad it must be on the Gulf side of Captiva.

Time to get to shelter.

Past time, really.

Waiting for a lull between waves, Lennox rushed along the dock and climbed aboard his boat, hoisting the remaining rolling duffel bag behind him. The wind blasted him, but he braced himself against it and dragged the bag into the wheelhouse. He set it down along with the overnight bag he had stolen, the latter of which he took great care not to jostle too hard.

Back on the deck, he again waited for a lull and then he cast off from the dock. His heart hammered in his chest. Hot rain plastered his hair to his scalp and soaked through his clothing, but all he could think about now was gunning his boat across the sound. On the deck, he took one last glance at Captiva and saw something that made his breath catch in his throat. Half a foot of water came flowing around the home he'd just robbed, cascading across the carefully manicured lawn and spilling off the edge of the property into the sound. Captiva had begun to flood. The Gulf of Mexico was washing across the island.

Lennox had stayed out too long.

A wave lifted his boat and smashed it against the dock. Only the bumpers saved the craft from being shattered there, as he hung on for his life. As the wave passed and the boat dipped into a trough, he bolted for the wheelhouse and fired up the engine. The boat tilted to starboard, slamming into the dock again, and he heard a crack that he prayed was only the fiberglass ridge along the deck.

He spun the wheel, aiming directly into the next wave, and throttled up hard. The boat speared through the wave as he rocketed away from the dock. Lennox cranked the vessel around and headed for Buck Key at top speed, the engine roaring and choking as he forced it over the waves. His chest ached and his knuckles hurt from the grip he held on the wheel and the throttle. Once a wave caught him sidelong and he thought he'd capsize, but the boat seemed to fly in that moment; and when it slammed into a trough, he saw the opening into Buck Key and aimed for it.

Lennox roared into Buck Key with the hurricane at his back, the boat propelled forward by the tidal surge. All around him, the mangrove trees were swamped, but the thick tangle of the woods blocked the worst of the wind, and he navigated back to the spot in Braynerd Bayou that he had chosen that morning. There were half a dozen other boats taking shelter there, but he saw nobody on deck. The owners and captains had moored their vessels and left them, heading back to safer havens, which suited Lennox just fine. No witnesses to his late arrival.

Of course it also meant that he would have to ride out the hurricane right here on his boat, in what shelter Buck Key provided. But when the storm passed, if he and his boat were still above water, his life would have changed forever.

All he had to do was wait, and try not to sink.

Deputy Hayes sat in her patrol vehicle and stared out at the storm. The engine hummed and the wipers squealed across the windshield, but she could barely hear them over the wind. Even the rain pummeling the roof became background noise as the wind tugged at the car, rocking it back and forth. The emergency lights flashed blue ghosts all around her, transforming the road into a haunted place, which seemed only right to her. People had died today. If they were lucky, perhaps there would be no additional fatalities, but she had no doubt there would be others who would be foolish or unlucky in this storm, someone she ought to have evacuated earlier . . . like the thousands who even now were hunkered down on Captiva, waiting.

Her police radio squawked, the burst of static cutting through the wail of the storm.

"Deputy Hayes, this is Sheriff's Official, please respond."

She glanced at the radio, then sighed as she picked it up. "This is Hayes."

"Hang on, Deputy," said the voice on the other line, the words tinny and hollow amidst the din.

A moment later, another voice came on. "Where are you, Agnes?"

She'd know that voice anywhere. Arturo Reyes had been Lee County Sheriff for only two years, but he had been in the department for nearly twenty. Even now, there in the dark with the blue ghosts spinning around her in the storm, she could picture his stern, craggy face and his kind eyes. He had been hard on her over the years, but they had developed a bond of trust that she found difficult to describe. Other people might say Sheriff Reyes had become a father figure to her, but Agnes disliked the idea of father figures. Her own father had been a garbage human being. Just because she had met an older man who had been kind and wise and set an example for her—who had expectations for her—that didn't make him a father figure. It made him decent.

Under oath, though, she would have had to admit that sometimes Sheriff Reyes acted as if he were a father. Now, for instance, with that admonishing tone. She glanced out across the parking lot at Blind Pass, jammed with cars that had been abandoned by the people who had made it across the pass before the fishermen had given up their efforts as too dangerous. That had been hours ago. Now waves crashed into the parking lot and swamped the cars. One Prius near the edge of the lot had already been swept over the edge, tumbled down the rocks, and carried through into Pine Island sound. If the storm surge rose any further, more would follow.

In the glow of her headlights, water washed across the road.

"Dammit, Agnes, are you listening? Are you there?" His voice held a tinge of worry, and she felt suddenly guilty for causing it.

"I'm here, Sheriff."

"Where's here?"

"Blind Pass. Just making sure nobody else tries to make it across. I turned two cars away in the past half hour, people finally realizing how dangerous it is on the island and trying to make a run for it now."

Sheriff Reyes swore loudly. "What is wrong with these folks? Every news station has reported that the bridge is closed."

"Power's out, Artie." She smiled to herself, knowing how much it grated on his nerves when she used his first name over the radio. "Some folks didn't try to leave when it went to mandatory evac. Now they're scared. Storm surge is on the streets and they're panicking."

Static blasted through the radio and she flinched at the sound. She could practically hear Reyes thinking.

"You need to take shelter now, Deputy," he said. "Water's still rising. I'm not risking one of my deputies for anyone stupid enough to make a run for it now. Get somewhere safe."

The storm screamed around her, almost as if it were laughing at the suggestion that anywhere might be safe. She wondered if there was anyplace on Captiva that might fit that description.

"Will do, Sheriff," she said. "I'll check in when I'm stationary."

He replied, but the words were lost in the roar of a wave that crashed into what remained of the Blind Pass bridge. Water smashed down onto the parking lot, swept cars into one collision after another, setting off shrieking alarms. The remains of the bridge buckled outward and then simply collapsed in relative silence, slabs tumbling into the water and washing away.

Deputy Hayes flinched as if she'd been slapped awake. Heart racing, she threw the car into Drive, skidded into a U-turn—tires sending up their own waves from the water on the street—and started back down Captiva Drive. The wind buffeted her vehicle. Branches littered the road—long since vacated by the cars that had waited in vain to escape the island. It had taken her hours to get them all turned and headed back to find shelter.

A coconut thumped the hood, dented it, then struck

the windshield and bounced up over the roof as she drove. Her lips moved, and Deputy Hayes realized that she had begun to pray. Ahead of her, a pair of trees had fallen across the road, one atop the other like lovers in a last embrace. She jerked the steering wheel to the left, went off the road into the brush at the front of some millionaire's property, took out the flamingo mailbox—and then a wave came flooding across the driveway. Debris rolled in the wave and it swept up bushes as it came onward. Deputy Hayes cut the wheel to the right and hit the gas. The wave hit the car broadside, lifting it, turning it, and she cried out with her hands locked onto the steering wheel.

The car was swept across the road, thrown hard against the trees on the other side. Both passenger windows shattered and cracks spider-webbed the windshield. Deputy Hayes screamed something that wasn't a prayer at all, but a cry of anguish.

The wave subsided enough that her wheels touched the ground, some on pavement and some on dirt and grass. The engine coughed but continued to run. Her headlights picked out another brightly painted mailbox, this one on the right side of the road. She hit the gas, drove fifty feet through water that had to be halfway up her tires, and turned into a driveway also partly underwater.

All sound went silent. She had blocked it out. Even her vision narrowed, so that all she could see was the dark silhouette of the house at the end of the driveway and the screened lanais, which she knew must contain a swimming pool. Deputy Hayes drove, knowing there must be better choices but aware that all of those had now been taken from her. The driveway curved and dipped, and for a few seconds the car sank and slewed sideways, but momentum carried it forward and then she found herself skidding to a halt in front of the house.

She flung the door open, slammed it shut, and ran for the front steps through water already nearly knee deep. A smaller wave rolled into her from behind, knocked her off her feet, and washed her up against the front steps. With a wild laugh, she ran up the stairs, tried the front door, and began knocking urgently when she found it locked.

Nobody answered.

Just her luck. These people had been smart enough to leave.

Deputy Hayes then broke and entered. She kicked the door in, shielding her eyes from the splintering wood of the frame. Inside, she dragged a heavy chair up against the door to keep the wind from blowing it open, due to the damage she'd just done to the lock.

She sunk into the chair, head against the door, soaked to the skin, hair full of shards of safety glass. Her heart kept pounding hard and fast, and she waited for it to slow down, waited for her breathing to even out.

At last, the wind screaming outside, she rose and went to the back of the house, stood and looked out at the trees and bushes in the backyard, at the dock there, and at the sound beyond. The water raged, waves crashing in all directions, as if the sea had come alive with rage, and she thought of the ancient stories about the rage of the gods. For the first time, she understood them.

With luck, she thought, she would be safe here until the hurricane blew over.

But she feared for what Captiva Island would look like then.

Broaddus knew right away that he had made a mistake. The trouble was that he didn't know how to fix it. From the outset, his plan had been to set the sharks free. He had known that the Institute would eventually be able to round them all up, but had intended to send anonymous emails to local and national reporters. There were all kinds of things the Institute could hide while the sharks were inside their walls, but if they were out in the Gulf with a bunch of marine biologists tracking them, an enterprising journalist could get great video of that. Add in the military research contracts and the information he would include in his emails, and he knew he would do lasting damage to their Frankensteinian efforts here.

But he'd screwed it all up.

With the hurricane blasting in from the Gulf, an umbrella would have been ridiculous, so he went out to the shark pool in his raincoat and bent against the wind. Hurrying, cursing his own stupidity, he fought his way through the storm and stood at the edge of the pool. The moment he had opened the tunnel for the sharks, the underwater lights had blazed on, so despite the rain and the chop on the surface of the water, he could see the sharks perfectly fine.

They were trying to kill one another.

"Goddammit!" he roared, turning away from the wind, shouting at the sky but really screaming at himself. "You stupid son of a bitch!"

The researchers had implanted the triggers inside the sharks' brains and built the computer program that controlled them. Maurice Broaddus recognized his own intelligence—he knew he was smart—but he wasn't a marine biologist and he wasn't a computer programmer. He had learned the application as best he could, thought he'd understood; but he had not anticipated needing to use that knowledge. When he had opened the tunnel and the sharks were too passive to swim through, he had amplified their aggression a little.

Except it turned out that either the program had malfunctioned, or he had—and he knew which was more likely.

"Shiiiiiiiit!" he screamed into the storm, shaking his fists in frustration.

Broaddus turned and stared into the pool. Blood fogged around one of the sharks and the others twisted toward it, knifed through the water, and attacked, tearing enormous chunks of its flesh away.

"No," he said to himself, so quietly the wind stole the word from his lips.

Frozen in indecision, he could only watch the shark die. He glanced toward the still-open tunnel they'd come through, and then at the seawall at the far end of the pool. The underwater lights showed the large steel panel that was phase one of a three-phase mechanism that would open the pool to the Gulf so that anything in the pool could swim out. It had been designed to bring sea creatures in, and occasionally to set one free, certainly not with any intention that anyone might one day start a mass exodus of their test subjects. But it would work, he was sure of that.

Or it would have, if only he could have used it.

A huge wave smashed over the seawall, as if the Gulf had flowed right in. A piece of the Institute's dock tumbled in the water, blasting across the deck toward Broaddus. He turned to flee and the water struck him from behind, took his legs out from under him, and slammed him on his back on the concrete as the wave subsided around him. With the wind tearing at him, he sputtered rain and sea from his lips as he wiped his face and stumbled to his feet. Whipping around, he wondered why the dock hadn't killed him, then saw that it had caught in the pool. As the wave spread— most of it caught inside the seawall—the broken dock settled into the pool with the sharks.

Another wave smashed the seawall, pouring over the top, but smaller this time.

A gust of wind blasted at him and Broaddus bent into it, jacket flapping around him. He fought it, but another blast knocked him backward and he lost his footing, hit the ground, and rolled several times before he managed to get onto his hands and knees. Behind him, the door to the Institute beckoned. He was soaked through, but there would be a dry sweatshirt at least in his locker. He could change, go out to his car, and leave forever. Put Sanibel and the sharks in his rearview mirror.

But there were the sharks. They suffered. They had been turned into weapons, and now he had made it worse for them. Struggling to his feet, Broaddus looked again at the tunnel, but as long as their aggression remained amplified, they would be hyper-aggressive and there would be no way to force them back through that tunnel and into their tanks without making them docile again. Broaddus did not have the first clue how to accomplish that.

Idiot, he thought. *Of course you do.*

The wind shrieked and he shouted in frustration at the power of it, the way it fought against him as he moved to the pool again. The sharks were still eating the first one to bleed, but as he looked on they began to nip at one another, to dart and bite, and he knew more would die and it would be his fault.

The researchers had to be able to control their aggression levels remotely. They didn't have to be in their tanks to be triggered to behave a certain way, or turn a certain direction, because that behavior would be useless to the military without a way to control it in the field. Broaddus didn't know if he could figure it out before they all killed one another, but he owed it to them to try.

Son of a bitch, he thought. He would regret this night for the rest of his life.

He turned toward the building just as the generator failed and the building went dark. The underwater pool lights went out with an audible pop. Night was still hours away, but the storm was so dark that it might as well have been midnight.

Broaddus wanted to run. What he'd done might not be able to be fixed. He had to try, but already he knew that if it didn't work, he would just have to leave the sharks as they were and get out of there, hide on the island until the storm subsided, and then get the fuck away from Sanibel, away from Florida entirely. He sure as hell couldn't release the sharks out into the Gulf with their aggression amplified like this.

As he started toward the building, another wave crashed the seawall, the biggest yet. It poured over the top and raged across the property, swamping the pool deck. Broaddus met it head-on, let it carry him backward toward the door, but this time there was too much water. He kicked his feet, paddled with his hands, fought the churning white surf, reached his shoes down to try to get purchase on the concrete as the wave began to draw back, pulling him with it. Broaddus fought, tried to swim, and as the wave lost its power he finally managed to stop himself from being swept away. His shoes dragged on the concrete and he stood up, fighting the water.

He shifted his right foot and found nothing beneath it. The world fell away. The wind rocked him and he pinwheeled his arms. As he fell, he saw the pool, saw the sharks and the blood in the water that told him at least one more had already been torn apart. Then he plunged beneath the surface and he tasted the salt water as it jetted up his nose.

His heart thundered in his chest, thrummed in his head. Terror became a scream for which he could find no voice. He swam, broke the surface, and whipped around in the water in search of the nearest pool edge. Blood fogged the water twenty feet away. Sharks tore at dead flesh in a frenzy. Fins slashed the water all over the pool, but he saw his opening, off to his left, clear swimming to the pool's edge only a dozen feet from him.

The next wave shattered the seawall.

Broaddus managed a scream as he saw the massive wall of water pouring toward him, carrying tons of concrete and granite his way. Something pounded his chest, crushed his ribs, pushed all the air out of his lungs just as the wave dragged him under. Unable to breathe, pain burning his every thought, he managed to surface.

Hanging in the water, he saw fins headed toward the opening in the seawall. *No*, he thought, and then *Yes*, because if they all left the pool, he might still live.

Slowly, in agonizing pain, he began to swim one-handed toward the edge of the pool. But then the undertow grabbed him and hauled him toward the broken wall, toward open water.

Just as he began to surrender, the pain too much for him to fight his fate, he saw the shark—saw its black eyes as it surfaced. He prayed it would be quick, that it might kill him so mercifully fast that the pain would be over swiftly. But the shark had no gods, did not understand prayers. It took his left arm first, as both were swept out into the Gulf. And then the others smelled his blood and came to rip and tear and fight for their share.

In the end, a final, errant, lunatic thought shot through his mind. In a way, he had been successful.

The sharks were free.

CHAPTER 7

———

By morning of the next day, the cleanup had begun.

Jenn Hautala sat on a beach chair with an iced coffee half-buried in the sand beside her and watched the island start to come back to life. It felt surreal, the most unearthly hours she had ever experienced. The worst of the hurricane had passed through by early evening, and by midnight it could have been any ordinary storm. Sunrise had given them an angry pink sky striated with dark, lingering cloud fingers. Now, with the morning halfway over, the humidity kept the sky opaque but the wind had returned to its ordinary Gulf breeze.

The island did not recover so easily. Trees were down everywhere. Most of the homes and buildings had damage from the wind and rain and the storm surge. The wind had torn the storm door off their porch, and a piece of debris had broken a taillight and dented the side of their rental car. The spring-breakers next door had more significant house damage—their Gulf-facing porch had been obliterated by a falling tree—but nothing that would endanger them now, as long as they used the front door.

Chainsaws growled in the trees and echoed from other spots across the island. Jenn could hear hammers banging nails and voices shouting to one another as people came together to begin repairs. In Sunset Captiva, she had seen a crew already sweeping up broken glass. She and Matti had walked down Andy Rosse Lane this morning. One of the restaurants had been flooded so badly that Jenn doubted it would ever reopen, but most of them had been built up off the ground. They would recover in time.

Aside from the noises related to work, the island seemed quieter than ever. There were fewer people, of course, since those who had managed to evacuate could now not return. But this was something different than ordinary quiet. The island had an awed hush, an awareness that they had all faced the force of nature yesterday and it was only good fortune that allowed them to live to see the sunrise. Had the hurricane made landfall as something more than a category 2, they might not have been so lucky.

There were no WaveRunners out this morning. Nobody had opened the little shop that rented them, and there would be no parasailing. For the people who lived and worked here, there would be only sweat and frustration now, whereas the vacationers were going to just have to make do and be patient.

Boats lined the beach, people from the island and mainlanders just there to help. Some had driven right up onto the sand while others were anchored just offshore, despite the water still being choppy in the aftermath of the hurricane. Though she remained aware of the other boats, her interest had been piqued by the single craft that really wasn't supposed to be there at all—an old wreck that had been washed ashore by the hurricane and now rested on the sand, crusted with old seaweed and shells. Jenn did not recall ever seeing a ship like it, for this one had both a paddlewheel and a smokestack, although the smokestack had broken in half at some point. For that matter, so had the ship. What had washed ashore must have been only half of the vessel, the rest of it still at the bottom somewhere.

From the look of it, the boat had been out there in the Gulf for a long time.

As if the police and emergency services didn't have enough to worry about, they had been here very early, staking out an area around the beached vessel with bright yellow tape. Several people had been left to look after the wreck, including a deeply tanned guy in a bright orange lifeguard swimsuit and Deputy Hayes, the woman who had come to the house the day before to listen to Rick Scully's embarrassing rant about the spring-breaker who'd flirted with his wife.

The thought made Jenn glance over her shoulder at the path that led to their rental house. Trees had fallen across it. Leaves and coconuts and other debris were scattered everywhere. A big yellow umbrella dangled from the trees, from one of the rentals, that someone had foolishly left under a house. She had seen another floating in the water that morning.

Rick and Matti were still up at the house, calling the property manager and the car rental agency. They had managed to get the generator going. Jenn could have done it herself, but she never minded letting Matti feel like she needed him.

She smiled to herself and dug her iced coffee out of the sand, took a sip, and then shielded her eyes to get a better look at the no-longer-sunken ship. Corinne and her girls were down at the police line, watching as a photographer took pictures of the wreck inside and out. Jesse had joined them, and Jenn knew her son wanted to slip under that tape and get a closer look, but she also knew he wouldn't dare. Even out here in the sunshine, in vacation paradise, and with people responding to so many other troubles, he knew better than to break the rules. There were always people who would get angry, always police who would shoot first and make up their own story later. Even here.

As she studied him, Jesse turned to look back at her, almost as if he could sense her focus on him. He said something to the Scully girls and started up the storm-ravaged beach. There were other people out there, but Jenn noticed nobody had dared to go into the water, afraid that the undertow would drag them out.

"What do you think?" she said as Jesse approached. "Pretty spectacular, huh?"

"Incredible," Jesse replied. "Like something out of a storybook. Pirate ship washes up on shore in a storm."

Jenn narrowed her eyes. "It's a pirate ship?"

"I wish. Can you imagine? Everyone within a hundred miles would be out here looking for treasure on the beach," Jesse said. "No, I overheard a couple of the guys photographing the wreck talking about it being something they called a blockade runner. I guess it was a Civil War thing."

She felt a rush of recognition. It seemed she had seen that boat design before. "I think I studied them in college. When the South seceded from the Union, they had no navy, so they had ships built in other countries, including England. The North blockaded the whole perimeter of the country to keep anyone from helping, but the South had these blockade runners that got supplies through."

Jesse looked impressed. "So that thing's really been down there since the Civil War?"

"Seems that way."

"Wow," he said, and it sounded as if he meant it.

For a few moments they stood there, mother and son, taking in the way the storm had resculpted the beach and all of the shells and seaweed and debris that had been left behind in its passing.

"You'll never forget this vacation," Jenn observed.

"Will you?"

"Not a chance."

A comfortable, companionable silence fell between them as they watched the activity buzzing around the shipwreck. It was strange to look out across the Gulf and not see a single boat on the water.

"It was pretty bad, I guess," Jesse said somberly.

"People were saying the cleanup is going to take a long time, but nobody seemed that surprised."

"This isn't the first bad hurricane these folks have dealt with. I'm sure it won't be the last one, either. As bad as it was, by the time it made landfall it was only a category two. One of these days they're going to get a category five and the devastation will be unbelievable. The house we're staying in—no matter how well it's built, it's up on those stilts. A storm that powerful might knock it over. The whole island might be scoured clean in a storm like that."

Jesse shook his head. "I don't get why they stay. Why even own property here?"

Jenn smiled, thinking of the stunning beauty of the Greek island of Santorini. The people had settled on an island that was part of the rim of a massive, active, underwater volcano. Someday it would erupt again and the entire city, all human activity there, could be burned away.

"It's paradise, babe," she told her son. "People will sacrifice a lot for a place like this."

Before Jesse could reply, Jenn heard voices and turned to see her husband coming down from the path with a fiftyish white woman, bleached blond and definitely not dressed for the beach. She wore white pants and a yellow silk shirt, and her shoes slung from one finger of her right hand. She walked like she owned the island.

"How's the house looking?" Jenn asked.

Matti nodded, though his focus shifted to the shipwreck on the beach. "Some minor damage. Someone will be over by the end of the day to board up the broken window, but otherwise, it's business as usual."

"Well, we're not miracle workers," the woman replied. "It'll be a few weeks until we've got it all cleaned up. Crews are out clearing the roads now, but the big concern is the bridge. The car rental companies will work with guests to sort out transportation at the end of a vacation, but now there will be a shortage of available vehicles off island, and the people who drove their own cars onto Captiva are in even worse shape. It's going to be chaos for a while."

"Trouble in paradise," Jenn said.

"There always is," the woman said with a thin, polite smile. Then she turned to Matti. "So, when am I going to meet your beautiful family?"

The confusion clouding Matti's features was understandable, but Jenn understood immediately. The property manager had seen a black woman and a black teenager and there had been a mental disconnect. If part of her brain had expected to find Matti's wife and son here on the beach, her presumptions had turned Jenn and Jesse invisible.

Matti fumbled for the right words.

Jenn didn't need to fumble. She fixed the woman with a withering stare as she put a hand on Jesse's shoulder. "We *are* his beautiful family."

The woman blinked as if still trying to make sense of this revelation. Then she smiled thinly. "Of course you are. How silly of me."

"Silly" was not the word Jenn would have used.

"Sandy, meet my wife, Jenn. And this is our son,

Jesse," Matti said, much more formally. His spine had stiffened and his voice had taken on an uncharacteristic chill. "Jenn, this is Sandy."

Jenn smiled. "*Sandy.* Of course you are."

A small voice called out and they all turned to see Kelsey Scully running up the beach toward them, sand flying behind her. Emma and their mother followed at a less-manic pace. Kelsey raced up, chattering excitedly about the shipwreck, and Jesse turned on his natural charm, responding to her enthusiasm with his own.

When Corinne walked up, Matti quickly introduced her. Rick Scully had remained inside the house, at least for now, but the property manager had the whole picture of the two families now. The Scullys were white enough to haunt an old castle. Jenn had skin almost as dark as her natural hair, which she'd tied back into a high puff this morning. With his Finnish heritage, Matti was maybe the whitest human on planet Earth, but their son was still brown enough to get "randomly selected" for additional TSA screening at most American airports.

While Corinne and Sandy talked amiably about the hurricane, the concerns of the homeowners—which restaurants might reopen when, and how the collapsed bridge might effect the local economy—Matti gave Jenn a quiet look of apology. She had seen that expression on his face so many times, the expression that said that he wished he could understand what the world looked like through the eyes of his wife and son. Though sometimes she wished for the same, Jenn was glad that Matti could never really understand. He was a sweet man, and maybe too soft for the harsher realities of the world. She envied him the luxury of never having to know.

"So what you're saying is that, for the moment, we're trapped on Captiva?" Jenn asked, studying the woman.

"For now, yes," Sandy said. "When you have to leave, I'm sure we'll be able to help you arrange transport by boat to Sanibel or Fort Myers, so you can get back to the airport. Call me if there's anything I can do, but for now, you'll have to make the best of it."

Jenn looked up and down the beach, saw all the shells, the scattering of people who had not evacuated, the waves, and the palm trees, and she reached out and took Matti's hand. He smiled and gave her a squeeze.

"I think we can manage," she said.

Matti nodded. "We'll survive."

There was more conversation. Something about the owner and possible repairs, but Jenn turned to Kelsey and Emma, who looked painfully bored. She whispered to get the girls' attention. "Psst. Hey. Race to the waves?"

Emma gave her a surreptitious thumbs-up.

Kelsey hemmed and hawed. "I don't know. Maybe we should . . ." she began, trailed off a moment, and then snapped her head up. "Go!"

The youngest of them took off running toward the surf. Emma and Jenn shouted about how she'd tricked them, but caught up to her anyway. They reached the water just steps apart, with Emma the first one to the waves. She halted in the white foaming surf, celebrating her victory. Kelsey did the same, coming in second, but Jenn blasted past the two of them, took half a dozen stomping strides, and then dove into a massive wave that broke above her, pushed her under, tried to drag her back toward shore.

She broke the surface, feeling the undertow, not caring. It wasn't strong enough now to drag her out. They were prisoners of paradise now. Castaways on a tropical island. Like Sandy said, they would just have to make the best of it.

As Jenn watched, Jesse joined Kelsey and Emma in the surf, and then all of them were swimming, laughing, splashing.

The storm had passed. The worst was over.

Kelsey splashed Jesse, putting on her best evil grin. Emma swam a few feet away, trying to act all cool around him the way she always did lately. Kelsey might only be in the third grade, but she recognized Jesse's overall cuteness. His face had changed, his jaw somehow stronger, and just this spring he had suddenly developed muscles he had never had before. The effect was enough to make Emma into a babbling idiot half the time. When Kelsey teased her about it, her mother told her to leave her older sister alone—that Emma just had a little crush. But it didn't seem very little to her.

What annoyed her more than Emma getting all swoony about Jesse was that she seemed to have forgotten why they had both always loved him. Kelsey loved his laugh, and what a dork he could be, no matter how handsome he might turn out. He was just fun.

"Time for a little swim," Jesse said now, stalking toward her, arms up like a monster on the attack.

"Don't even think about throwing me in!" Kelsey warned.

Emma splashed them both. "Do it!"

Kelsey started splashing with both arms, sweeping first her left and then her right across the waves to send sheets of foamy water spraying at Jesse's face. He lunged for her, roaring, and Kelsey squealed as he hauled her out of the water. Jesse lifted her over his head and she kicked a little, but not too much, before he hurled her as far as he could. She screamed, then clamped her mouth shut and her eyes closed as she plunged deep.

The undertow grabbed her. Her heart lurched and panic seized her as she remembered how strong it could be, but then her feet touched bottom and she shoved upward and broke the surface, and Jesse was there, wading toward her, still playing sea monster.

"No!" Kelsey said. "Throw Emma now! I dare you."

She saw her sister's face blanch. "Try it, boy, and I'll drown you."

Jesse laughed and turned to march toward her.

Kelsey grinned, knowing how crazy Emma must have been feeling in that moment, loving and hating the attention from Jesse all at the same time. She glanced around, searching for her mother, and saw her a little farther out, swimming with Jesse's mom.

Beyond them, she saw the shark.

Kelsey went completely still in the water. The waves were tall, but she watched the fin slice through a trough, watched a wave roll over it, and then watched as it emerged on the other side of that swell.

A wave struck Kelsey, knocked her backward. She spun around in the water, kicked and swam, and wiped the water from her eyes as she turned to search for that fin again, her heart racing.

"Mom!" she called. "Mom, look!"

But even as she pointed, she could not spot the fin again. Her mother and Mrs. Hautala scanned the waves to see what had alarmed Kelsey and then both women were working their way closer to her in the water. Kelsey heard splashing behind her and turned to see Emma and Jesse crashing across the waves toward her.

"What's the matter, kid?" Emma asked.

Kelsey would normally bristle. She hated when her sister called her "kid." In that moment, she barely noticed.

Her mother said her name, but Kelsey continued to stare out at the Gulf, scanning the surface, a chill spreading through her in spite of the warmth of the water.

Her mother put a hand on her shoulder, sunk into the water so they were side by side and almost face-to-face. "Hey, honey. What is it?"

"A shark." Giving up on finding that fin again, she turned to look at her mother. "There's a shark out there. I saw it swimming."

Her mother make the trademarked Corinne Scully you're-imagining-things face. "Kelsey, there are all

kinds of sea creatures out here. Manatees and stingrays and tons and tons of dolphins. If you saw a fin,
I'm sure that's what it was—a dolphin."

"Mom, no—"

"Honey, trust me. I kind of flipped out a little the
other day myself, but it was a dolphin. Of course it was.
I know it's scary to think there might be a shark, but
trust me. The dolphins are super-friendly, and even if
there was a shark, the dolphins would beat the crap out
of it and scare it away. That's what they do. They're
not afraid."

Kelsey glanced back out to where she'd seen the fin.
It was nowhere in sight, but she started backing away
toward the sand regardless.

"Maybe they're not afraid, but I am."

She practically backed into Emma, who dropped
into the water and started swimming toward her, making the noises from the movie *Jaws* with her mouth
halfway in the water, so bubbles shot up. It might have
been funny, but Kelsey didn't feel like laughing when
Emma reached for her under the water, baring her teeth
as she tried to bite her sister.

"Stop!" Kelsey shouted, slapping her arm.

Her mother snapped at her, then glanced embarrass-
ingly at Mrs. Hautala. "We never should have let her
watch that movie. She's too young."

Whatever Mrs. Hautala said in response was drowned
out by Emma doing her *Jaws* music again and diving
after Kelsey.

"When did you get to be so scared of everything?"
Emma teased her.

Kelsey fixed her with a murderous glare. "About the same time you started drooling over Jesse."

Emma's jaw dropped and her eyes went wide. Her face had gone pale beneath her Florida tan, and she stood swaying in the waves as if she had abruptly frozen. Jesse stood just behind her, over Emma's left shoulder, and he had heard Kelsey's words with crystal clarity. Kelsey stared back at his sister and at Jesse, knowing that she could never put the words back into her mouth.

"Kelsey," their mother said. "I think that's enough."

For her part, Emma continued to gasp like a fish on the shore sucking air. Jesse didn't look amused the way Kelsey had expected. Instead he seemed awkward and embarrassed and uncomfortable.

"Fine," Kelsey said. "Don't believe me."

Maybe it had been a dolphin, like her mother said. That did make more sense, but the way she had been dismissed had stung, and now Emma looked like she wanted to strangle her. Kelsey turned and waded toward the shore, wishing she could do a bit of dramatic stomping and storming away but feeling impeded by the water.

When she reached the sand, she was surprised to see her father sitting on a beach towel, watching her with a smile on his face. What surprised her even more was the absence of his cell phone. It was just Rick Scully in a vintage Soundgarden concert T-shirt and a bright-orange, tropical-patterned bathing suit, and a pair of a sunglasses to protect his eyes. No hat, no flip-flops, no book or beer or any other distractions.

"Hey, Dad."

"Hey, pumpkin. You and your sister fighting again?"
He asked without judgment, without admonishment.

Kelsey smiled. "I saw a shark. Mom says it was a dolphin—which it probably was—but Emma decided to be her usual cranky self."

"Well, you can hang here with me," he said, and then a shadow crossed his features and he hesitated. "If you want to, of course."

Kelsey had always resented how much her father worked and how often he was on the phone when he should have been paying more attention to her, or Emma, or their mom, but she had never realized just how much it had bothered her until the rush of pleasure she felt now at its absence.

"Sure!" she said happily, and plopped herself down beside him, sharing the towel. They sat for a minute or two, just watching the family, and Jesse and his mom.

"That shipwreck is so cool," he said. "I'd like to get some photos before they remove it."

"How do you think they'll do that?" She frowned, trying to imagine it.

"They'll tow it away somehow, take it somewhere to study. But it's going to be a while. They have a lot more important things to worry about. Repairs and injuries and getting people off the island who need to go."

Kelsey stared at the shipwreck, wondering if she could get inside. She would have loved to take a closer look. Once they towed it to wherever they would tow it, she figured the best she would be able to do would be to look at pictures that would eventually show up online.

Her dad nudged her. "Hey. I'm really sorry this happened in the middle of our vacation. It's a scary thing, I know, but we're all going to be fine."

"I know. It's not your fault. You can't control Mother Nature. And we have days to go. There are tons of things I still want to do, but . . ."

Her words trailed off as she gazed back and forth along the Gulf and saw the cleanup and the small number of people, and remembered how desolate and damaged Andy Rosse Lane had been that morning.

"What's tops on your list?" he asked. "The one thing you really don't want to go home without doing?"

She thought of that fin. "Dolphin watch! That sightseeing trip where you go to the island and gather shells, and do the dolphin watch along the way."

"Dolphin watch," he repeated. "Okay. As soon as the boats are running again, we'll take one of those tours."

Kelsey smiled. The fin she'd seen still made her a little nervous, no matter what her mother said, but as long as her parents were with her, she knew she would be safe. They'd already made it through a hurricane— and dolphins weren't scary, they were sweet.

Just a dolphin, she thought again.

Just a dolphin.

* * *

Nadia throttled the WaveRunner and felt the thrum of it run up her thighs and throughout her body. Her ribs rattled and her teeth chattered as she bounced the machine over a wave, and its bottom smashed back down onto the water. Spray hit her face and she laughed as the engine sang. She nearly let go of the throttle but managed to hold on. Her sunglasses were covered with droplets but she didn't dare lift a hand to wipe them.

Heart pounding, Nadia glanced over her shoulder and spotted Simone racing along in her wake. It had felt like a race until that moment, because instead of chasing, Simone had decided to play, zipping back and forth in Nadia's wake.

Something struck Nadia's WaverRunner and she let out a cry. Her grip weakened and the engine screamed as she nearly flew off the back of the machine, barely holding on by her fingertips as it tipped to the left. In an instant, she had her grip again and turned out to sea, heading straight for the next wave even as she realized she had almost capsized because she hadn't been paying attention. While she had been looking at Simone, she had let herself get parallel to a big wave.

Stupid, girl, she thought. *You told the GulfDaze guys you knew what you were doing.*

Her heart skipped along like the WaveRunner, but she had wrested control back—both of the machine and of her emotions. It had surprised her that the rental business had been willing to put WaveRunners in the water so soon after the hurricane, but she figured that people marooned on Captiva needed something to do and the owners weren't averse to making a buck. The ream of indemnity documents she had signed would let them off the hook if she crashed or drowned or if a fucking comet fell from the sky and obliterated her.

Also, she had begged. Simone had teased her mercilessly about it afterward, but they had gotten their WaveRunners. The absurdly handsome, shaggy, bearded, and tanned beach bum at the counter had even brought them down to the beach himself. The hurricane had been moving fast, he'd said, and the surf had calmed down considerably even since the morning. Now it was mid-afternoon and they were open for business thanks to Nadia's pleading.

Something brown flashed below her, visible in the clear water, and Nadia circled back to get a better look. A trio of stingrays—one nearly the size of her WaveRunner—swam beneath the surface, beautiful and alien in their slow progress. A shame, she thought, that the others were missing this. Tyler and Kevin had walked over to the other side to rent kayaks, which while calmer, was at least its own brand of adventure, but Marianna and Rashad had chosen to stay behind entirely. Rashad claimed it was because he wanted a better look at the shipwreck and to talk to anyone who came to investigate it, but Nadia thought he had stayed behind only because Marianna was the world's most massive wimp, too scared for a kayak, never mind a WaveRunner. And maybe because Rashad wanted to get into her pants, though if so, he hid it well.

She had slowed down. Now she spun the Wave-Runner around and throttled up again, scouting for Simone. She spotted her friend in the distance and aimed the nose of the machine toward her. Zipping over the waves, she scanned the beach, and the view tarnished her happy buzz a little. From this vantage point it was easy to see some of the damage: downed trees, a roof torn right off a house, The Mucky Duck's still-boarded-up windows. There were so few people out there and no umbrellas, just some hardy, stranded souls and the old shattered boat that had washed up in the storm.

Nadia shook off the worries—there was nothing she could do about their situation except make the best of the rest of their vacation, and she intended to do that. She spotted Simone again and adjusted her path to head straight for her. As she did, she saw Simone waving a hand, trying to get her attention, as if she wasn't already headed that direction.

Nadia let out a long, ululating cry of triumph as she bounced over the water, but her hands had started to ache and her butt hurt from smashing down onto the seat. They had another twenty minutes or so, and she wanted to head farther out to sea, but first she would see if she could recruit Simone.

She throttled down. The engine's whine softened and then began to putt and choke as she slid over toward Simone.

"Having fun?" she called.

Simone gestured to a churning bit of water about fifty feet away. A wave rose and the WaveRunners crested over it and slid down the other side, and then Nadia saw what had gotten her friend so excited. A pod of dolphins circled and submerged and rose again, as if the entire group were in some kind of aquatic dolphin ballet.

Delighted, Nadia held onto the handlebars and stood up on the WaveRunner, not wanting to rev the engine again and scare them off. "Oh my God," she said. "They're so adorable!"

Simone didn't seem to share her delight. Instead of a smile, she knitted her brows and pointed. "No, check it out. There's something going on. They're up to something."

The waves undulated beneath them, rocking the WaveRunners, and Nadia gave the engine a little gas, nudging closer to the dolphins. One after another, they darted forward, diving deeper, then swimming quickly away. Nadia smiled in wonder, thinking it must be a game. Dolphins were playful and curious and intelligent, and all her life she'd felt a special bond with them. As a little girl, she'd seen them at the aquarium and from that day on she had cherished them, from her first plush stuffed dolphin to the small tattoo on her left thigh.

"Oh my God," she said in delight. "I'm in love."

"No," Simone said sharply. "Something's wrong."

Nadia rolled her eyes. She loved Simone—the girl was like a sister to her—but when she was in the wrong mood she could bleed the fun out of anything. Why had Simone even called her over here if she was going to be such a buzzkill?

"Don't be like that," she said. "They're just—"

But they weren't *just* anything. Nadia saw the other fin, the one that didn't look anything like a dolphin's—

larger and thicker, the body below displacing more water—and she felt herself go numb. A sound issued from her lips that might have been words or just a whimper. Her grip tightened on the handlebars and her right hand tensed, ready to twist the throttle.

"Simone," she said, half-turning away from the dolphins and that other fin. "Do you see—"

The second shark erupted from the water with such force that it created its own wave, tipping Nadia's WaveRunner hard to the left. She lost her grip, began to flail, and would have fallen off if the shark hadn't reached her first. Its jaws struck her with such force that she felt the impact more than the rending of its teeth. The air blew out of her lungs as its massive body traversed the air *above* her WaveRunner and then plunged her down into the churning water.

The last sound she heard was Simone screaming.

Eyes wide, shrieking into the ocean as the shark dragged her deeper, she tried to suck in air and choked as she began to drown. Teeth tore deeper, her own blood fogged the water around her, and the shark whipped her back and forth, its jaws ripping her apart. The panic and sorrow, the single moment of understanding her fate, were worse than the pain.

Her last thought was that she could taste her own blood.

Darkness claimed her, but the shark had claimed her first.

CHAPTER 8

Simone heard herself screaming and stopped.

She began to tremble, sitting on the back of her WaveRunner. "Nadia? Oh my God," she said, entirely to herself, as she leaned forward, breath hitching in her throat as she stared at the blood clouding the water, spreading out in the sunshine, diluted and fading. Deep in that cloud, something floated that could only be a part of her friend, and then Simone could not look any more. She dropped her eyes, staring at the seat of the WaveRunner between her legs.

The machine surged beneath her. Her breath hitched and she held on tightly as it rolled; she whipped around, telling herself it had been a wave. But there had been a slight bump, hadn't there? Her heart skipped and raced and her lips pressed into a thin line as tears came to her eyes.

"Nadia," she said again, but this time the word

sounded like a requiem on her lips. It couldn't have been real, what she had just seen. Sharks only behaved that way with seals and dolphins, and yet she had witnessed it.

The rational core of her mind had retreated but it had not been erased.

The dolphins had begun to swim away, the whole pod racing across the water, leaping from the waves with an urgent speed that had nothing to do with play and everything to do with survival. A second cloud of blood blossomed beneath the water near where Nadia's WaveRunner rocked back and forth. A dolphin had died there, and the others had taken the moment of distraction to run as far and as fast as they could.

Simone's heart went still.

But I'm still sitting here.

She saw the fin surface twenty yards away and she knew the second shark must be close.

Her hand twisted the throttle without any conscious thought. She cranked the handlebars to the right and opened up the engine. The machine nearly leaped out from beneath her, but she held on, turning toward shore.

In her peripheral vision, she saw the second shark burst from the water only feet from where she'd been idling. Shaking, whispering profanity, she watched it crash back down and knew how close she had come.

Simone bent her head and aimed for the beach.

* * *

Sheriff Arturo Reyes drove his Jeep down the rutted road to the Institute, surprised at how quickly the downed trees had been cleared. Sanibel was a beehive of activity, emergency crews and locals all working quickly to repair the damage, clear the roads, and limit the long-term economic impact of the storm. Captiva hadn't been so fortunate. Without the bridge at Blind Pass, it would take much longer for the restoration the island required. But even with Sanibel's comparative good fortune—if millions of dollars in damage could produce anything positive—the Institute had been especially proactive in keeping their operation going.

Reyes reached the end of the road and entered the parking lot. All the gates were open, but as soon as he passed through, an engine roared to life and he glanced to the left to see a van pulling in to block the entrance. It bore the Institute's logo on one side.

There were only half a dozen other vehicles in the lot, and the trees that had fallen here had not been cleared.

Once he had parked and climbed out of his Jeep, Reyes saw a man emerge from the Institute's front doors and hurry toward him, hands stuffed in the pockets of his white lab coat. Despite the fact that he lived year-round in Florida, the guy looked pale as a ghost, but as they approached each other, Reyes didn't think it had anything to do with lack of a tan.

"You Dr. Tremblay?"

The man in the lab coat put out his hand. "Sheriff, thanks for coming. I didn't know what else to do."

Reyes shook his hand, studying his face. Dr. Tremblay seemed to be trying to maintain his calm, but he had a tightness around his eyes and mouth that gave him the look of a man on the verge of cracking.

"You could've called the Sanibel Police," Reyes said. "This is really their jurisdiction."

Dr. Tremblay glanced back toward the building. "It's not, though. Technically the Institute is county land, which puts it squarely in your lap, I'm afraid. If you want to bring in Chief Smalls after we talk, that's up to you. But I happen to think Rodney Smalls is a grandstanding buffoon who wouldn't know how to handle any crisis worse than running out of beer during the Super Bowl—and maybe not even that."

Reyes smirked. There was no love lost between himself and Chief Smalls. "You don't hold back, Doc. And I appreciate the faith in me, but there's a hell of a lot calling for my attention today, so why don't you introduce me to your crisis and we'll see what we can do."

The man nodded, turned, and led Reyes up the steps without another word. Dr. Tremblay had a certain grimness about him that belied his otherwise relaxed appearance. His beard was brown and gray and he wore glasses that drew attention to his expressive eyes. As they entered the Institute, he shook his head as if admonishing himself.

"So, you wanna tell me what's going on, or am I supposed to guess?" Sheriff Reyes asked.

"It's show-and-tell, Sheriff. The show part comes first," Dr. Tremblay said.

Reyes rolled his eyes, his thoughts wandering to the dozen other calls he needed to answer at the moment, most of them related to Captiva. He had deputies all over Lee County facilitating the recovery effort, but the only one on Captiva Island was Agnes Hayes, and as competent as she might be, that was where he needed bodies the most.

Silently, he promised himself he would give Dr. Tremblay ten minutes, no more. He followed the research scientist. *Was he director of this place? Was that how he had introduced himself on the phone?* Reyes couldn't remember, but obviously he had the run of the place, because Dr. Tremblay used a key card to allow them through doors marked Authorized Personnel Only. They passed entrances to labs, including one where some kind of control center revealed multiple observation screens, one of them shattered as if in anger. The whole place smelled like smoke and something else, some acrid odor.

At last they reached a raised foyer, all glass and smooth plastic, like some 1970s vision of the future, where they were greeted by a tall woman with a long face, who turned to stare at them from beneath severely disapproving eyebrows.

"Tali, meet Sheriff Reyes," Dr. Tremblay said. "Sheriff meet Dr. Tali Rocco." Without another word, he turned and walked back the way they'd come.

"Dr. Tremblay?" Reyes called. "Hey, Doc! What the hell are you doing?"

Tremblay kept walking, let himself through a security door, and was gone.

"What the hell?" Reyes said, turning on Dr. Rocco.

She held up her hands. "Follow me, please, Sheriff," she said, and started walking the opposite direction.

He took a deep breath and followed, anger simmering. "Dr. Rocco—"

"Tali."

"I don't have time for this shit. You have any idea what happened here the past couple of days?"

"I'm not sure *you* do, Sheriff. That's why we need you. You're probably aware that the Institute does government work. Some of our research is funded by the Department of Defense, and most of that requires security clearance that you simply don't have."

She glanced back at him. "Dr. Tremblay left because he needs deniability. Everything I tell you now, I will deny having told you. He likes to have a clear conscience, so he didn't want to hear me tell you these things."

"What things?"

"Let me be clear, Sheriff. I can't be certain that this even needs to concern you. But given the possibility for something to go very, very wrong, we thought it our obligation to bring local law enforcement in. People may die, and we're hoping you will be able to prevent it."

Reyes went cold. "'People may . . .' What are you talking about, Dr. Rocco?"

"Tali."

"I'll call you whatever the hell you want if you'd speak plainly."

"I promise you that I will."

She turned and pushed out through a pair of heavy, automatic doors that were slow to kick in. When they swept open, they did so with a grinding noise that could not have been normal. Damage from the storm, Reyes figured.

Beyond those doors, the corridor was soaked. At the far end, where the glass exit doors had shattered despite the metal shutters that would have been drawn down to protect them, inches of water remained pooled by the threshold. Tali walked right through the water and stepped out through the doorframe, ignoring the fragments of glass still sticking from its edges.

"Enough of this crap," he muttered as he followed her outside.

Reyes stopped short, staring at the Gulf of Mexico. Whatever had been behind the Institute had been obliterated. There had been a seawall here, he knew, but now the water came nearly all the way up to the shattered rear doors. He exhaled, nodding in appreciation of the power of the storm.

"One of the most significant projects here," Tali said, standing off to his right, "one of the projects the DoD had the greatest interest in, involved sharks. I had a lot of them here, Sheriff. Thirty-two. During the storm, someone—a security guard with an extreme animal-rights agenda, we believe—released those sharks into an outdoor research pool. We also believe that before he did that, he triggered certain behavioral modifications that were part of our research for the military."

Tali did not seem to notice that she had said 'military' instead of 'government.' Reyes did.

The wind rippled across the water that had flooded the Institute's property. The sun gleamed, beating down warmly, almost as if the storm had never come at all, as if nothing had changed.

"The security guard. Where is he? Can I question him?" Reyes asked.

"When the storm passed, there was no sign of him."

"Then how do you know—"

"We have larger problems, Sheriff," Tali said, and for the first time he noticed the same fear in her eyes that he had seen in Tremblay's. "The outside pool . . ." She pointed straight ahead. "It was right there."

Reyes reached up and massaged the bridge of his nose. "And your thirty-two . . . behaviorally modified sharks?"

"Now you see the problem."

Reyes swore. How could something like this happen? His thoughts raced and he reminded himself that the population of the two islands had diminished drastically because of evacuations, and most people were too busy to be at the beach while the recovery was going on. But there would be swimmers. It was fucking Florida, after all.

And there was more to the area than Sanibel and Captiva. Pine Island, Cape Coral, Fort Myers Beach. . . Reyes felt a migraine building behind his eyes.

"So . . . *Tali*," he said, "what exactly can you tell me about these sharks?"

She stared at him, seeming to mull over the words to come.

"I'll say this, Sheriff. In some states, they're virtually harmless. In others, they're ruthless, murderous, unstoppable killers."

Reyes glared at her. "If you've got some way to control them—"

"We did. But the storm didn't do us any favors. If we can fix the system, get the program running properly again, we might be able to regain control. But until then . . . well, we just wanted you to know. It could be nothing. They could be just out there swimming contentedly."

It was clear she did not believe that.

"Can you track them?"

"Once the system is back online, we'll let you know. We'll coordinate an effort to find them. Hunt them if we have to, though of course that's a last resort. Our . . . financers will not be happy if we have to destroy our research."

Reyes turned to leave.

"Oh, and Sheriff," Tali said. "You can't tell anyone what I've told you."

"That there are nearly three dozen sharks roaming around that weren't out there a couple of days ago?"

"By all means, warn them to keep an eye out for sharks. But nothing about the work we do here, or who we do it for." She smiled. "Trust me. You don't want to upset them."

"You talking about the sharks or the Department of Defense?"

Tali shrugged. "Both."

Reyes started back toward the shattered doors, but Tali reminded him that he'd need a key card to get through the building. He wanted to rage about it, but he had done enough talking. The hurricane recovery had suddenly become his second priority. He turned and started around the perimeter of the building, and he pulled out his cell phone to call Deputy Hayes. The Sanibel cops had sent a boat over to help her out, but she was the only person out on Captiva with any legal authority. He needed to give her a heads-up, let her know that as bad as the hurricane had been, the danger had not passed.

It was swimming out there in the Gulf.

In the aftermath of the storm, Lennox had certain regrets. Not about the crimes he had committed—on the contrary, just thinking about the items he'd stashed in his boat made him feel giddy. But walking along Captiva Drive in search of a place to buy coffee, he had started to think about the moment he'd almost fallen into the water, the moment the boat had nearly shattered itself against some rich asshole's dock, and that giddiness turned to a strange, sick dread in his gut.

What the hell had he been thinking?

Thinking about robbing some people, obviously. About getting away from Captiva and setting up somewhere he would never have to think about his ex again. Yeah, of course, but once upon a time Lennox had known where to draw the line between risk and reward, and in the middle of a goddamn hurricane, he had somehow lost that ability. The third house had turned up the most valuable goods—the jewelry, the vase, all of that—but it had also taken him time that the hurricane had used to gain strength, to spill a little bit of the Gulf of Mexico across Captiva and nearly sink him.

It gave him a chill to think about navigating across the channel to Buck Key and finding his way into the bayou there. In the moment it had felt wild and brave, the kind of shit that real outlaws did, the kind of outlaws who had inspired him all his life. But he had been out there alone, and even in the bayou the water had nearly swamped his boat. The rain had been brutal. Lennox figured the only blessing was that the hurricane had moved through so quickly. If it had stalled at the coast it could have dumped a hell of a lot more rain. All in all, they'd been fortunate, but he still wondered how he had convinced himself to risk so much.

Temporary insanity, he thought.

But that temporary insanity was going to buy him a fresh start—and with any luck, the BMW he'd been coveting for a long while. He had been dropping hints for months to Dallas, his occasional drinking buddy who worked at the marina, that he wanted to sell. By now, he knew Dallas would be ready to pull the trigger and buy the boat, the business, everything—if Lennox wanted to go that way.

For the moment, though, he was frozen in place. With the bridge out, he couldn't leave the island except by boat, and he didn't want to draw any special attention. If he just abandoned his business instead of selling, he would raise quite a few eyebrows. Fingers would eventually point in his direction. The only upside of the bridge being out was that until it was replaced, the people he'd robbed would not be able to return to the island unless they sailed over, which meant they would likely send someone to check on their property, and Lennox had been careful to make any damage he'd created in breaking in look as if it had been caused by the storm.

He had time. Not a lot, but enough. Still, he was anxious to be gone, to begin his new life.

Lennox reached the little strip mall across from South Seas Plantation where some genius had put a Starbucks. The telephone landlines weren't working, so he had rolled the dice on the place being open and was rewarded with the bold OPEN sign in the window. He paused in the mostly empty parking lot, staring at the few heads he could see through the plate glass windows. Anxiety needled at him, though he understood the absurdity of the emotion. None of those people could tell just by looking at him that he'd become a criminal the previous day. He'd read so many stories in which characters had guilt "written all over their faces" and he knew people could create suspicion through their behavior, but as long as he acted normally, no one would be the wiser.

As he started up the steps toward the Starbucks, his phone began to vibrate in his pocket. Lennox dug it out and studied the unfamiliar number. It took him a moment to realize that the call had been diverted from his business line—this was a potential customer, the day after a hurricane.

"Captain Len's Boat Tours. How can I help you?"

"Oh, hi. I was sort of expecting an answering machine," a man mumbled on the other end of the connection.

"Nope. You've got the real deal. What's on your mind?"

"Well, I know maybe it seems a little nuts right now, but we're sort of stranded with nothing to do and I thought I'd see if you were still operating tours in spite of the hurricane."

Lennox smiled to himself. What better cover for his crimes than to be able to say he kept working, trying to salvage whatever he could of his business post-hurricane?

"I'm not running my regular schedule, but under the circumstances, I could reinstate my two p.m. dolphin watch and shelling adventure, if you're interested. How many in your party?"

"Seven, but I'm not sure everyone will come. I could give you a call back in fifteen minutes or so, once I know. If you really don't mind doing a trip for such a small group. I know there's a lot of damage on the island."

Lennox glanced up at the Starbucks, thinking he might need extra shots of espresso. "No worries. I'm sure you won't be the only call I get. And the seas may be a little rough, but at least out there the mess on the island isn't going to disrupt our travels. Once you know how many in your party, please go and book on the web page. I can't process payments over the phone at the moment. What was your name, sir? So I can keep a lookout?"

"Scully. Rick Scully."

"Fantastic. See you at a quarter to two, please, Mr. Scully. We're going to have a great afternoon. Nothing out on the water but sun and stunning wildlife."

"Sounds perfect," Rick replied. "I can't wait."

Corinne stood in the living room, surrounded by tropical artwork in pastel colors, beneath a bamboo ceiling fan. All she needed was a Mai Tai to complete the picture of the island vacation. Instead, she stared at her husband and tried not to wish he hadn't come along on this vacation.

"That's a terrible idea," she told him, instantly regretting the sting in her voice. "It can't possibly be safe."

Rick winced. She could see that he wanted to snap at her, but instead he nodded. "I get why you'd be concerned, but think about it. If there's any danger, it's here on the island. What could be safer right now than being on the water?"

Corinne frowned. "I can't believe this guy is even operating his tours today. What if there are sunken boats? He could hit something. How many paying customers can he hope to get?"

"Zero if he cancels everything." Rick threw up his hands. "Babe, listen, this vacation is over in a few days. The storm is a disaster for the people here, but once the cleanup is finished, they'll still be here. We'll be gone. I'd like to salvage as much of our time here as we can, and that means—"

The front door opened and the kids tromped in. Emma led the way, loudly running down the list of her teachers at school and how much she hated each one on a scale from one to ten. Jesse trailed behind her, beach towel draped around his neck, patiently listening to her rant. Kelsey came last, still brushing sand off her feet.

"Is there food?" Kelsey asked, turning hopeful eyes to her mother.

"If you mean 'Are you making lunch?'" Corinne said, "sure. I'll make you a grilled cheese. Who else wants one?"

Jesse's hand shot up. Emma raised hers apologetically, at least courteous enough to realize she was old enough to make her own damn grilled cheese sandwich. Corinne didn't mind. She had taught her kids a certain amount of independence, and they were pretty good about everything except preparing a meal. Unfortunately, they were expert snackers, so she didn't mind cooking for them if it meant preventing them from eating too much junk.

Across the glass coffee table from her, Rick raised his hand, smiling innocently.

"Seriously?" she asked.

"Well, I mean, if you're going to get the grilled cheese assembly line fired up."

Corinne rolled her eyes. Times like these, she could almost forget how often she wanted to strangle him.

"It's a good thing you haven't forgotten how to be charming."

The door opened again, allowing Jenn and Matti inside.

"What's up?" Matti said, glancing around at them.

"Mom's making grilled cheeses!" Kelsey said happily.

Jenn grinned and cocked an eyebrow at her. "Is she? That's so sweet of you."

Corinne shook her head. "I'm going to murder you all."

"I'll help," Matti said. "With the sandwiches, not the murders. The kids need to get plates and serve drinks."

"Fair enough," Jesse replied.

"We'll have to make it quick if we want to see the dolphins," Rick said.

Corinne shot him a dark look. "I'm not—"

"Dolphins!" Kelsey said, head whipping back and forth to look at her mother and father. "Where are we seeing dolphins?"

Rick sat on the arm of the plush sectional sofa and clapped his hands together. "Well, most of the boat tours aren't running today, naturally, but I found a guy who's willing to go out. Captain Len. It's a dolphin watch and shelling trip, like we talked about."

"I don't know," Jenn said, brows knitted.

Corinne crossed her arms. "Me either. I was just telling him that when you guys came in. I'm not sure it's a good idea."

"I think it's a great idea," Rick teased. "Seriously, though, what's happened on the island is awful. But who knows when we'll be back down here, if ever? I think we need to scratch as many fun things off our to-do list as possible."

"Plus, dolphins!" Matti said happily.

Corinne facepalmed. "Not you, too."

"When does the boat leave?" Matti asked.

Rick glanced over at the time blinking on the front of the cable box. "We have to be there in about an hour."

"Plenty of time for grilled cheese sandwiches," Matti observed.

"I just need to know how many of us are going."

Corinne still had reservations about safety, but she supposed Rick was right, that being out on the water wouldn't be any more dangerous than being on the island. Still, after the hurricane, she just wanted to sit on the beach and read the Karin Slaughter novel she'd brought with her.

"I'm in!" Kelsey announced as she opened a cabinet and stretched to reach for plates.

"Me too," Matti said with a grin. "I mean, who doesn't love dolphins?"

"I love dolphins," Jenn replied. "But I prefer to see them from the beach. Or to fall asleep on the sand."

Corinne started pulling out the bread, cheese, and butter to make sandwiches. "I think I'll stay here too."

"Babe, are you sure?" Rick asked, and there was a twinge of hurt in his voice. Real disappointment.

Touched, Corinne glanced at him. "The next fun thing you want to do, I promise I'm in, as long as it's not parasailing. I'll hang back with Jenn and figure out if we have the fixings to make pomegranate margaritas tonight."

Jenn gave her a thumbs-up. "I approve, but what about dinner?"

"We'll let the guys worry about dinner."

Rick turned to Emma and Jesse. "What about you two?"

Emma had been staring down at her phone, texting or on whatever social media platform had been introduced this month. Now she looked around at them and gave a small shrug.

"I think I'm good."

Corinne saw the hurt look on Rick's face. Against her better judgment, she took up the cause.

"Are you sure?" she said. "You love dolphins."

Emma shrugged a second time, this one her apology-shrug. Teenage girls, it turned out, had an entire lexicon of shrugs that parents needed to learn to interpret. "I want to get a tan. And I'm kind of tired."

Tired from being up all night on your phone, Corinne thought but didn't say.

"Well, I'm definitely on board," Jesse said. "After yesterday, I definitely want to get out of the house and just do something."

Corinne saw the stung expression on Emma's face and realized she had expected Jesse to stay behind with her. Now she understood, just as she understood the way her daughter closed down in that moment. Emma would have gone along if she had known that Jesse planned to, but now that she'd made her choice so clear, it would be far too conspicuous if she changed her mind suddenly. Instead, she would spend the afternoon sulking and pretending nothing was the matter.

All of a sudden, Corinne wished she could change her mind, but like Emma, she was committed.

"Okay," she said. "These grilled cheeses aren't going to make themselves."

They set about preparing lunch. Jenn and Matti were laughing, teasing Kelsey, who pretended to be insulted though she secretly loved the attention they gave her. Jesse helped fix the sandwiches and then helped clean up. Emma ate half a grilled cheese and stared at her phone the whole time.

"Hey," Corinne said quietly, drawing Rick to a quiet corner by the stairs. "Please just be safe."

He smiled like the old Rick, the one she'd been happy to have married, and he kissed her forehead. "I promise I'll bring everyone back in one piece."

CHAPTER 9

Deputy Hayes couldn't remember ever being as exhausted as this. She stood in the sun, appreciative of the breeze off the water, but she desperately wished she could just strip down and dive into the waves. Sweat dripped down her back and beaded up on her forchead. She could have been wearing shorts—there was a version of the Lee County Sheriff's Department uniform that allowed for it—but sometimes it was difficult enough to assert authority without being undermined by short pants. They provided a visual that made people think of casual moments or childhood, so she nearly always wore long pants.

Today, she regretted it.

The shipwreck fascinated her. The old blockade runner had been on the floor of the Gulf for more than a century and now half of it had been dredged up by the storm. There were three universities that were sending people to take a look. After the police tape had gone up, a news photographer had appeared, followed by Wayne W. Randall, a crime novelist who wrote Florida-set potboilers and lived year-round on Sanibel. According to the Sanibel officer she'd left standing guard, Randall had zipped over on a boat, beached it down the shore from the shipwreck, and then sat taking notes for twenty minutes. When Deputy Hayes had returned to the site after checking on a report of an elderly woman injured in a roof cave-in, Randall had asked if he could get inside the perimeter, even inside the wreck, and Hayes had snapped at him and sent him on his way.

Today was not the day. What the hell must be wrong with people for them not to realize that a tragedy should not be converted into an opportunity, even in the simplest way? But she supposed there were a thousand worse ways in which people were even now exploiting the destruction and human suffering. The prices of gas and groceries would be jacked up, not to mention lumber and other repair supplies.

She needed a meal and a drink and about twelve hours of sleep, preferably in that order.

A wave crashed against the shipwreck, causing a little hollow boom to echo inside. Deputy Hayes knew her presence was wasted here. Even the Sanibel cop who had been on sentry duty before her should not have been using his time this way. But they weren't the people in charge, so they did not get to make that decision.

The wind gusted and brought a sound to her ears, the noise of someone shouting. Urgent, desperate, maybe even afraid. Deputy Hayes turned and spotted three people rushing along the beach toward her. The two lanky, tanned men wore the bright-orange GulfDaze swim trunks. One was shirtless, while the other wore a faded purple T-shirt bearing the company's logo. The guys were shouting at her, running on the beach, sand kicking up in their wake.

Deputy Hayes barely looked at them. They wore fearful faces contorted with alarm as they shouted to get her attention, but her attention focused on the young woman racing alongside them, farther away from the water. The woman—the girl—wiped at her tears. And when the three of them came skidding to a halt on the sand just a dozen feet short of Deputy Hayes, the girl shook and wiped furiously at her eyes again. She glanced out at the water, desperately searching the waves.

"Officer, you gotta help this girl," one of the beach bums said, his concern every ounce genuine.

Deputy Hayes didn't correct him about her rank. Looking at them, at this honest fear and the girl's panic, she knew this wasn't any ordinate dispute. The girl kept shaking, so Deputy Hayes reached for her arm and steadied her.

"Hey," she said. "I'm Agnes. What's your name?"

The girl—one of the college kids renting in Sunset Captiva, she remembered—glanced out at the water again and raised a hand to cover her mouth, as if to keep from screaming.

"Oh fuck," she said, her voice muffled by her hand. "Oh my God. Nadia."

"Is that you? Are you Nadia?"

The girl's eyes flared. "No, I'm not Nadia! I'm Simone! Nadia's dead!"

Deputy Hayes felt a sick twist in her gut. She shot a quick look at the two GulfDaze dudes, who had been hanging back respectfully. Now the bare-chested blond gestured toward Simone.

"She and her friend took out a couple of Wave-Runners," he said, his eyes soft with sympathy. "The other one . . ."

Simone erupted. "Her name is fucking Nadia!" She pointed out at the waves. "We were out there checking out a pod of dolphins, and a shark came right out of the fucking water, ripped her off the WaveRunner. There was . . . Jesus, there was blood everywhere. I saw two sharks at least, and they started after me, bumped my WaveRunner, and I got the hell out of there."

Deputy Hayes felt her eyes go wide. She knew she had to stay professional, but could not contain her horror. "It came out of the water? What do you mean—"

The girl turned on her, slightly bent, as if she had suddenly become stooped with age. But this was grief, an entirely different pain.

"I mean it jumped. Out of the goddamn water. Ripped her off the seat and . . . and it fucking . . ."

Simone didn't finish the sentence. Her lips trembled and fresh tears fell, and it was clear she could not continue. But in her mind, Deputy Hayes felt sure she knew the words that would have come next—*ate her.*

"I'm so sorry," she said, releasing Simone's shoulders. "I can't imagine how shaken you are right now. I'm going to get you somewhere you can rest, and hopefully get an EMT to look you over—"

"I'm fine," Simone said, wiping at her tears and looking at Deputy Hayes as if she were crazy. "I don't have a scratch on me. I'm not the one who . . ." She cleared her throat, stood a bit straighter. "I'm fine, okay. But you've got to keep people out of the water until something's done. I've always heard people say sharks don't attack humans unless it's an accident, like they mistake a person in a wetsuit for a seal or something, but this was no accident. You hearing me? Those sharks didn't think we were fucking seals or dolphins. We were on WaveRunners. They came for us."

Deputy Hayes tore her gaze away from Simone and turned to scan the waves, unnerved by the girl's words. She didn't see any fins cruising the water, no dolphins arcing out of a wave or sharks slicing the Gulf. But she had no doubt, after the haunted look in Simone's eyes, that they were out there.

She unclipped the radio from her belt. Nodding to the two GulfDaze dudes, indicating that they should keep an eye on Simone for a moment, she turned her back and clicked her radio.

"Sheriff, you there? This is Deputy Agnes Hayes for Sheriff Reyes."

A crackle on the line, and then his voice. "I know your first name, Agnes. You don't need to remind me."

He was trying to lighten the mood, but his own voice sounded tight with anxiety. Neither of them, Deputy Hayes thought, were finding any of this day funny.

"Sheriff, we've got a new problem. There's been a shark attack out here. A girl is dead."

Static hissed on the radio. Deputy Hayes glanced back at Simone and the GulfDaze dudes.

"Sheriff?"

A click, a hiss, and finally a response. "Agnes, listen. I'm on my way to you. I'm taking a Sanibel Police launch. I'll explain when I see you, but as of this moment, all the beaches on the Gulf side are closed."

She walked away from them so they wouldn't overhear any more of the conversation. "Yes, sir, but are you saying you were already on the way here?"

"Give me fifteen minutes. I'll be there."

A click, and she realized the conversation was over.

Deputy Hayes turned and scanned the beach for swimmers, saw a few people in the water, and turned to the GulfDaze guys and Simone.

"If you're willing, I could use your help getting people out of the water." She looked at Simone. "I understand if you don't feel you can do this right now—"

Simone shook her head. "I'm good. I can help. I don't want anyone else to get hurt."

Deputy Hayes thanked her, and the four of them spread out across the sand, hurrying toward those few people who were swimming. But something niggled at the back of her mind.

When she had told Sheriff Reyes there'd been a

shark attack, and a girl was dead . . . he hadn't seemed at all surprised.

Matti stood on the deck of Captain Len's small sightseeing boat and marveled at the quiet, aware that perhaps "quiet" wasn't the word he sought. With the engine rumbling, the world had certainly not gone silent, but the wind had died down and the seas had begun to calm, and the shore of Cayo Costa looked like the apocalypse had come and gone. The trees were skeletal, arcing at strange angles toward the sky like the gnarled, crooked fingers of witches. They weren't all bare, but the hurricane had stripped many clean, while others had been bleached so white that they seemed to have been the victims of much older storms. Some were newly fallen and lay across the narrow beach, some partially in the water.

"Hey, Len?" Matti called, turning just as the captain cut the engine and dropped the anchor. "You sure it's safe here?"

The man might look tired, scruffy, even a bit strung out, but he knew his small passenger boat. The current continued to turn the vessel a bit, until it bumped the bottom, rocking on the waves just fifteen feet from the shore.

"Dad, look!" Kelsey cried. "More dolphins!"

Matti saw her pointing north, and sure enough the water churned with so many dolphins that it was hard to fathom that they were simply there, in the wild. That they could swim anywhere they liked, but they had decided to choose this moment to frolic off the coast of Cayo Costa. It emphasized the impression he already had—that there must be many hundreds of them in the area, perhaps even thousands. Captain Len had already given them a tour around North Captiva and into Pine Island Sound, where he had managed to locate a few manatee, despite many of them having retreated to safer water during the hurricane. The dolphins, however, seemed fearless. This was the third pod they had seen in just over an hour, but their omnipresence had not diluted Kelsey's excitement at all.

"Daaaaad," she said, dragging Rick over to the railing. Kelsey seemed very nervous about getting near the water, but she was okay as long as her father was with her.

Or Jesse. It made Matti grin to see the way the young girl's eyes sparkled when she looked at his son. Kelsey had grown up with Jesse almost an older brother to her, and she adored him, always wanting his attention.

The other passengers began to drop into the surf, wading through the crystal clear water. Captain Len had ignored Matti's question and gone to the rear of the boat, helping those who needed it to climb down the metal ladder. On an ordinary day, Matti figured this trip would have been loaded, with at least forty passengers jammed onto the boat, but today there were only ten, including himself, Rick, Jesse, and Kelsey. Most everyone had worn a bathing suit, except for one heavyset white guy with a shaved head and tattoos and flab that looked to have once been muscle. He wore baggy cargo shorts, but dropped into the water and stumbled to shore nevertheless, more focused on his small cooler of beer than on his wife and son. The other three were a trio of moms about a decade older than Matti and Rick and who appeared to be on a "girls' vacation." One of them, a ponytailed Latina with a gym-sculpted body, had glanced at Matti several times, not turning away when he noticed. He had decided to stop noticing.

As Captain Len helped the three moms at the ladder, Jesse and Rick dropped off the back of the boat. Kelsey jumped into Rick's arms, leaving Matti alone at the stern, looking down at the captain.

"You didn't answer my question before."

On his own now, Captain Len could not ignore him. "Sorry, what was the question?"

Matti dropped down into the waist-deep water. A wave swept in, soaking the bottom few inches of his T-shirt, but he hadn't expected to stay dry. He turned to Captain Len, assessing him anew. According to his business card, his real name was James Lennox, but he went by the amiable, somewhat-too-cheerful "Captain Len" for what Matti presumed were marketing purposes.

The man had to be in his fifties, but it was difficult to tell with any accuracy given how weathered and leathered his skin had become after years in the Florida sun. He was deeply tanned, his skin lined, and he had blond and white stubble on his face that made the tan seem even darker. He was thin, but his arms were

ropy with muscle from the work he did. His shorts
were spattered with different-color paints, and Matti
wondered if the man was an artist or had run out of
clean laundry and decided to put on clothes he normally wore to paint his walls.

"Is this place safe?" he asked again. "With the trees
down, and nobody around, I wondered."

Captain Len shrugged and glanced ashore. "It's as
safe as it usually is. Keep an eye on your little girl—"

"She's not my girl. She's my friend's. Jesse is my
son."

The captain blinked, maybe taking that information
in. If he had an opinion about Matti's son being black,
he kept it to himself, which Matti felt was wise.

"You're safe enough, Mr. Hautala," he said. "The island has residents, just a handful of them, but they all
went to the mainland for the hurricane and I'd be surprised if they'd already come back."

Matti nodded. "Thanks."

He waded ashore, where Kelsey had already com-
mandeered Jesse's attention and run ahead of the rest
of the group to search for the best seashells. The sun
beat down without mercy. What breeze there was hung
heavy with humidity, but Kelsey had zero interest in
anything that would have stood between her and the
huge, magical conch shell she now hunted. They had
found at least twenty in the past few days, but most of
them were small or broken or both.

Rick had waited for him. He wore a brand new T-
shirt emblazoned with a Captain America shield,
which Matti found amusing. Neither of them had

grown up reading comic books, but Rick loved the movies and had adopted Captain America as his personal avatar somehow. Maybe he thought he was fighting injustice instead of pushing paper. Matti did not want to be unfair to his friend, but he could not help wishing Rick would face his unhappiness instead of sublimating it.

"Hey," Matti said. "You want to follow the kids?"

"Yeah, but we don't need to hurry." Rick smiled. "Jesse's always been her best baby sitter."

"Kelsey doesn't need a sitter any more."

Rick nodded. "True. But let's face it, she likes him more than she likes me."

"He's much better-looking, and he's not her dad."

"There is that."

They started following their children along the shore at a distance. The three moms had stripped off their cover-ups and gone for a swim. Matti made an effort not to let his eyes linger on the woman who had been checking him out, focusing instead on the tropical foliage and those skeletal trees.

"What would it be like to live out here, totally isolated?" he said aloud.

"Paradise," Rick replied, scanning the trees. The island was quite small, but they could see a rooftop in the distance. "Or maybe Hell, I'm not sure which. If I was this alone, I might turn into Jack Nicholson in *The Shining.*"

"It'd be nice for a while, though," Matti said.

Rick sighed, and Matti did not have to ask him to elaborate. The guy worked so much and was under so much pressure that the idea of escaping his obligations had to seem like a dream. He knew he ought to strike up a conversation about it, ask Rick about his marriage and the tension with Corinne, but though they had been friends for a very long time, that was simply not the way their relationship worked.

Up ahead, the big shambling guy had perched on the edge of an old, fallen tree and cracked a bottle of beer while he watched his wife and son searching a field of seashells for perfect specimens. The shells had been spread into a fan shape here, thousands of little ones and hundreds of larger ones driven to this one spot by the way the currents collided.

"We should have brought our own cooler," Rick said.

"Next time," Matti said. "I'll tell you this much, though. I hope like hell that the store will be open later and we can pick some up. I think even Jenn might get a little buzzed without much encouragement."

"Say it ain't so," Rick joked.

Jenn had never been much of a drinker, but Matti figured that after the past couple of days they would all be in the mood.

The tattooed guy must have seen them eyeing his cooler. He lifted his beer to hail them. "Come on over, fellas. I don't mind sharing. We're castaways, right? We gotta stick together."

Matti glanced at Rick, who pointed at the man.

"You, sir, are a hero," Rick said. "Generosity is sorely lacking in the world."

They joined him on the fallen tree. He handed each

of them an ice cold bottle of something called Swamp Monster Ale, and used his opener to pry off the caps.

"I'm Ernie."

They introduced themselves to Ernie, and gave him the lowdown on their families while he talked about his own. When he began to comment on the three women who were swimming out by the boat, Matti shifted uncomfortably.

"What do you think about our captain?" he asked.

Ernie arched an eyebrow. "He's not my type. I guess his bathing suit's pretty cute though."

Rick laughed. Matti grimaced a bit, but when Ernie raised his beer to clink a toast, Matti did not refuse. All three tilted their bottles back and drank. Matti had never been comfortable with the way men tended to talk about women, even if it seemed nothing more than idle chatter.

"So, you guys staying on Captiva?" Rick asked.

"Yep. Down at South Seas Plantation," Ernie replied. "Didn't bother with a rental car, and I figured since we were on the third floor and facing the mainland, we'd be all right. Mostly that turned out true, but there's no power in our building, so I'm trying to keep us busy till they sort it out or till we go home on Saturday."

The conversation went on like that, with Rick engaging Ernie about the storm and its aftermath. Matti glanced up along the beach and saw Jesse standing with Kelsey about a hundred yards farther along the sand. Kelsey stood on the sand and walked parallel to Jesse, who had waded knee deep into the water and bent over, peering through the clear surf in search of shells. Jesse had his T-shirt pulled out in front of him, creating a basket in which he had undoubtedly been tasked with carrying the girl's shells. Kelsey seemed reluctant to go into the water and was instead directing Jesse's search. A sudden rush of love for his son swept through Matti. He was a good kid—a fine young man—and Matti knew he would never be prouder of anything in his life than he was of being Jesse's father.

He had always been sentimental and only grew more so with each passing year. He figured by the time he turned fifty he would be weeping at TV commercials like his own father had at that age.

Along the shore, a wave crashed in and Kelsey retreated up the sand. Matti frowned deeply. He had seen children flee from incoming waves a thousand times, many shrieking gleefully, but what he had just witnessed did not appear to be a game. Kelsey had looked genuinely nervous, glancing over her shoulder as she raced up the sand.

Matti looked at Rick, but he had been too wrapped up in his conversation with Ernie and had not been paying attention. Whatever had turned Kelsey so skittish, her father hadn't noticed at all.

CHAPTER 10

Jesse spotted the conch and a huge grin spread across his face. It was just laying there, a massive shell, bigger than any he had ever seen outside of a store. He had always wondered where they came from. Even most of the smaller ones ended up smashed, but the hurricane had swept in so many beautiful shells that his T-shirt hung heavy and wet and sandy with all of the ones Kelsey had demanded he keep.

This one, though—he glanced at her, saw her noticing his hesitation—the kid would lose her mind. He was happy Emma had stayed behind. Jesse liked her well enough, but Kelsey always seemed to take the brunt of her older sister's moods, so it was nice for her to be away from Emma for a while.

"What is it?" she called to him.

Jesse gave her a sly smile. He shifted in the water so his back was to her. Carefully cradling his shirtful of shells, he bent and hefted the massive conch, lifting it up, doing the best he could with one hand to brace it against his leg and search it for holes and jagged edges. The shell felt smooth and, if not perfect, at least close enough to be sold in some beach store.

He dropped it with a splash and let it sink to the bottom.

"Oh my God, what was that?" Kelsey asked. "Jesse?"

"Come find out," he replied, giving her a small shrug. "It's going to make your whole week. I promise."

Kelsey hesitated. She stared at the water where he had dropped the conch, glanced out at the deeper water, and then glared at him.

"That's not fair."

"I've been doing all the work out here."

"'Cause you're supposed to be a nice guy, and you're my friend."

He couldn't argue with that. "At least tell me what you're so freaked out about."

Kelsey glanced at her feet in embarrassment. "The shark I saw earlier. Everyone said it was a dolphin, but I don't think so."

His mouth dropped open and then he laughed at her.

"Hey!" she snapped. "That's not nice. I can't believe you're laughing at me. It just made me nervous, okay? Jeez!"

Jesse held up his one free hand, trying to wipe away his grin. "That's not why I'm laughing. I'm laughing because you are an evil kid."

She crossed her arms. "Me? I'm evil?"

He cocked his head. "You're afraid if you come in the water you'll get eaten by a shark, so you send me in to hunt for shells? Like, oh, it's only Jesse. If he gets eaten, that's totally fine."

Kelsey couldn't even argue. She tried to fight her smile, but then it blossomed into a giggle and she shrugged. "Well, when you put it that way, it does seem a little evil."

"Do you want me to dump all these shells?"

Her smile turned into panic. "No, please!"

"Then come on in here and get this absolutely massive conch shell that nobody will believe we just found in the water. I mean, it's so huge, you will keep it as a souvenir from this trip forever. But you have to come in and get it."

Kelsey kept her arms crossed, frowning nervously at the water around him. She glanced up and down the beach, out at the waves, and then sighed dramatically and threw her arms in the air. "Fine!"

As she reached into the water and lifted out the beautiful conch, Jesse heard his dad calling for them. When he looked over, he saw people heading back to the boat.

"Oh my God," Kelsey said, staring down at the shell in her hands.

"Come on, kid. We've gotta go."

As he led the way out of the water, she didn't complain about him calling her "kid." And she seemed to have forgotten her fear of imaginary sharks altogether. Jesse felt good, walking beside her. He had no siblings of his own and had always enjoyed the big brotherly relationship he had with the Scully girls, but Emma had become distant and a little strange, even skittish, over the past year or so. With nine-year-old Kelsey, he could still feel like a big brother, like he was helping. His parents wanted him to work hard, to get good grades or excel on the baseball diamond, so he could feel proud of himself, but those things never felt to him like sources of pride. Making Kelsey feel better was different.

"They better not leave without us," she said, picking up her pace on the sand.

Jesse smiled. "Race you back?"

She started to reply, then bolted in mid-sentence to get a head start, laughing the whole way. Kelsey looked absurd, jogging with that huge shell cradled against her abdomen, but Jesse knew he must have appeared even more ridiculous as he tried to catch up with her. The sagging belly of his shirt, laden with shells, made him look and run like a pregnant woman.

The three middle-aged women were still swimming, extending their stay on Cayo Costa for a few extra minutes despite the scowl of Captain Len. The massive, rotund guy talking to Jesse and Kelsey's fathers shuffled over to admire his kid's sand castle and help his wife pack up. Despite their burdens, and with Jesse calling her a cheater the whole way, he and Kelsey managed to reach the boat first. They waded into the water—Jesse noticing Kelsey's wary glances out at the waves, in search of fins—and carefully climbed aboard.

"That's a hell of a prize," Captain Len said as he

helped Kelsey up. "Best conch I've ever seen somebody find out here. You must be the luckiest kid alive."

Kelsey beamed. As Jesse followed her up onto the deck, clutching his wet, sandy, shell-laden shirt against him, he nodded his gratitude to the captain. The guy had seemed like a bit of a jerk earlier, but he'd been very kind to Kelsey and that went a long way.

"Excuse me," Jesse said, as Captain Len called out to the others that it was time to depart. "Any chance you have a plastic bag or something, so I can get these shells out of my shirt?"

The captain barely looked at him. "Not sure. If you wanna check the cabinet in the head, you might find something."

Jesse went across to the enclosed area of the deck. Kelsey had already gone inside and as he walked past her, he smiled again. She had put the conch on the seat beside her as if it were her favorite pet. If she had been any younger, he thought, she would have started holding conversations with it.

"I'll be right back," he told her, and he went carefully down the narrow steps to the cabin area, where a rope bearing a Crew Only sign hung across the passageway.

As he opened the door to the head, he saw the narrow space, the toilet, and the tiny cabinet above it. A frown creased his forehead. His chances of finding anything useful in there were almost nil, but out of the corner of his eye, he spotted something that drew his attention. Beyond the head, beyond the Crew Only sign, another small door stood open. It was some kind of utility closet. A canvas bag lay half-spilled from the partly open door, some kind of gray shopping bag jutting out of the canvas.

Jesse glanced over his shoulder. "Crew Only" meant "Crew Only," but Captain Len had seemed nice enough, happy for Kelsey, and Jesse just wanted to take a quick look. If one of those bags was empty, surely the captain wouldn't mind.

He stepped over the rope. The sign swung a bit when his leg brushed against it. He could hear Captain Len calling to the others, getting agitated now. With a thump, someone boarded at the back of the boat, so it wouldn't be long now. Jesse opened the door a bit farther and crouched to look at the canvas bag and the plastic one sticking out, but the bags held what looked like snorkeling equipment.

Beyond the canvas bag, he spotted a pastel-green beach duffel with a flamingo stitched onto the side. Halfway zipped, it had another plastic bag sticking out of it. Jesse knew the moment he reached into the closet that he had crossed a line, but all he wanted was a bag, after all. Kelsey's shells were weighing down his wet T-shirt, stretching it out, and he wanted to divest himself of that burden.

Inside the plastic bag, he found an array of women's jewelry. Expensive looking. The bag contained two wads of cash and three cell phones.

Jesse held his breath. He glanced to his left, but the narrow stairs were in shadow. Voices called out up on the deck, but he was alone. He pulled the flamingo duffel toward him and positioned it on top of the canvas bag he'd first seen, and he unzipped it all the way. There were two other plastic bags inside, as well as several expensive-looking items. One seemed to be an ornate, antique hand mirror badly wrapped in a clean facecloth.

For a moment or two, he struggled to find an explanation that didn't involve Captain Len being a thief, but unless someone else had stashed this bag here, he could come up with no other rational answer.

Jesse rocked back on his heels, staring at the bag. He whispered to himself, wondering what he was supposed to do now.

"Little shit," a voice growled. "I guess you can't read the sign."

Jesse turned to see Captain Len on the narrow steps, staring at him, only the rope and the CREW ONLY sign between them. He stood up quickly, hands dropping to his sides. All of Kelsey's sandy shells showered to the floor at his feet.

"Mister, I—"

"Can't mind your own business? Obviously," the captain said. "Now why don't you put that back and shut the door, then get upstairs with your family?"

Jesse could only stare. His breath had caught in his throat and his heart tapped a rapid rhythm in his chest. Wasn't the guy going to hurt him? Threaten him?

"Come on, buddy," Captain Len said.

Warily, Jesse grabbed the flamingo bag and pushed it back, deeper into the utility closet. Was there some other explanation after all? Could these things belong to him? Had he been helping someone move?

Then again, what was Captain Len supposed to do, attack him now? Kill him, with his father and Mr. Scully and those other people on board?

Jesse stood. He shut the door. At first it didn't click, swung back to halfway open the way he had found it, and he had to lift the handle and give it a shove to make it latch.

"It does that," Captain Len said. "Pain in my ass."

Jesse stepped over the rope. For a moment, Captain Len wouldn't get out of his way, but then he shifted aside and gave him just enough room to pass. As Jesse slid by him, the man leaned over and whispered to him, his breath reeking of garlic.

"You forgot something," the man said.

Flinching, Jesse realized he meant the shells. They had spilled on the ground and he had just left them.

"Go upstairs. I've already pulled the anchor up and we're starting to drift. When we're under way again you can come back down and clean up your mess."

Jesse nodded and pushed past him, climbing the narrow steps.

When he reached the top, that was when the screaming began. Jesse saw Kelsey's panicked expression, saw the way Mr. Scully turned toward the rear of the boat, and then they were all rushing to the back, out onto the aft deck.

Jesse's dad stood at the top of the ladder. The fat guy's wife had climbed on board and now his little son was on the ladder, his father behind him in the water. They had also turned to look off the starboard side.

Two of the women traveling together were knee deep in the water, frantically scanning the surf. One had her hands over her mouth but the other stood partly bent, as if she might vomit, or as if she needed to search for something very small that she had lost in the waves.

The third woman had vanished. A pool of blood spread in the water, eddying and swirling, just a part of the ocean now. Something bobbed to the surface perhaps thirty yards away and began to float—a small scrap of brightly colored material, a swatch of the missing woman's bikini.

The other two screamed again.

Mr. Scully jumped off the boat, rushing to those women. Jesse's dad followed suit, wanting to shout for his father to come back, because Kelsey had been right.

Kelsey. Jesse glanced around, worried for her, and saw her rushing at him. The little girl wrapped her arms around him and held on tight.

"I told you," she said. "I told you."

One of the women went silent. The other started shouting, pointing to where the missing friend had been swimming. Jesse scanned the water, watching his father and Mr. Scully start to wade out farther.

A fin appeared, fifty feet away, and that changed their minds.

They turned and rushed for shore, escorting the two grieving women up to the sand, too late to save their friend.

"Nosy little fucker," a voice growled in Jesse's ear.

Strong hands slammed into his back. Kelsey screamed as Jesse went overboard, flailing, trying to reach for the railing. He saw Kelsey's wide, terrified eyes as he fell, saw Captain Len grab her by the hair and tug her toward the front of the boat.

Jesse splashed into the waves, deeper than he thought he would be. His feet couldn't touch bottom. Submerged, trying to swim, trying to figure out which way was up, all he knew was that the water felt warm, the current strong, and that the sharks were down there with him. Down there in the swirl of a dead woman's blood.

Rodney Smalls had been chief of the Sanibel Police Department for seven years. In all that time, there had never been a murder on the island, rarely been an act of violence of any kind. There had been precisely one accidental drowning and a number of deaths by natural causes. He liked the sound of the job—Chief Smalls—but he had never fooled himself into thinking it was anything but a cushy one. As chief, he didn't have to do any of the bullshit policing work. No speeding tickets, no parking citations, hardly any domestic disturbances. The job consisted mostly of paperwork, public relations, and keeping the peace amongst the various small-town roosters who strutted around trying to lay claim to what little power could be had over their fellow islanders.

Hurricanes turned his whole life upside down. This wasn't his first one and he figured it would not be his last, but those assholes who had raced their boat into Blind Pass as the hurricane had been blowing in had made it a much bigger headache than it had to be. If they hadn't died on impact—or in the resulting gas-tank rupture, or crushed by falling debris, or whatever had been their actual cause of death—he would have drowned them with his bare hands.

Instead, he stood on the rocks beneath the wreckage of the short-span bridge and watched men scrambling at the water's edge. A small boat had been anchored there, with divers investigating the remaining supports to see if they could still be used. Up on the Sanibel side, a crane waited to lower new beams into place. A short way to the east, through the pass, cleanup crews dredged the debris from the water.

For a little bridge, it was a massive effort, and Chief Smalls was impressed. The governor of Florida might be a shit-sucking weasel willing to take a bribe from just about anyone, but he had certainly gotten on top of this repair quickly. Smalls figured that was partly because he wanted to be reelected and partly because Sanibel and Captiva were havens for wealthy foreigners and less-wealthy vacationers who were willing to spend money they didn't have. The local economy depended on tourism.

Chief Smalls tapped the package of Camel cigarettes in his front pocket. He knew he shouldn't smoke, but the knowledge never interfered with the temptation. With a grumble, he turned his back on the workers and started to climb back up the way he'd come, to the Sanibel side of the pass, where a snobby

little restaurant looked out over the Gulf with a view
so fine they wouldn't let families with children in to
appreciate it. On the one hand, Chief Smalls usually
wanted to fling the little rug rats off a balcony when
he was in a public place with screaming kids and parents who wouldn't silence them. On the other hand, if
you owned a restaurant, he figured you had to be a
pretty confident asshole to alienate such a huge percentage of your possible customer base. But that was
their business.

As he crested the hill, he saw a vehicle rocking
along the road toward the pass. For half a second,
Sheriff Reyes seemed about to pull some kind of 1980s
movie stuntman jump across the pass, but then he cut
the wheel hard, skidding a little as he drew to a halt
thirty feet from the crane, and the repair workers gathered around it. Some of the men hooted, two applauded, and one—who'd been startled by the Sheriff's
arrival—gave Reyes the finger.

Sheriff Reyes climbed out, spotted Chief Smalls,
and jogged over to him. Reyes was a big man, and
Smalls often forgot how big when they hadn't crossed
paths in a while.

Chief Smalls grimaced. "Fuck's sake, Artie, you
drive like a prick. What are you doing out here?"

"We may have a problem," Reyes said. "I didn't
want it over the radio till we discussed it."

Chief Smalls threw open his arms to take in the hurricane damage around them. "You think we *may* have
a problem?"

Sheriff Reyes narrowed his eyes angrily. "You think now's the time for busting my balls?"

He glanced around as if to make sure they weren't going to be overheard, and then walked a few steps closer to the rocks the chief had just scaled. Waves rolled through the pass. The small boat anchored below rocked on the water. One of the divers poked his head up and glanced around, then submerged again.

"Okay, Sheriff," Chief Smalls said. "You've got my attention."

Reyes watched the horizon for a moment, then looked at him. "Short version. Turns out the Institute has been researching how to control shark behavior for years, trying to turn them into military weapons, maybe put cameras on them, turn them into spies or something."

Chief Smalls cocked his head. "Okay, well, that's fucking weird."

"One of the things they figured out how to do is make them meaner. Hungrier, too. Or at least make them *feel* hungry all the time."

Smalls frowned and shook his head. He tried to picture some Navy sailor in a dark room navigating the course of a torpedo, but instead of a torpedo, the sailor was controlling the path of a shark as if he were playing a video game. The kinds of things the military invested billions into would always baffle, but never really surprise, him.

He scoffed, nearly asked the question . . . and then the answer sprang into his head.

"You saying what I think you're saying?" Chief Smalls asked.

Sheriff Reyes glanced back at the water, and Smalls knew just from the worried crease of his brow.

"These pissed-off sharks," Chief Smalls said. "They got out?"

Reyes nodded. "In the hurricane. They're out there."

Smalls had two reaction settings—curmudgeon and smartass. But there were no wisecracks for him to make and he could not settle into the grumpy persona he had so patiently crafted. A hurricane he could handle. Destructive as the storm had been, he understood its power and its aftermath, knew how to calm the public and orchestrate recovery efforts. This was something else. Military-grade sharks were something that should not exist in his predictable world, and the news shook him. "What the fuck do we do?" he asked.

Sheriff Reyes must have seen how rattled he was, but to his credit the man went on as if he hadn't noticed. "Deputy Hayes is on Captiva. She has a few of your people out there, but she's going to need some more help."

Chief Smalls stared at him. "We can get some of the state police out there, but you're talking about reacting. You wanna just wait till people get attacked?"

"I want to keep people safe, Chief," Reyes said. "We need to close the beaches and put out a 'no swimming' order. It won't be easy getting people to comply, but that's our best option. Keep people out of the water while we go out shark hunting."

Smalls nodded slowly. A small laugh escaped his lips. "This is nuts."

From down in the deep current of Blind Pass, a voice called out. At first, Chief Smalls barely noticed. Reyes was in the middle of saying something about the researchers at the Institute and the way they planned to help with the search for their missing sharks, but then that voice from below cried out again and the hair on the back of the chief's neck bristled. He turned away from Reyes and stepped to the edge of the rocks, staring down at the boat moored down there.

One of the divers had pulled off his mask. Treading water, he held onto the back of the boat, looking up at the team working on the dangerous wreckage where the bridge had torn away. With the wind and the water, the workers couldn't hear him shouting, but Smalls had heard him.

"Hey!" he shouted down into the pass. "What's going on?"

The diver redirected his focus. "Chief? Did you see Dunwoody get out of the water?"

"That's your partner? Dunwoody?"

"I can't find him!" the diver called. "I'm worried he maybe got injured on some debris or something. He's not answering me. Hasn't surfaced. And there's no sign—"

"Shit," Reyes hissed. "Get him out."

Chief Smalls didn't need to be told. He had started scrambling back down the rocks toward the water before Reyes got the words out.

"Get in the boat," he called, wracking his brain to remember the diver's name. "Acevedo . . . David! I need you out of the water now, okay?"

Now just Acevedo, either. Chief Smalls thought about the workers on the east side of the pass, dredging debris. How were they supposed to do the job if they couldn't be in the water?

"What about Dunwoody?" Acevedo asked, still hanging on to the back of the boat.

Smalls scanned the rushing water, thinking about the deep channel, and what might be hiding there. He feared that if they ever saw Dunwoody again, he wouldn't be in one piece.

CHAPTER 11

—

Emma didn't mind being out on the beach by herself. Her mom and Mrs. Hautala had gone up to the house to see what kind of dinner they could cobble together with the groceries on hand, and to see what restaurants had reopened if there wasn't enough. It felt nice to be alone—it felt adult. Mature. Though of course she wasn't entirely alone. A handful of people were scattered on the beach in either direction, just a few dozen. The day had waned into late afternoon, the hour when families tended to vanish off the sand to begin taking turns in the shower and making dinner plans. The hurricane had turned this into anything but an ordinary vacation, but the rhythms seemed to have remained the same. Emma had been ruminating on this phenomenon. She understood that she was young and that, despite how ruffled her feathers became when her mother suggested it, she did not know everything. But she doubted she would ever figure out why people in a crisis insisted on behaving like nothing was amiss.

They had been through a hurricane. Yes, it could have been much worse, but water had flooded parts of the island and then receded. There was a frickin' hundred-year-old shipwreck on the beach where they'd been swimming a few days ago, and aside from her mother and father at each other's throats, everyone behaved as if this was literally just another day at the beach.

And if she were being honest with herself, she would have to admit that tension between her parents was nothing new. Another example of people shrugging their shoulders and continuing on. If a meteor had crashed onto the house next door, she thought everyone would just go all bug-eyed, shout "Holy shit, a meteor just killed those spring-breakers," and then her mom would ask if they wanted pizza or burgers.

A shriek tore along the beach, followed by a ripple of giddy laughter. Emma looked south and spotted a family playing at the water's edge. The dad chased his daughter into the waves. Emma felt a little frisson of fear for the girl, since her own parents had warned her about the post-storm riptide, but then she figured the father was right there with her. The girl would be safe with her father watching over her.

With a peal of laughter, she splashed her dad. He raised both arms and stomped into the surf in pursuit, grabbed her, and lifted her into his arms. She squealed with delight as he spun around and hurled her farther out. Arms and legs flailing, the girl plunged into the water. A wave swept over her and she vanished, then bobbed up again. When her arms flailed this time, they were reaching out in alarm. At this distance, Emma could not make out her expression, but she imagined panic there before the dad waded closer, plucked her from the water, and hugged her closely. She wrapped her arms around his neck with a ferocity of love that made Emma's chest hurt. Part of her wished she had gone with her father and Kelsey out on the sightseeing boat, but then she remembered the sour person her dad was becoming and she felt cast adrift by her own emotions.

Better to be alone, she thought. The words felt convincing in her head.

Emma lay down on her beach towel, enjoying the feel of the sun on her skin. The temperature had dropped, so when the breeze kicked up she actually felt chilly. But then it would subside and the sun would bake again. From somewhere far off she heard the sound of a police siren, but with all the damage that had been done, she knew emergency crews were at work, so the siren didn't worry her.

She felt herself slipping into the warm, soft cradle where sleep seemed only a moment away. The sound of the surf lulled her. She heard a gull caw as it flew overhead. Down the beach, the little girl's laughter erupted again and Emma felt herself smile as she drifted off.

Flinching, she inhaled sharply and opened her eyes. It took her a moment to realize she'd heard a noise nearby, but then the voices came again and she let her head loll to the left and squinted through her sunglasses to see two of the spring-breakers on the beach. Rashad and one of the girls—Marianna, she thought—and wondered if the two of them were hooking up. He wore a purple T-shirt with a palm-tree logo on the back and a black bathing suit. Marianna had a white tank over her tiny bikini, but the bottoms didn't cover much more than a thong. Emma thought the girl was overdoing it a bit. She had the body for it, but it just seemed a little *extra*.

As she watched, Rashad and Marianna walked down to the shipwreck. They glanced surreptitiously to the left and right, and then quickly ducked under the police tape with a confidence that suggested this had been their sole purpose in coming out onto the beach. Emma hadn't moved, but she kept watching. Whoever had been meant to guard the wreck had left their post, but it hadn't occurred to Emma to cross the line. A lifetime of having the rules drummed into her head had stifled her curiosity.

Rashad whispered something to Marianna. He hesitated, but she tugged at his arm, and he looked around one more time before they began moving alongside the wreck.

Holy shit, Emma thought. They weren't just examining the shipwreck. They were searching for a way inside.

That got her up off her towel. She stood, brushed sand off her butt, and started straight for them, glancing around in a self-conscious imitation of their behavior from moments before. She tugged up the police tape and ducked under. As she did, she caught a glimpse of the father and daughter farther down the beach. The little girl had spotted her and now started toward her—toward the wreck—as if she too felt its curious lure, and seeing Emma cross the line had given her permission to do the same. Unfortunately for the little girl, her father grabbed her, shaking his head, and tossed her in the water again.

Emma smiled to herself. The shipwreck was no place for a little girl to go exploring, so it was better that she have her dad around to play with her. Emma, though, was fourteen, and not a little girl anymore.

"Hey, what do you think you're doing?"

She glanced up sharply to see Rashad and Marianna staring at her. They stood thigh deep in the water, at a place where the hull of the old blockade runner had broken in half. The rest of the ship had never come out of the Gulf, but up close, just half of the vessel seemed massive to Emma. The darkness inside the broken ship seemed to whisper with the noise that she had always heard when holding a seashell to her ear, as if this were the sound of the ocean itself and the ship had been on the bottom long enough to learn it well.

Waves rolled even inside the hull. The sound shushed and echoed in there.

"I'm coming with you," Emma said. "I want to see what it looks like in there. Get some pictures."

The old wreck rocked a little with the waves, tipping toward shore, then tilting back as the tide rolled.

"That's a terrible idea," Rashad told her. He frowned, his profile in sunlight, although the rest of his body was wreathed in the shadow of the old hulk. "You stay put. I've got enough trouble with your father already."

Emma rolled her eyes. "Please. You're the one who was flirting with my mother. Which, by the way, is disgusting."

"She's right," Marianna said, then quickly shot an apologetic glance at Emma. "Not your mother. She's gorgeous."

"But she's old," Emma said.

"And married," Marianna added. "Sorry, kid. Rashad thinks he's charming."

"Hey! I'm standing right here." Rashad splashed her.

"Don't start," Marianna warned. She smiled at Emma. "Anyway, come with us if you want. Just don't tell your parents. We're neighbors for a couple more days. I'd rather not talk to that cop again."

"Deputy," Rashad said.

Marianna rolled her eyes. "Whatever." She had tucked her cell phone into the elastic band at her hip. Now she plucked it out and flicked on the flashlight function, then stepped into the darkness of the shipwreck's hull.

Rashad glanced at Emma. "Do what you want. But if you're coming, watch your step."

He followed Marianna. Emma hesitated a moment, thinking about how long the ship had been at the bottom of the Gulf and what kind of damage there might be. There was no telling where a piece of metal or wood might be broken or twisted out of shape. Every step could prove treacherous.

Her heart pounded.

She glanced back along the beach and saw the little girl and her father floating together in the waves.

Emma stepped into the darkness.

Tyler told himself it would be easier paddling the kayak on the way back. He and Kevin could have rented a double, but they had tried that once before and found themselves bickering whenever their paddles would get caught up together. Kevin always laughed about that sort of thing and declared the two of them an old married couple, but Tyler had never liked that comparison. They were neither old nor married, and Tyler didn't like the suggestion that the bickering was healthy, or even normal. No rule said they had to fight in order to stay together. Separate kayaks helped avoid petty arguments.

On the other hand, separate kayaks allowed them to indulge their natural competitive spirit.

"That the best you can do?" Kevin said, grinning at him. "I might have to trade you in for a younger model."

Tyler dipped his paddle into the water, racing smoothly across the sound. Kevin had gotten ahead of him, but sweat sheened the smooth skin of his back, and Tyler could see the effort involved.

"I'm pacing myself," he said. "You're going to burn out fast and then I'll have to wait for your tired ass."

"We still talking about kayaking?" Kevin asked, huffing between strokes.

"Ha ha."

Tyler wanted to tell him racing wasn't necessary, but they had been dating for seven months and he had grown accustomed to the tension that competition created between them. Most of the time, it was all in good fun. Sometimes it ended in an argument and other times it ended in bed, but it all seemed to balance out in the end.

The wind swept across the Roosevelt Channel, the water that separated Captiva from Buck Key Preserve. The sun felt warm and the salt air filled Tyler's lungs. He could smell the coconut scent of his sunscreen as he bent into his paddling, and a beat of sweat ran down the center of his back. He glanced at Kevin and smiled at the sight of him, grimly serious in his efforts. "Isn't this supposed to be a leisure activity?" he asked.

"Fuck that. We can paddle leisurely inside Buck Key. Winner takes all."

"Winner? What are we racing for, again? Normal people do not race kayaks."

Kevin dug in with his paddle. A few feet off to the south, a pair of fish jumped out of the water. "Who wants to be normal? And as for why we're out here . . . to get away from your friends."

"You love my friends! And they're *your* friends, too."

"Love is a strong word. I like Rashad and Simone, but Nadia and Marianna get on my nerves."

"You never told me that."

Kevin laughed. "You don't listen."

Tyler resisted the urge to defend his friends further. No matter how loyal he might be to them, the stress of the past couple of days had put too much pressure on them. Going on vacation with them in the first place had taken some persuading, but the way the tension and awkwardness had grown in the midst of the storm and its aftermath, Tyler had seized the opportunity to do something alone with his boyfriend.

Up ahead, Buck Key Preserve seemed like a tangled, impenetrable jungle. Mangrove trees grew at strange curves and odd angles, as if they had their own minds and had spread and twined their branches with the purpose of preventing human beings from moving amongst them. Tyler scanned the mangroves for some hint of the entrance into the river that would take them to the lagoon at the center. The trees created an illusion that hid the entrance, but one of the inlets revealed itself to be more than a curve in the key's perimeter.

"There it is," he said.

Kevin didn't reply. Tyler felt a flicker of alarm and turned to check on his boyfriend, just as Kevin used his paddle to sweep a blast of water into his face. Tyler sputtered and swore, lost his momentum and the rhythm of his stroke, but Kevin had kept pace the entire time and now his kayak sped past, overtaking Tyler yet again.

"Oh, you son of a bitch." Tyler bent his back into it, chasing after him. "That is so not fair."

"We never established rules of conduct!"

Tyler fell silent, but his smile widened as he redoubled his effort. They followed the opening in the trees, where the inlet turned into a winding river that would lead to the broad Braynerd Bayou. They'd paddle across it, then to the narrow, winding path on the other side. The current had already exhausted Tyler, but he comforted himself with the fact that they would have its strength behind them on the way back. Otherwise he would have surrendered now.

Halfway along that winding river trail, he kept his breathing even as he came abreast of Kevin again. He could not help thinking how much more fun they would have had on this trip if they had come alone. He loved his friends, but this vacation had hammered home that there was a limit to how much group time he was capable of enjoying before people began to get on his nerves.

As the nose of his kayak edged ahead of Kevin's, he saw something from the corner of his eye. In a fraction of a second, his brain interpreted it as a storm-felled tree jutting up out of the water, but then it struck the side of his kayak and he realized the dark shape beneath the water had moved.

The kayak tipped. Tyler got halfway through a shouted profanity before he plunged into the water. He swallowed salt water, started to choke as he kicked his legs, and surfaced. Coughing, hacking, he glanced around for his kayak and saw the paddle floating nearby. The kayak bobbed and drifted, already swiftly carried back the way he had come, twenty feet away. Twenty-five. He coughed again, and water sprayed from his lips. Frustrated, he swam after the paddle, though he had no further use for it without his kayak.

As his hand closed around the paddle, he realized he hadn't seen the downed tree, and now he glanced around for it. Part of a thick branch had been visible above the water, but now he found no sign of it, and when he scanned the edge of the mangroves on both sides, he saw no broken trunk, no felled tree.

Confused and angry, it took him a moment to hear Kevin crying his name.

When Tyler turned toward him, all of his questions vanished. A fin had broken the surface and now carved through it, circling around behind Kevin's kayak. Kevin whipped his head back and forth, torn between staring at the shark and shouting for Tyler to swim.

"Goddammit, Ty! Swim for the trees!" Kevin screamed as he started paddling furiously, bent over, panicked and flailing.

Tyler inhaled sharply, frozen for a moment with the impossibility of that shark. It couldn't have been real. This could not have been happening, and yet it was, and he turned and swam. All the tightness in his muscles vanished. His weak arms found new strength as fear fueled him. The stories he had always heard about sharks not attacking humans whispered in the back of his mind like ghosts, but those whispers didn't take into account the fact that this shark had just knocked him out of his fucking kayak and all he could think about was the fact that sharks had rows of teeth that would grow back if they fell out or were torn out eating prey. He didn't want to be the grist stuck in some shark's teeth, and so he kicked his legs and his arms turned to limp spaghetti, but he kept swimming.

His left hand struck rough bark. He popped his head up to see the dense shadows of the mangroves only inches in front of him. Tyler grabbed the branches of two skinny, gnarled mangroves, and a dozen tiny tree crabs showered down on top of him. One crawled along his right hand while he hoisted himself out of the water, scrambling into the copse of trees. His back and legs and shoulders scraped against the trees, but he hurled himself into the strange, tangled cage of mangroves. Beneath him, water and reedy moss were the closest thing to land. A few more feet and there was actual ground, soft and spongy, and vanishing as the tide rose.

He heard Kevin screaming his name and turned to see the second kayak gliding into the trees, empty of any passenger. The mangroves blocked his view and he hung above the water, twisted around and spotted Kevin just a few feet from the trees, hip deep, wielding his paddle like a baseball bat as the shark sped toward him.

Tyler screamed his name and dropped back into water, taking two steps toward him.

Kevin jabbed the paddle into the water, maybe aiming for an eye, but the shark smashed it aside and lunged at him.

Tyler froze as he saw Kevin go under.

Blood churned up behind the shark, and then it turned toward him. Tyler snapped back into action, turned, and clambered once more into the mangroves, where he slumped like a cut-string puppet and whispered his boyfriend's name. Sorrow carved into his chest and he felt hollow, so torn by shock that he could not even cry.

When he heard the splash, and the grunt, he turned. In disbelief, he watched Kevin pull himself from the water and climb into the mangroves just a dozen feet away. The shark sped through the current, ripping through the space Kevin had occupied only seconds before.

"Oh, my God," Tyler said, staring at him. "I thought . . ."

Breathless, Kevin nodded. Then he winced in pain, his face contorting, and Tyler saw the torn flesh of his left thigh and the blood that trickled into the water.

Out in the channel, the second kayak drifted quickly after the first.

They were safe, for now. But Kevin was bleeding badly, and they were stuck here, with no way back.

Mangrove tree crabs scuttled along his arms and shoulders, but Tyler hardly noticed them as he made his way through the branches toward Kevin. They were alive, and right now that was the only thing that mattered.

Matti Hautala saw it all unfold. Just as he and Rick jumped into the water, wading toward the screaming women and the dark-red stain spreading on the waves, Captain Len shoved Jesse off the boat. He heard Jesse cry out, heard Kelsey shout, and then saw his son plunge into the water. Fear lit up his mind with electric clarity. One of the three women who'd been traveling together had been attacked by a shark—killed by a shark, because nobody lost that much blood and lived.

Two fins carved the water, circling ominously, and then both submerged as if they had planned their attack. Which was impossible, wasn't it?

"Rick!" Matti shouted. "The boat!"

He didn't wait for his friend to put it all together. Instead, he grabbed Rick by the wrist and tugged him toward the boat, even as the engine roared and Captain Len started turning out toward open water. The husband, Ernie, stood waist deep in the water looking a bit like a confused sumo wrestler. Ernie didn't see the third shark breach the shallows behind him, but Matti caught sight of the fin and pointed, shouting for him to get out of the water.

But the big man was a stranger, and Matti could not afford to spare him more than a moment's thought. Jesse had plunged into water too deep for him to stand. The boat began to pull away, and Matti saw Kelsey standing on the deck with Ernie's wife and son, all of them confused and scared, but they were going to have to be Rick's problem.

Matti had to reach his son.

His heart hammered in his chest and a terrible dread began to choke him. He and Jenn had talked many times about what they would sacrifice for their son, and they had agreed that nothing held more importance than Jesse's life and freedom and happiness. If their house had caught fire and he could only save one of them, Jenn had told him it had better be Jesse, and Matti felt the same way.

His son.

He felt the presence of the sharks. As he plunged

deeper into the water, he knew the two that had submerged might be anywhere, but it didn't matter. If they killed him, and that gave Jesse precious minutes to reach the shore, he would gladly surrender himself. None of it made any sense to him—sharks simply did not behave this way. The world had made them the villains of the sea, painted by urban myth and pop culture as killing machines whose hunger never waned, but Matti knew that was an illusion. Sharks were predators, but humans were not their usual prey, and they were creatures of instinct, not malice.

And yet . . . a woman was dead, the sharks were near, and his son was in the water. Logic and reason seemed a luxury he could not afford.

Off to his left, the big man shrieked in pain and then his voice cut off. Matti glanced in that direction and saw Ernie on his side, face halfway under water, one arm being tugged into the surf. A wave crashed over him and the big man's face vanished, followed by the rest of him. One arm thrust up and then hammered back down, trying to fight off the shark, but a cloud of blood spread around him.

Cold certainty gripped Matti. These were no ordinary sharks. They were vicious, savage, swift, and starving. They were grim with dark purpose, hunting instead of casually feeding. As one of the other two women screamed, he knew they were all going to die.

Then he saw Jesse burst from the water. For a heartbeat, Matti stared at him, searching for that blood cloud on the water that would say he'd been bitten. Instead, Jesse stretched into an Olympic-speed swim, striking out for the turning boat. The motor roared and it began to pick up speed, but Jesse caught hold of one of the bumpers hanging by a rope on the port side, even as Rick reached the back of the boat and grabbed the ladder.

Matti saw a shark swim across the boat's path. Knowing Jesse would be safe, he considered making a break for the shore of Cayo Costa. Then he remembered Captain Len pushing his son into the water, and he recalled that little Kelsey was on that boat, and he hurled himself forward, swimming hard. If the boat had already begun to pick up speed, he would have had no chance at all, but Captain Len had turned her around, aiming the bow toward Captiva, and those precious seconds were everything. Matti had taught Jesse how to swim—both had been competitive swimmers, a generation apart—and he stretched into his stroke, aiming to cut across the boat's path.

Gasping, he plowed through a wave, kicked and lunged and angled his body so that when he reached out, his fingers slid across the smooth side of the boat as it picked up speed, roaring by him. Matti felt a scream building, a primal fear for his boy that hooked deep into his chest and made him kick into one last ferocious effort. As the rear of the boat slipped past, he surged toward the ladder. His fingers grazed it, caught onto a step. He barely held on, but then he got his other hand on the ladder.

With a deep, ragged breath, Matti hugged the metal steps in relief. He heard shouts on the deck and pulled himself upward. He climbed high enough to see across the deck—to make out Ernie's wife and son—and he spotted Rick and Jesse outside the wheelhouse, facing off against Captain Len, who had Kelsey in a one-armed chokehold. They were all shouting, but over the engine Matti could not hear a word.

He climbed higher.

From the corner of his eye, he saw movement, as a shark burst from the water. Its jaws tore off the bottom half of the ladder, ripping metal and cracking fiberglass as it scraped past. Matti hurled himself backward onto the deck so the twisted metal would not snag him. The mother and her son only huddled more tightly together and stared at Rick as he rose to his feet.

Matti scanned for the shark. He spotted a fin further out, not the one that had nearly gotten him.

Behind him, Kelsey screamed. Rick and Jesse brayed threats at the captain.

To starboard, a shark surfaced. The boat picked up more speed, but the shark cut so swiftly through the water that the boat barely seemed to be moving. He thought it would pace the boat the way dolphins did, but the shark arrowed straight at them. Matti tracked the fin, waited for it to submerge, as it surely must.

But the shark struck the hull head-on, full speed.

The shouting on board stopped. Even Rick, his daughter still in the hands of a stranger, turned at the sound of the collision. The boat rocked. It tilted slightly to starboard. Matti went to the railing and hung over, staring down at the hull. Fiberglass had spider-webbed all along the starboard side. He knew that was impossible, that no shark had the strength or speed to do that kind of damage, but he could not deny the cracked fiberglass . . . or the sound the collision had made, like wood splintering.

The boat listed a bit further, even as the motor careened them across the waves.

When a second shark struck, from the port side, Matti was not even surprised.

Shaken, enveloped in the surreal strangeness of it all, he turned and started straight toward the wheelhouse. The woman hugged her little boy and asked him questions, but Matti barely heard them. He had been a pacifist his whole life, but he knew how to fight if it came to that.

Something cracked on the side of the boat. The fiberglass splintering further, he figured, as the boat took on water.

But Captain Len needed to be dealt with before Kelsey got hurt. Captain Len, who had pushed Matti's son into the water filled with impossibly strong man-eating sharks.

Fucking Captain Len.

CHAPTER 12

—

Emma felt like the world had turned upside down, but it was only the shipwreck. Voices drifted and slid across the interior surfaces like ghostly moans inside a haunted house. Just Rashad and Marianna, she knew, but it still gave her a chill. There was something so strange and otherworldly about being inside the broken vessel, as if she had just smashed her way inside someone's tomb, and she supposed that in a way that was precisely what all three of them were doing—not breaking in, perhaps, but certainly trespassing.

The ship rocked slightly, and with each large wave outside water rushed into the lowest parts of the wreck. At this angle, what had once been a wall had become the floor. She ducked her head slightly as she walked, wary of rusty doors that hung open above her. The water rushed in again and the boat rocked, and it all sounded to her as if the wreck were one enormous iron lung, breathing in and out.

Emma felt a frisson of fear run through her, or perhaps that was excitement. She found she could barely tell the difference between the two. Fascination prickled the little hairs on her arms as she walked away from the daylight streaming in behind her and stepped carefully around a door in the floor-that-had-been-a-wall. At an iron stairwell that went off to her right but would once have led upward inside the ship, she paused to listen for voices, wondering which way Rashad and Marianna had gone. The sounds bounced off the walls, difficult to pinpoint, but after a few moments she realized they had gone through the stairwell, so she followed. With the ship at this angle, Emma only had to walk alongside the steps and then duck way down to creep through the doorway.

Inside the next level—what would have been the deck above where she'd entered—the light had dimmed dramatically. In a yellowing gloom, she spotted dark figures farther along the corridor and a glow from someone's cell phone. She stumbled a bit on something affixed to the wall beneath her feet, but with the creak and tilt and hush of the water ebbing and flowing inside the wreck, her little noise did not attract attention from Rashad or Marianna.

"This is so eerie," Rashad said, his voice slithering back along the corridor, echoing off the walls and the water underfoot. It seemed disembodied, as if the words came from somewhere other than those two dark figures.

Emma thought of a dozen horror movies she'd seen and then smiled to herself. There were no ghosts or demons or curses inside this old, rusted hulk, but from his words, it was obvious Rashad was just as creeped out by the wreck as she was.

"Don't be a wimp," Marianna told him, her voice also disembodied and far away. "You'll never do something this cool in your life. Think about it. This boat has been at the bottom of the Gulf for a century and a half. Nobody's been in here except us and a lot of fish in all that time. There's no telling what we could find in here. Civil War secrets. Nineteenth-century whiskey. Confederate Army gold."

Emma decided she liked Marianna. Her own thoughts had been running along the same path. Her heartbeat had quickened and she found herself glancing back and forth, wanting to take in every inch of this piece of history. It seemed in that moment that she had spent her entire life just drifting through the world with no real purpose and no passion. For the first time, she felt ignited, desperate to learn more, to see more, to discover, and Emma wondered if this was what it felt like when a spark caught fire. Her mother had often talked about that feeling, when you realize that something is more than an interest . . . it's a calling.

Was history her calling? Archaeology? She didn't want to end up just teaching people about stuff like this, but being one of the first people to touch a piece of the past stirred an interest in learning that she'd never before experienced. Certainly none of her middle-school teachers had inspired that interest, but in a matter of weeks she would leave eighth grade behind forever, and in the fall she would start high school. Maybe high school would be different.

The boat tilted toward the beach.

Emma stumbled, went down hard, and banged her knee. She swore loudly, scraping her hands as she caught herself. Along the corridor, she heard Rashad and Marianna cry out. Rashad groaned.

"My head," he complained.

Marianna shushed him. "We're not alone."

"You're shushing me? I just smashed my head. I think I'm bleeding."

The boat tilted back in the other direction, the water that had gathered beneath them cascading side to side in a little wave of its own.

The whole wreck shifted.

Emma held her breath, thinking that it might have been best if she had listened to her mother's instructions, or gone with her father and Kelsey.

Those dark silhouettes down the corridor played out a strange pantomime as Marianna began to ignore Rashad, peering into the darkness around her. Rashad started climbing to his feet, touching the back of his skull with one hand.

"I'm not kidding," he said.

"Neither am I."

The moment the words were out of Marianna's mouth, the next waved rolled in, taller and more powerful than any she'd felt so far.

"Hey, kid!" Marianna yelled. "I didn't think you'd really follow this far. Listen, we can't be responsible if you get hurt in here. No crashers at our party."

Emma felt anger flare inside her. She hated being told what to do, hated being treated like a little kid— by anyone. It wasn't like they were talking to Kelsey. They weren't *that* much older than she was, college or no college.

"It's not your fucking property," she said quietly, her own voice carrying along the tube of the sideways corridor. "We're all trespassing."

Rashad laughed. "She's got you there."

In the gloom, Emma smiled.

The wave receded, rocking the wreck back out to sea, and Emma stumbled. Both knees hit the floor hard, but this time she kept going. The water sloshed as the ship rolled nearly upright. Emma's shoulder hit the floor—the actual floor—and water washed around her, deeper than before.

Down the corridor, Rashad and Marianna tried to catch each other and both tumbled over instead, tangled in each other's limbs. He shouted that she was trying to drown him, sounding only half-joking, and Marianna cussed him out.

Emma felt the wreck lurch and slide and sway, but this was nothing like before. The boat dragged and bobbed, and its weight shifted, and she flushed with alarm. "Rashad!" she called. "We're moving!"

Marianna laughed at her. "We've *been* moving, honey."

Emma had started to like Marianna, but now she wanted to throttle her. "You want to drown, have fun," she said.

As she started back toward the stairs—which were now beneath her the way they ought to be, water pouring down from this level into the next—she heard them arguing behind her.

Rashad could feel it too, the motion of the wreck, but Marianna doubted anything Emma had to say.

Emma reached the steps and started down, even as the wreck began to tilt in the opposite direction. The boat rolled. She smashed her ribs against the railing and started to fall. Emma shot her hands out, grabbed hold, and felt her shoulder wrench, flaring with pain at the same spot where she had smashed into it moments earlier. Crying out, she fell through the space between the railing and the stairs and plunged into the water that had collected there.

Panic seized her. Emma flailed in the water, held her breath as she got her feet under her, and tried to stand. A wave rolled through the wreck as the tide dragged it deeper, for she knew that must have been what happened. The tide had risen and lifted the wreck off the sand, and now the sea had begun to reclaim the ruined half of the lost vessel.

The water knocked her over. She tried to lash out with her arms to right herself, but pain burned in her shoulder and again she tried to get her feet beneath her, stunned to find the water up to her abdomen now, when it had been only to her knees before.

"Are you okay?" Rashad called, as he scrambled

through the stairwell opening. He hung from the railing as the boat rocked, and let himself drop into the water with a splash. "Shit, this is deep now."

"You think?" Emma said. "We're being dragged out. We're going to sink."

Marianna appeared in the stairwell opening now. She moved down more awkwardly, more carefully, partway hanging and partway climbing, like some kind of Spider-Girl.

"Not necessarily," Marianna told them. "Not immediately, anyway. There's enough air in here that we'll float for a bit, but you're right. Unless we hit a sand bar or someone takes enough interest to tow the wreck back to shore, it's going down soon."

Another wave rushed in. Rashad took Emma's hand to keep her from falling.

"I'm not interested in studying a shipwreck while it sinks," she said.

Marianna glanced around. "I'm with you."

Rashad braced his hand on the wall. The ship listed even more. The three of them took hold of one another, working together for the first time, and started wading toward the sunlit opening at the end of the corridor. The opening had narrowed, the hole filling with water, and as they were dragged out farther it might submerge completely—but they would be out by then. Only an idiot would stay inside a sinking ship if she had a choice, Emma knew.

"Do you think the crew survived?" she asked, turning to Marianna, who seemed to know about things like this. "When the boat went down, would they have abandoned ship? Maybe whoever sunk them rescued them from the water."

"Maybe," Marianna said. "I'm sure some of them didn't make it."

"No underwater skeletons on board," Rashad said as they stumbled together through the water.

"Not that we found, anyway," Emma said.

Marianna laughed. They all held one another more firmly, wading, ducking beneath a door that dangled open overhead. Emma made them stop, feeling ahead with her feet for a door or hatch that might be beneath them.

She scooted forward in the water.

Rashad's hand tightened on her arm. "Stop."

Emma winced and turned to snap at him, but when she saw Marianna's expression—frightened eyes, parted lips—she whipped around to follow her gaze. That's when she saw the shark entering the narrowing opening at the end of the corridor.

A shark. Inside with them, as the wreck began to sink again. Emma's breath caught in her throat and ice crept through her chest, like frozen spiders crawling on her heart. She shuddered, shaking her head in denial. She squeezed her eyes shut as if the shark might have been her imagination, but when she opened them she saw its fin and the ridge of its back above the water, limned by sunlight.

Out beyond that, she saw another fin.

"Oh my God," Marianna said at last. "This is . . . we're fucking dead."

Rashad spotted the shark at last—spotted both of

them, probably—because he turned and grabbed Emma's arm. "You've got to—"

She shook off his grip and hurled herself through the water, rushed back to the stairwell, and scrambled along the metal steps into the next deck. It should have been above them, but with the ship tilted so hard to one side it was now nearly parallel. Up would have been better, but at least she had a metal floor between herself and the sharks.

Emma ducked her head back through the stairwell opening in time to see Rashad leap up to grab hold of the doorframe above him. The door hung open, and he braced his feet against it as he hauled himself up through the doorway.

Marianna stood halfway between the doorway and the stairwell. She seemed frozen by indecision as the first shark glided along the corridor and the second fin entered the wreckage of the ship. Rashad shouted her name, but as frightened as Marianna seemed, Emma could see the swift calculus taking place in her eyes. Going up, through the doorway in what was now the ceiling, might be safer than moving sideways through the stairwell into the next deck, but the doorway was closer to the shark, and if she didn't make it on the first jump . . .

She turned and waded toward the stairs.

Emma shouted, urging her on. Marianna lunged and the shark seemed to do the same, as if it sensed what it was about to lose. Rashad called out, urging her on, and Marianna reached the steps. Now that the wreck had tilted, water poured from the lower deck to the upper, and Marianna hurled herself through the opening with that cascade.

The shark struck the submerged portion of the stairwell as it went by. With a metallic shriek, bolts snapped and the steps tore away from their moorings, twisted and bent. Emma had stood aside when Marianna rushed through, but she'd kept her eye on the shark, peeking around the entryway, and now she saw a tiny light blinking red, part of a thin silver band on the left side of its head, only inches back from its eye.

"Oh my God," Marianna rasped. "Oh, God."

Emma took her hand. The other girl was older, but fear affected people differently, and for Emma it provided one clear message—stay alive. She glanced up and down the corridor as more water poured in, and she knew they had to find a way to get on top of the newly sinking wreck, and signal someone if they were too far from shore.

"Let's go," she said, squeezing Marianna's hand.

They started down the corridor. Behind them, the sound of shrieking metal came again, as if the shark—either shark—had attacked the ruined steps a second time, trying to pursue them. Trying to get through. Marianna began to pray aloud, glancing around frantically as if she feared she was alone, as if she no longer realized Emma was with her despite the grip of her hand.

Emma squeezed her hand hard and gave it a tug, forcing Marianna to look at her. "Get it together!"

Marianna exhaled sharply and nodded.

The ship rose on a swell, the waves lifting it high.

As the swell subsided, the wreck listed hard. Emma and Marianna tumbled together and slammed into what had once been the ceiling of the corridor. Emma struck her injured shoulder and pain stabbed through muscle and bone. Blackness swam at the edges of her vision, and for a moment she lost any sense of self or place. Then she began to choke and cough, and she lurched up from the water pouring down around her, growing deeper by the second.

"Holy shit," she said, staring at the waterfall rushing down through the opening to the stairwell above. The ship had turned upside down, and all along the corridor, water poured in from above. She felt suffocated already, unable to breathe just knowing they had no way out.

Marianna grabbed her arm, wrenching that injured shoulder again. Emma cried out and used her good arm to shove the girl away, fighting the pain.

"What the hell are we going to do?" Marianna asked.

Down the hall, at the next stairwell, a shark slid over the edge and plunged through the waterfall into the rapidly flooding, upside-down corridor.

Emma twisted around, frantically scanning for an exit that would lead them back up. Up was down, now. The bottom of the ship was now the top, so she wanted some way up into what had once been the keel. But her thoughts would barely coalesce, because she knew the quiet, hungry, persistent monster swam down there with them, that somehow it had spilled through from above.

As she held her breath, the fin surfaced, the shark gliding toward them. Panic burned inside Emma, but she fought the urge to scream. Screaming would keep her from finding a way out.

Without a way out, even if the shark didn't get them, they were going to drown.

Corinne stared at her phone. "Jenn, are you seeing this?"

On the sofa, her friend stuck a finger in the paperback she'd been reading and glanced up with a sleepy expression. "I'm not seeing anything except words on a page, and they're blurring at the moment. I keep nodding off."

Corinne got up from the chair where she'd been curled up for an hour. "They've closed all the beaches. No swimming anywhere in the area, not the islands, not Fort Myers. And there's a small-craft advisory."

Jenn folded down the page and put the book aside, a frown creasing her forehead. "What are you talking about? A small-craft advisory is for a storm. The hurricane's passed. The bad weather in its tail went through in hours."

"Right?" Corinne replied. She went to the sliding glass door and looked through the ruined porch and the trees at the beach and the Gulf of Mexico gleaming in the sunlight.

Unable to exit through the back, she turned toward the front door. "The story I'm reading doesn't say anything about why the beaches are closed. I'm going to walk down there. See if anyone has an explanation."

Jenn slipped on her sandals. "I'm coming. And I'll try calling Matti. The small-craft advisory is so fucking weird, but it worries me. How big was that sight-seeing boat they were taking today?"

"No idea."

They didn't bother to lock the house as they went out and down the front steps. The moment Corinne reached the sandy driveway, she spotted the sheriff's department vehicle parked at the house next door.

"What's this, now?" Jenn asked.

Corinne didn't reply. If Deputy Hayes was at the spring-breakers' rental house, she would have the answers they sought. She picked up her pace, strode between houses and then up the steps next door. As she raised her hand to knock, she thought she heard sobbing inside but it didn't stop her fist from falling.

"You hear that?" Jenn asked.

Corinne nodded. "I do."

She knocked again, and a moment later Deputy Hayes opened the door. When they had met before the storm, the woman had seemed relaxed and confident, formidable, and put together. Now she had frayed somewhat. Dark circles underlined her eyes. She looked tired and pale and more than a little sad.

"The neighbors," Deputy Hayes said. "What can I do for you?"

"We're wondering . . ." Corinne began, but she let the words trail off as the sound of a woman crying reached them from the kitchen. They couldn't see who might be there, but the noise could be mistaken for nothing else.

"The beaches are closed," Jenn said, taking up for her. "We hoped you could tell us why."

Deputy Hayes looked more tired than ever. The crow's feet at the edges of her eyes crinkled as she glanced toward the kitchen, then nodded silently and began to step out to join them on the stoop.

"It's all right," a cracked, broken voice said from within. "Let them in."

Corinne felt uneasy. Her skin prickled and something about the air did not feel right, like the sunshine and calm winds were a lie and there really was another storm on the way. Deputy Hayes swung the door inward, and they could see one of the spring-break girls stepping out from the kitchen with a cup of coffee in her hands, warming them on the mug. She wore a neon-blue Captiva Island sweatshirt and bikini bottoms, as if she'd started to change her clothes from the beach and forgotten halfway through.

"There's been a shark attack," Deputy Hayes said. "Simone and her friend Nadia were on WaveRunners and encountered multiple sharks. Nadia did not make it back to shore."

Corinne felt sick. Hollow inside.

"Oh my God," Jenn said. "I'm so sorry."

"Is there anything we can do?" Corinne asked. "Where are your friends?"

The girl, Simone, shrugged. She tried to speak, but emotion stole her words and she turned her back to them, sipping coffee with shaking hands.

"We're trying to locate them now," Deputy Hayes said quietly, using her body to try to diminish the sound. "But we're shorthanded, as you can imagine."

"They must be on the beach," Corinne said, her thoughts shifting to her eldest daughter. Emma had been down on the beach alone. She'd wanted to wander and read, and Corinne had thought that would be fine because of course there would be other people there. Not many, but enough.

"WaveRunners," Jenn said softly. "That's the reason for the small craft advisory?"

Deputy Hayes glanced at the floor. "Not exactly."

"So what is it, exactly? Because our husbands and two of our kids are out on a small sightseeing boat and it'd be nice to know if there's something to be concerned about."

The deputy steadied her gaze, looked back and forth between them, and seemed to make a decision. "If I were you, I'd contact them and tell them to get back here as soon as possible."

"You want to explain that?" Corinne asked.

"I do want to, yes, but I'm afraid I can't."

Corinne looked at Simone, who stood over in the kitchen staring toward the Gulf, even though their sunroom had been ruined by a fallen tree. She ignored them, as if to her mind they had vanished entirely.

"You've got this, Jenn?" Corinne said, stepping back out the door. "I've got to find Emma."

She did not wait for her friend to reply before rushing down the steps. If there was anything she knew she could rely on in the world, it was the determination and utter competence of Jennifer Claire Hautala. She was a woman who accomplished things, who took on a task and made it happen in ways that forced others to recognize just how woefully inadequate they were at getting shit done. Jenn would get in touch with the guys and make sure all was well.

But Emma was Corinne's responsibility.

She walked between the two houses and hurried along the path that led to the beach, picking up speed with every stride. By the time she emerged from the palms and underbrush onto the open sand, she had nearly broken into a run, but now she skidded to a halt and glanced up and down the shore. There were people to the south, just a handful who dotted the beach, reading under umbrellas or drinking beers. A beer-bellied, bearded man in a sun hat stood in the rippling surf with a fishing rod, looking more content than she ever remembered being.

In the other direction, she saw two police officers talking with a couple of the employees from GulfDaze, as a third one attached a trailer of WaveRunners to a fat-tired four-wheeler and towed it up the beach to Andy Rosse Lane. Corinne did not have to wonder what might be going on over there—a young woman, had died in the water. There would be no body for the coroner to examine, at least not yet, and if any of the dead girl's body did show up, it would be in stomach-churning shape.

Corinne forced herself not to think about it.

She could not allow herself to think about it, because she could see no sign of Emma on that beach. She scanned the water, searching for the bobbing heads of swimmers. The only thing out on the water aside from the buoys the hurricane hadn't uprooted was that shipwreck. She narrowed her eyes and strode down the sand. One of the stakes the police had put in the ground remained, but the tide had come in and washed the others away, along with all but a single streamer of yellow police tape that lay in the water, attached to that one stake, flowing back and forth.

The tide had come in. Of course it had. The police would have known that, should have anticipated that the wreck would be lifted off the sand. Perhaps they had expected it, or perhaps there had simply been no choice but to tend to more urgent issues. Marine historians and archaeologists would stamp their feet, Corinne assumed, but that shipwreck returning to the Gulf floor felt like the least of anyone's concerns.

"Emma?" she called, feeling foolish.

Again she glanced either way along the shore, evaluating every person she could see, wondering who amongst them would have noticed Emma. She settled on the fisherman. If he had been there long enough, a man just standing on the sand seemed most likely to have taken notice of a girl on the beach by herself.

As Corinne started toward the man, she heard a cry. Or thought she did. It sounded far away, almost hushed, as if the wind had brought it to her from somewhere far away. She turned and looked back up the beach toward the police and the GulfDaze staffers, but realized the sound had not come from that direction.

She glanced out at the water, at the buoy, at the

broken smoke stack and the rickety remains of the paddle wheel on the back of the shipwreck, but she saw no one.

Just her mind and her hopes playing tricks on her, she knew.

Emma had gone for a walk, that was all.

But she kept looking up and down the beach for any sign of her daughter, and dread gnawed at her gut.

Shark attack, she thought. A girl was dead, a girl they had seen on the beach all week. Corinne had always told her daughters that anything could happen in life, and they had to be prepared. She'd meant for them to be ready to embrace opportunity, but now her own words took on a much grimmer meaning. Anything could happen . . .

Even the worst thing.

CHAPTER 13

~

Rick watched Captain Len's arm tighten across his little girl's neck, watched him pull the black-handled knife from its sheath at his hip, and a dam silently burst inside him. He saw the gleam of that blade—a knife the captain probably used to clean fish—and he saw the glimmer of unshed tears in Kelsey's eyes. It felt as if his consciousness lifted out of his body, as if he saw them all there for the first time. Matti and Jesse Hautala. The woman and her little boy, Emilio. Captain Jim Lennox. And his sweet girl Kelsey, who would never look at the world the same way again, would never truly put this day behind her. Every day at the beach, every unknown man, would be cast in shadow by this one moment. That much damage had already been done, no matter what came next.

"Daddy?" Kelsey said, her voice cracking, her eyes

pleading with him. She was brave, but how brave should one child have to be?

"Let her go," he said. No threats, no insults, no tough-guy profanity. He didn't want to antagonize the captain. He just wanted his little girl. "Please. I don't know you, but this can't be what you want."

Captain Len laughed, his voice as cracked as Kelsey's. "Damn fucking right it's not. We're sinking, you asshole. We're—"

An impact rocked the boat. The splintering noise from the starboard-side hull was louder than before and came with a terrible crunch. The ship listed hard to starboard.

"That's a hole," Jesse said, rushing to the railing even as the boat listed further. He looked down into the water, then turned to Matti. "Dad, there's a—"

Little Emilio began to wail, the kind of child's cry that carves a hole into the chest of anyone with a heart. His mother held him more tightly but said not a word, just waiting and watching to see what the rest of them would do. Waiting and watching to find out if they were going to die.

Captain Len moved toward the wheelhouse, half-dragging Kelsey with him. The tears she'd been fighting back began to spill down her cheeks. Rick started to follow, and Captain Len pointed the knife at him.

"Really? You've seen too many movies, Mr. Scully. You're not some action hero. Let's all just follow captain's orders and all will be well."

Jesse shouted something about the sharks, but Rick barely paid attention. His only focus was Kelsey.

"You!" Captain Len shouted to Jesse. "The goodies of mine you found below. Go and get them and bring them topside before we sink to the fucking bottom."

"Mister," Jesse said, hands up, moving toward him, "you don't need to do any of this. Don't you see the sharks out there? Something's going on. We've all got to get off the boat and nobody here cares if you stole a bunch of stuff."

Rick shot a hard look at Jesse. "Just do what he says!"

"But—"

"Jesse," Matti said. "Please. Just do it."

Rick saw the indecision in the kid's face, but then Jesse nodded and went below.

"Good. We're all working together here," Captain Len said.

Matti went to sit with the woman and her crying son, but watched the captain the whole time. "My boy's right, you know."

The boat listed further. The aft end tilted so hard to starboard that waves began to dump water onto the deck. Rick saw no sign of the sharks now, but little Emilio's mother held her son even more tightly and began to cry along with him. She spoke in quiet Spanish, something that might have been a prayer or a curse, and suddenly Rick remembered that he knew her name after all: Paola. He'd heard her husband use it while they were ashore, and suddenly Paola and little Emilio were more than just people on the periphery of Rick's own story, of the damage being done to Kelsey and the danger she was in. Paola loved Emilio as much as he loved Kelsey, had probably been a better parent than he'd been. The woman had anguish in her eyes, but also a brilliant light, intelligence, identity.

"Paola," he said, and she snapped her head around, surprised to be named. Their eyes met. "It's going to be all right."

She gripped her son more tightly still, raised a hand to point at Captain Len, and spat her words in perfect, sharp-edged English. "Not if that motherfucker keeps wasting our time."

Captain Len actually laughed. Something seemed to give way in him, as if he had been working from only confusion and Paola had given him clarity with that single, pointed finger.

"Scully," the captain said, "get to the wheel. I'll tell you what to do. We'll get to shore before we go under and the rest of you can do what you like. If you feel like going for a swim, that's up to you."

Paola stood up, holding her son. "There are sharks in the water. Crazy fucking sharks."

Her son wiped at his tears, blinking in surprise at her. "Bad words, Mami."

"Bad men bring out the bad words, Yo-yo."

Captain Len ignored her, gesturing for Rick to get into the wheelhouse. Rick watched the knife, tried to reassure Kelsey with his eyes, and did as the captain wanted. He had never piloted a boat before, but if Len instructed him, he was sure he could do it, and he would do it.

Jesse came up the steps from below with two heavy-looking bags in his hands. "Now what?"

"You just wait on deck," Captain Len said, the knife approaching Kelsey's throat again. "I'll let you know when I need you."

He made Rick go first, then followed him into the wheelhouse with Kelsey at knifepoint. Rick thought about lunging then, but could not bring himself to risk it. Kelsey began to breathe in little sips of air.

"Just let me go," she pleaded. "I promise I won't run. I just need to—"

"Stop," the captain said, jerking her against him. "I don't like this. Never wanted this. A few minutes, that's all, and then you'll never see me again." He gestured to Rick. "Okay, Mr. Scully. North Captiva's off to starboard. We're taking on water too fast to make Captiva itself, but I ought to be able to steal a little boat from one of the residents there. No choice. It's that or sink."

"How do I—"

Captain Len interrupted him, barking sharp commands, and moments later they were headed for North Captiva. Rick steered the boat, controlled the throttle, kept adjusting for the water they were taking on and the way it listed. Off to the port side, just ahead of them, he saw one of the shark fins surface.

"It's headed right for us," he said.

They were dragging now. The engine coughed and sputtered and would not get up to full speed, but they churned toward North Captiva. The island looked much like Cayo Costa, with the same mix of fallen, skeletal trees and the local greenery that seemed almost primordial.

"Dad," Kelsey said quietly, "do sharks do this? Do they attack boats? I didn't know—"

"They're doing it," Captain Len interrupted. "Never seen it before. What does it matter?"

In Rick's pocket, his phone buzzed. His heart ached. He knew it must be Corinne, wondering when they would be back, but he could not answer. Captain Len would never allow it.

"Coming up on North Captiva," Rick said.

"Throttle down and back away," Captain Len answered, a snarl on his lips.

As he did, the boat rocked from another impact. This one seemed less direct, as if the shark had only grazed them. Rick stepped back from the wheel, hands in the air. Captain Len kept his grip on Kelsey as he took the wheel and guided it toward the shore of North Captiva. Rick felt as if he might have overpowered the man then, when the knife was away from his daughter's throat, but he still did not want to take the risk. Letting the captain get away with his ill-gotten gains was the safest path for all of them.

"It's going to be okay, honey," Rick told his daughter.

Kelsey had been gnawing her lip, fighting her tears, and now she looked at Captain Len. "I hope the sharks eat your face."

"I can't say I blame you," Captain Len replied.

He backed away from the wheel, taking Kelsey with him, and stared at Rick as they made their way out of the wheelhouse. Out on deck, he turned, knife still hovering near her throat, and focused on Matti and Jesse, Paola and Emilio.

"Folks, we're gonna run aground. Brace yourselves."

Waves splashed over the starboard side. The boat listed so hard now that in moments the aft end would dip underwater completely, and Rick wondered if that would drag them down before they even hit the sand. How deep was the water here? Not very, surely. He looked out toward North Captiva as the boat limped toward shore, and they all heard the engine choke and a grinding of metal as the water that had poured through the holes in the hull finally swamped it, seawater mucking up the works. With a pop and then the quiet thump of an underwater explosion, the engine quit.

They all looked at one another, the fear tangible, but the boat continued to glide toward the sand. Long moments passed during which Rick watched the twitch of every one of Captain Len's muscles, praying he would be as good as his word, that he would not harm Kelsey.

The boat ran aground. They all cried out, stumbled, nearly fell. Paola crashed to her knees, alarming little Emilio, and she grabbed the boy and hushed him as the water finally swamped the aft section of the boat, a wave splashing over them.

Captain Len dragged Kelsey to the edge. They were a good thirty feet from the sand when the captain turned toward Jesse. "Kid, you're coming ashore with me. Just long enough to get those bags onto the sand.

Then you and the girl will come back aboard and you'll all wait till I'm out of sight."

Rick wanted to call him on poor strategy. Once Jesse and Kelsey were back on board, how could he make them do anything? But he had higher priorities. "You're not taking my daughter off this boat. Go, take your bags. Nobody will stop you. None of us care."

This last was a lie. The man had held his daughter at knifepoint. Had terrified them all and given Kelsey a lifetime worth of nightmares. They were all reeling from what the sharks had done, from the blood in the water and the screaming and the terror of that splintering sound in the hull, but they would all have been on shore already if not for him.

Jesse went to the railing, knee deep in water, moving at an angle on the tilted deck. He turned to look at Captain Len.

Then he threw the bags over the side, into the water.

"No!" Captain Len screamed, lowering the knife. "What the hell is wrong with you? You stupid fucking kid! Jesus Christ!"

Rick started toward him, but now the captain changed. His face lit with fury, eyes welling with his own tears. He touched the knife tip to Kelsey's throat and she screamed.

The scream tore Rick apart.

"Now you're gonna jump in the water and get those bags," Captain Len told Jesse. "You and your dad over there." He nodded toward Matti.

Matti put a hand on Jesse's shoulder and stepped forward. "I'll go."

"Dad, no," Jesse said.

"Someone's gotta go," Captain Len said, hatred and a lifetime of bitterness on his face. "Should be the kid, since he was the asshole who decided to make a point. Things were going so well."

"You want your bags. Just leave us here," Jesse said, with fire in his eyes. "Go, man. The boat is sinking. Just fucking go!"

Rick should have been proud of him, but with Kelsey in danger, he wanted to throttle the boy.

Kelsey stared at Jesse in horror, then looked at her father with an expression full of sorrow, devoid of hope.

"The sharks are out there," Paola said.

They'd been so focused on Captain Len that Rick had ignored her. She held her boy and pointed to port, farther along the North Captiva shore. One fin cruised through the water. A second surfaced briefly, then submerged again.

"I'll go," Rick said.

"Me too," Matti replied.

Paola hugged her boy. Kelsey begged her father not to go, but what else could he do? Jesse had been shortsighted, too confident, thinking Captain Len would do the smart thing, the expedient thing.

"Do it," the captain said.

Rick and Matti moved into the water at the starboard railing. They weren't going to sink any farther, at least not till the tide rose higher and lifted them off the sand. Then they would drift and sink, slowly but surely. For now, they had a little time. He could see the bottom through a cloud of sand stirred up by the boat. One of the bags had bright colors visible even through the swirling brown cloud.

"Daddy, no!" Kelsey screamed. "The sharks will get you!"

She lunged, tried to get away from her captor. Captain Len shouted for her to stop, grabbed her around the throat with one arm, but as he did, the knife blade nicked her face, right along the jaw, drawing a stripe of bright-red blood.

Kelsey cried out in pain.

Captain Len drew back from her in shock at what he'd done.

Rick roared and charged up the tilted deck. Only ten feet separated them and he crossed that in a blink. The rest of the people on board vanished from his sight, leaving only Kelsey and the captain. Rick barreled into the man, grabbed his wrist and twisted the knife away from his daughter, shouting at Kelsey to *go*! Screaming at Matti to protect her.

Captain Len's eyes were wide with fear now, still damp with tears, but his rage had extinguished.

"No!" the captain said as Rick slammed him against the railing. "It isn't supposed to . . . that goddamn kid—" he muttered as he struggled to fight back. "Back off!"

Captain Len tried to shove him away. Rick hauled back and hit him so hard he felt knuckles break in his hand. The captain's head rocked back, and when he twisted upright there was only hopeless fury in his eyes. He ripped his right hand free. Rick tried to grab for the knife again, missed, and instead wrapped his hands around the bastard's throat.

The knife went in.

Rick exhaled loudly, gasping at the bright pain in his side, but he thought of the slice on his daughter's jawline and he kept choking with his left hand as he began punching with his other. Captain Len stabbed him again. Rick got both arms around the man, pinned him in a bear hug to keep the knife from striking again, and hurled the captain backward.

They tumbled together into the railing.

Kelsey screamed. Little Emilio kept shrieking. From the corner of his eye, Rick saw Matti and Jesse rush forward to try to prevent what was about to happen, but it was too late.

Rick and Captain Len went over the side together and splashed into the water, where Rick's blood spilled out, stolen away by the seawater clouding around them. Rick felt the water envelop him, tasted the salt even as he held his breath, and the pain of his wounds sang louder than before. He tried to wrest the knife away one last time, only to find that Captain Len had dropped it. The man's hands were empty.

Bursting to the surface, Rick grabbed the captain's hair. The captain kicked him, swimming away. He paddled in the water, staring downward, and then dove under, and Rick realized he was still trying to retrieve the things he had stolen.

A wave of weakness washed over Rick. Kelsey was safe. That was all that mattered. One hand on his side, pressing against his wounds and hoping they were not as bad as he feared, he turned to swim the few feet to the beached, sinking craft. The others were lined at the railing, Matti and Jesse, Paola and her boy, and Kelsey, with little droplets of blood trickling from her chin into the water. She gave him such a hopeful look that he forced himself into a pained smile, more of a grimace.

Her reply was an expression of horror. "Dad, swim!"

Kelsey was no longer looking at him. She was looking beyond him, and Rick knew what that meant. He let go of his wounds, let the blood flow, and gritted his teeth against the pain in his side as he stretched into a swim. Matti and Jesse shouted for him. Paola turned away, holding her boy so he would not see, and Rick wished someone would do that for Kelsey, to spare her this.

Please, God or Satan or whoever is listening, spare her this.

He could feel the shark bearing down on him, practically feel the rush of displaced water as it sped up behind him. Matti stepped over the railing, held on, reached down for him. Rick touched the boat with his left hand, reached up with his right.

Matti's hand closed on his wrist and started pulling.

Kelsey screamed again. She put her hands over her eyes and turned away, and Rick had a heartbeat to feel grateful that she wouldn't see.

Then Matti dragged him out of the water. Jesse helped him get over the railing. They were all scrambling out of the sunken end of the boat, even Kelsey helping her father, when Rick turned to look back the way he'd come and saw the shark thrashing in the water. It threw its head back, and Rick saw Captain Len, still alive, mouth open in silent agony and terror. The captain hammered at the shark with both fists as its jaws closed around his pelvis and abdomen. Rick saw water spilling out of Captain Len's mouth from when he'd been submerged. If only he'd had the time to drown.

The shark whipped him side to side like a dog with a toy as it plunged into the water again. Blood showered the surf. The captain's scream cut off.

Moments later, they watched the shark swim away.

Part of Captain Len bobbed in the water. The rest was with the shark.

Kelsey climbed into her father's lap. Rick held her tightly, wincing at the pain in his side, knowing he had to bind his wounds. He watched his blood run in little rivulets down the deck and into the water at the sunken end.

"We've got to get to shore," he said.

Out in the water, the second shark had joined the first, and the two of them were now circling back toward the boat.

CHAPTER 14

Sheriff Reyes held a dark secret. He had never liked boats, never liked being out on the water at all. He liked to swim in the shallows, where his feet could still touch the ground. Whenever someone discovered this secret, it was assumed that he must be a poor swimmer, but in truth Reyes had been on the swim team in high school and he had made it all the way to the state championships. In a pool, or in the shallows, he swam like a fish. His fear of drowning did not trouble him there, or in the bathtub, of course, or even in a river. But in the ocean, or a large-enough lake, he had always felt like the water was waiting to drag him down, as if it called to him and had laid a claim on him as a child.

Reyes knew his fear made zero sense, yet he could not escape it. Most of the time he managed to forget all about it, even living so close to the Gulf, doing a job that gave him responsibility over several islands.

But there were times when he had to swallow his fear and anxiety and step aboard a boat.

The Institute owned a variety of research vessels. One of them had been smashed into the marina in Fort Myers during the hurricane, but the others had survived the storm well. It hadn't taken long for Dr. Tali Rocco to summon one of those vessels, and now Reyes found himself in his least favorite place in the world— on the water, in a boat . . . hunting sharks.

The research vessel was a fifty-footer, its hull as thick as a politician's skull. It was a monstrous thing, with a crew of six, not counting the researchers themselves. Tali and her assistant, Philip, were crowded around a circular table just inside the cabin belowdecks. The area served as a sort of conference room, and even now Tali and Philip argued with their boss, Dr. Tremblay, on FaceTime. The two shark hunters were on the deck, rigging a massive, deck-mounted harpoon gun as well as a cage, in case one of them had to go into the water. Neither of them looked keen on the idea.

"You can't just turn them off!" Tali snapped in a tone that might have gotten her fired on another day. "You know it doesn't work like that."

"Even if it did," Philip chimed in, "the software at the Institute is ruined. There's a backup, but the thing needs to be rebuilt and we're out here on the water. Someone familiar enough could do it in a few hours, but until then—"

"You just said yourself it wouldn't work," Dr. Tremblay said, his voice tinny as it came through the speaker in Tali's phone.

"Not fast enough," Philip replied.

"Sir, you have to trust us," Tali said. "They have to be stopped. People are going to die, and the word is already out. Do you really want the media knocking at your door and reporting that you could have helped but refused?"

They continued arguing. Reyes blocked it out. He did not understand the debate. These weren't ordinary sharks, but an imminent danger based on unnatural species behavior. The Institute had been cooperating thus far only because they feared the public and political fallout of doing the opposite, but Dr. Tremblay's military benefactors had put a lot of money into this research and development, and they weren't about to give up their investment in these creatures without a fight.

Reyes's phone buzzed and he slipped it from his pocket. Chief Smalls was calling.

"Rodney," he answered. "Are the beaches under control?"

Chief Smalls laughed. His voice sounded small and faraway and the line crackled. "You kidding me? The word is out and I've got my officers and the state police working with your team, but with the power out in so many homes, it's been a challenge. There've been three further reported shark attacks. At least two fatalities, including the girl your deputy called in."

"And the helicopters?" Reyes asked.

"Sheriff, I'm trying," the chief replied. "The governor is balking because the choppers are still surveying the damage and looking for people in need of rescue."

"Goddammit, anyone on the water could be in need of rescue. Say whatever you have to say, but we need some of those choppers reassigned immediately."

"I'm on it, man. Don't doubt it."

"I don't," Sheriff Reyes said. "Just frustrated. This is not the job we signed on for."

A bit of static burst onto the line, masking the chief's voice. "—kill order?"

"What's that?"

"Did you get the kill order for the sharks?"

Reyes turned his back on the steps down to the cabin to make sure Tali and Philip didn't hear. They knew the answer, but he didn't want to rub their noses in it.

"Yeah. We've got the green light. Now we just have to find them."

"How's that coming?" Chief Smalls asked.

Reyes turned and looked down the steps. He could hear the scientists talking in the cabin, arguing with Dr. Tremblay. Philip seemed to have worked out a way to track the sharks. They were on an Institute research craft, so all of their equipment was here. But so far, they hadn't managed to track anything.

"I think they've figured it out," he said. "Let me go and put some pressure on them."

"You think they're stalling?"

"I'm going to find out."

Chief Smalls signed off. Reyes said goodbye and studied the hunters for a second. The harpoon gun now affixed to the deck seemed more appropriate for a whaler, but it would certainly work if these guys knew how to aim—and if they could find the sharks. He just wondered how many people would die in the meantime. If the beaches were closed, if the waters were clear, maybe they would get lucky and the two deaths so far would be the end of it.

No more stalling. He had to get Tali and Philip to do their job, whether they liked it or not. Once you'd created a monster, it was your responsibility to destroy it.

He started down the steps but his phone rang again. Deputy Hayes, this time.

"Agnes. What's up?" he asked.

The clarity of this call seemed much sharper.

"I'm talking to a woman whose husband and daughter are out on a sightseeing boat with some friends. They're not answering their phones."

"A sightseeing boat," Reyes echoed. "We just had a fucking hurricane. Who operates a . . ." His words trailed off. Did it matter? Tourists were trying to enjoy themselves in spite of the storm and some guy whose business had taken a hit had decided to make the best of it. "Never mind, Agnes. Have you tried ringing the company?"

"The husband, Richard Scully, made the reservation over the phone and he's got the phone with him. Mrs. Scully doesn't remember the name of the company. I think we need to get them off the water, Sheriff. Can we get a ping off their cell phones, try to fix their location?"

Reyes massaged his temple, but he only pondered the question for a second. "They might all be just fine, but under the circumstances, yes. Absolutely. Let's get these folks on dry land, along with anyone else we can find."

"What about you, Sheriff? *You're* out on the water."

Don't remind me, he thought, the old fear bubbling up.

"We'll be fine," Reyes said. "Just hope we get these sharks quickly and quietly. Between hurricanes and red tide, killer sharks is the last publicity this region needs."

"And people will die," Deputy Hayes reminded him, like a mother whose son had forgotten his manners.

"Yeah," Reyes said. "That, too."

Rashad shouted for Marianna, and for the girl next door, Emma. He banged on the hull from within as a dreadful claustrophobia closed around him. He felt as if he could barely breathe as the wreck canted to one side and continued to slide deeper into the water. How had it come to this? An hour ago, he and Marianna were just enjoying the sunshine and now he was going to die. Marianna might already be dead.

He thought about his mother, and what his death would do to her. What it would cost his father emotionally to be strong enough to keep them both from falling apart. His dad had never been the strong one, not in the small moments. His mother had been the disciplinarian, the foundation the family had been built on, but Rashad knew what he meant to her. He knew that when they got the call and someone told them he had died . . .

Oh, God, please let them find out from a friend, or at least from the police. Not from the news. Don't let them find out from the fucking Internet, from some well-meaning asshole who gets it off Twitter.

His father would have to be strong then, because his mother would break.

Rashad banged on the wall. "Marianna! Emma!"

He didn't know why he was bothering. Thus far he'd heard nothing, and he'd been walking and stumbling and half-crawling his way through the corridors for ten minutes. The temptation to surrender became physical. His body flagged, all the energy leaving him, and he wanted to just sit down and let the water pour in, as it inevitably would. He could hear the ocean filling the spaces in the ship, hear burbling and pouring and shifting along with the creaks and buckling of walls and floors as the blockade runner sank for a second time. The hurricane had stolen the wreck from the sea floor, but the sea would now have it back.

"Marianna!" he screamed, one last time.

Rashad felt a strange cold descend around him. Within him. He would not let his mother break, would not give in to the temptation to surrender. He sucked in a breath and trudged onward, up a sloping corridor, walking on what had once been the ceiling as the wreck sank further, knowing he was going the wrong way—that the hull would be the least likely place to find an exit.

He reached an open hatch and stepped through. To his right and down, the water had filled a narrow, steep staircase, barely more than a ladder in a hole. But down that ladder, where water had flooded in, he saw daylight. Through the water, there had to be a hole.

In the upside-down wreck, Rashad hesitated only a second before going down that ladder. He took a deep breath and plunged into the water. The salt stung his eyes but he had to keep them open to find the way out. The light brought him to a hole, open to the outside, and the sun shone through. He had to go down to go up. Careful not to touch the edges of the hole, he pushed off the wall inside the submerged corridor and swam out.

The sharks would be there, but he didn't know how quickly, and he had to take the risk. His other choice was drowning, or suffocating when the air trapped inside the wreck ran out.

Rashad followed the sunlight, swam for the surface, burst into the air, and inhaled greedy gulps of oxygen. By instinct he grabbed hold of a cleat on what had been the deck of the ship, and began to pull himself up. The wreck had canted so badly now that he managed to climb at an angle, scrambling along the pitted surface that had once been the ship's hull. His heart thundered and his chest ached, but moments later when he dragged himself into a sitting position, he realized he had made his way on top of the wreck.

He stood, carefully, arms out for balance, as he turned to study his surroundings. The ship had grown smaller, the wreck shrinking on the surface as more and more of it sank. The aft section jutted out of the water. Half a wrecked paddle wheel stuck out at a strange angle on the starboard side. Rashad spun around and felt relief wash over him. The wreck rocked back and forth beneath him, but he was not nearly as far from shore as he had expected. A couple of hundred feet, that was all—at least for now.

There were several people on the beach. He waved his hands, cupped them, shouting for help, but they did not seem to hear him. The wind kicked up, a northerly gust that stole his voice. They wouldn't be able to hear him, but he kept shouting and trying to draw their attention anyway.

Glancing around at the water surrounding the wreck, he saw no sign of the girls, but he forced his grief down deep inside and gauged the distance to the shore. He could jump in and easily swim it, but how long would it take him to reach the beach? That might have been the most important question he had ever asked himself, because though he saw no sign of Marianna, he saw a shark cutting cleanly through the water, passing through the space between the wreck and the shore.

Rashad had no choice but to stay put, there on the sinking wreck.

Soon, though, that would change. When it did, his only choice would be to do the thing he did not yet dare to do. He would have to swim, and pray the girls would do the same.

* * *

Kevin Li had never been certain he understood love. He knew how the people who made movies and TV shows wanted him to see it, as something people felt deeply and with a staggering certainty. Mostly straight people, of course, but even most of the films he'd seen from LGBT writers and directors presented love as something concrete, something that people recognized when they felt it. By those criteria, Kevin had never been in love. He had met Tyler Follin at a bookstore reading by Eleanor Babineau, whose work they both adored, and they had found one another instantly fascinating. Drinks had followed, and drinks had led to a predictable finale. Seven months later, they were still together. Tyler talked about being in love with him, and Kevin returned the sentiment, but it felt hollow every time he said it. Each use of the famous three little words seemed like a betrayal, because he wasn't sure he meant it.

What the hell was love, anyway?

Only when they had agreed to come on this vacation did Kevin begin to think he might actually understand love—and might actually love Tyler. He really liked Simone and Marianna, and he felt fairly neutral about Rashad, but he found Nadia insufferable. Just being around her and her feigned stupidity made him want to scream. He could not stand intelligent people who pretended to be dumb just to get attention, and he was sure that was half of Nadia's daily life. She had spent way too many hours of her existence watching idiotic reality shows and did not seem aware that the behavior of the nasty women on those shows was not something to which she ought to aspire.

Kevin hated breathing the same air as Nadia, but he had come on this trip anyway. He figured that had to be love. A week in the same house with Nadia, just so he could get to know Tyler's friends better, blend in with the group, all to help build his relationship.

Even if that only hinted at love, it had given him an inkling of what this feeling in his chest might be.

Now, he understood even better than before.

He crouched in the mangrove trees, the twisted and tangled branches so thick that only slivers of sunlight made it through the shadows. Little tree crabs crawled up and down the mangroves, and tropical birds cawed. The water flowed by at the edge of the mangroves—only half a dozen feet from where he crouched—and Kevin held on to the trees and leaned forward as far as he could to get a look out at the little inlet.

"See anything?" Tyler asked.

"No," he lied.

A ripple on the water gave away just the tip of the shark's fin, but enough for him to know it had not left them alone.

"We'll need to move around to the west, try to flag someone down in the channel," Kevin said.

Tyler looked down at the sodden tufts of undergrowth, but he did not put his feet down. Instead, he stood on the strangely angled mangrove trunks and hung on like some lower primate. He looked ridiculous, but Kevin felt a pang in his heart. This guy had become his comfort, his home, and he would not allow anything to happen to him, even if that meant putting himself in harm's way. This was how Kevin finally understood what it meant to be in love. If that shark came for them again, he would do anything to make sure that Tyler was safe.

"Do you hear that?" Tyler asked.

Kevin cocked his head and frowned. He hadn't heard a thing . . . or had he?

Yes, those were voices. Mangrove branches rustled as Kevin shifted them out of the way. A tree crab scuttled up his arm but he ignored it. Others fell to plunk into the water beneath them.

"Be careful," Tyler said. "You're hanging out too far. We should go inland. Cross on stable ground."

It was a good thought, although deeper into the mangroves meant forging a path through a thicker tangle of trees. And now wasn't the time, not as those voices grew louder. He hung out over the water, watching for any sign of the shark, and got a glimpse of the kayak coming their way. A scraped-up yellow skiff with two passengers, a middle-aged couple who babbled to each other with the easy familiarity of years between them. Silly voices, splashing with paddles, the woman admonished the man for steering them into the mangroves, and they flailed as they tried to point the nose of their kayak in the right direction. She wore a Chicago Cubs baseball cap and the most enormous sunglasses Kevin had seen on an actual human face.

The guy had a bushy gray beard and the sort of beet-red suntan that had clearly started out as a burn.

The ripple on the water turned toward them and then vanished altogether.

Kevin cursed under his breath. "Hey!" he shouted. "Get over here!"

The couple slowed their paddling. The Cubs fan glanced around, trying to figure out where his voice had come from. Her boyfriend or husband, whatever he was, lifted his paddle out of the water.

"Hello?" the guy called.

Tyler took Kevin by the arm, nearly toppling him from his perch in the mangroves. "You're going to scare the shit out of—"

Kevin ignored him, hanging farther out of the trees. He shook the branches. "Hey, people! Cubs fans! Whoever the fuck you are, get into the trees. Get out of the kayak right now!"

They spotted him. The woman started paddling again, trying to turn so they could pass by while keeping as far away from Kevin as possible.

"Go," she said to the man. "Let's get out of here."

Their paddling was off rhythm again and the kayak began to turn, gliding beneath a fallen tree and into a small inlet. The woman swore and reached out her paddle to push off the trees. Kevin's heart sped up as he stared at the water behind them, watching for a fin, for any sign of the shark.

"Listen to me," he said, and he began to scramble through the mangroves, moving toward them. "There are sharks in the water. We were kayaking, too. We were attacked. Now we're stuck here."

"What are you doing?" Tyler rasped from behind him. "Stop. You'll fall."

Kevin ignored him. He moved as swiftly as he could while still being careful about his footing. His shoe slipped off and his leg plunged into the water up to the knee. His foot wedged between two mangroves but he pulled it up immediately, dripping, and kept moving, bracing himself. He spotted a clump of solid ground tufted with undergrowth and stood on it. In front of him there was an opening in the mangroves that gave the kayakers a full view of him, and he saw the way they stared as they tried to adjust their course.

"I don't see any shark," the Cubs fan said.

"There sure as hell isn't any room in our kayak," added her man.

"We don't want to get in. Aren't you listening?" Kevin said, glancing back and forth between the kayakers and the water. "A shark attacked us in our kayaks. We had to get off the water."

"Look," the guy said, "we'll tell someone as soon as we're back at the dock. They'll come out and get you, I'm sure."

Tyler appeared suddenly, hanging halfway out of a clump of mangroves to Kevin's left, farther from the kayakers. He looked comical, and Kevin smiled.

"Hi, folks," he said cheerily, and maybe a bit maniacally. "Look, we're trying to help you here. But by all means, stay in your kayak and get eaten." He shot a grim look at Kevin. "Now can you back the hell up and we'll go back to our plan? Let's not—"

Kevin saw the ripple beneath him, then the fin broke the surface. The kayakers shouted in shock. Tyler spotted the shark and sprang back into the mangroves, but it smashed through the roots and branches, still mostly underwater, thrashing the tree as if to shake him loose. Both feet slipped and plunged into the water beneath the trees and Kevin screamed, hurling himself through the mangroves. Branches whipped his face and arms and snagged him, trapping him as if in a spider's web.

He broke free just as the shark made a second try, but Tyler had thrown himself forward, onto a patch of scrubby but solid ground in the midst of the tangle. Kevin reached him, practically fell on top of him, and a moment later they were sitting together, cradling each other. Kevin felt Tyler's heart beating against his chest and held him even tighter, more determined than ever to get them both out of there.

They sat and listened to the kayakers screaming. Kevin could imagine them frantically trying to paddle together, to coordinate well enough so they could get out of there. Then there came a thump and a crack, followed by a splash and then screaming. In his mind's eye, he could see what had happened without even looking. The Cubs fan had been knocked into the water. Her mate shrieked, watching her die.

Tyler tried to turn and look, but Kevin cupped his face and they focused on each other as they heard the sound of the guy trying to paddle, maybe trying to hit the shark with the oar. Did he try to jump into the mangroves at the last second? Maybe he did, but it didn't matter. They heard a terrible crunch and a scream and then silence, except for the sound of water being pushed aside.

When it had been quiet for several minutes, Kevin stood and helped Tyler to his feet. They moved carefully, watching for the shark, until they spotted half of the yellow kayak floating on the water, drifting away. The mangroves were quiet except for the birds and the shush of wind through the leaves.

"What do we do?" Tyler whispered.

Kevin started to reply, but a new sound filtered through the trees. He grabbed a branch and pulled himself up, turning toward the unmistakable roar. Tyler rose behind him, grabbing hold of his arm.

"Is that what I think it is?"

"Helicopter," Kevin replied. "Looking for something."

"Us?"

"Too soon. Nobody knows we're missing yet. But they're looking for something," Kevin said. "We stick with the plan. Let's get over to the open bayside. There's more open sunlight there, more chance of being spotted by a boat or that helicopter, if it's making more than one pass."

"Anywhere's better than here," Tyler said, glancing toward the place where the kayakers had been killed.

Kevin agreed. Together, they began to move through the mangroves again, swiftly but carefully. He thought about Nadia, and wished he had hated her just a little bit more, enough for him to have ignored his desire to get to know Tyler's friends better, and to keep from hurting his boyfriend's feelings.

He guessed it was love, after all. He was just glad it hadn't gotten them killed.

CHAPTER 15

Emma wished she could just break down. She wanted to stop, to turn invisible, to pinch herself and wake up from a nightmare in her bed. Instead, she stared at the hand holding hers, then looked into Marianna's eyes.

"Pull!" Marianna screamed. "Pull me up!"

No point. Emma knew that. She had her right arm hooked inside a doorway, keeping herself from sliding down the corridor into the water that rushed to fill the empty spaces on board the wreck. The water would reach her in seconds and then the shark could get her, like it had already gotten Marianna.

The girl began to scream. Some of it came out as words, but most of the noise was pure pain and panic. Marianna tried to pull Emma down after her, but she had little strength left as the water rose around her and her blood bubbled up in the foam. The shark had turned away for a moment and taken a piece of Marianna with it, one of her legs, Emma figured. Or most of one.

Emma cried, her lips quivering. She gripped Marianna's hand more tightly and tried to pull her up, as she'd pleaded, but she wasn't strong enough. She watched the other girl's eyes glaze over with shock and studied her face as the terror leeched away, all expression vanishing.

For a moment, Emma thought Marianna was already dead. Then the shark rushed up again. Emma saw its black eyes staring as its jaws clamped around Marianna's torso, those eyes gleaming with a promise: *I'll be back for you.*

Marianna cried out one last time, weakly, just a bleat. Emma let go of her hand, startled. Terrified. The shark yanked and Marianna vanished down the gullet of that flooded ship's corridor, and Emma felt a wave of relief and guilt come over her.

The water kept rising.

Emma hauled herself up by the doorframe, managing the strange angle in that upside-down, tilted, sinking wreck. Through the door was some kind of galley kitchen, its furniture rotted after a century and a half on the Gulf floor, floating in pieces as the room filled up with water again.

A huge portion of the outer wall was gone, ripped outward by years of pressure on the paddle wheel on the side of the wreck. The mooring of the wheel had cracked a hole in the hull. Water rushed in through that rift, but she could see daylight, see blue sky and open sea, and though she would have nowhere to run out there, she would drown or be chum if she stayed here. The water rising in the corridor spilled over the lip of the doorframe, along with traces of Marianna's blood, and she knew that she had no choice. The shark would be back. Her only chance was to hope they had not drifted so far from the beach that she couldn't swim to the shore. And that the sharks would not get her first.

Emma pushed off from the doorframe, jumping as far as she could. She splashed into the galley room and began to swim, shoving aside the floating debris. A wave pushed in through the hole, lifted her, and pushed her backward, and she cried out in fear that it would hurl her back through the door, but then it reversed direction and carried her forward instead, out into the open Gulf.

Another wave caught her but she swam against it, kicking her legs and shifting to one side. The water threw her against the hull, but she was outside, away from the shark. Her heart pounding, her skin prickling with the sensation that shark teeth might tear into her at any moment, she glanced around for anything that might save her. The shipwreck blocked her view of the beach and, looking out over the Gulf, she saw a distant buoy and several boats on the horizon, but no hope of rescue. She had to get around the wreck and swim to shore, but that certainty felt like a dagger in her heart. Emma wanted to cry out, certain that she had escaped the wreck only to die in open water.

To the north, the torn-open end of the ship had

submerged completely. To the south, the tip of its bow jutted from the water and the ship canted to one side. She could see the railing, dripping water. The hull faced the sky. If she wanted to try to climb, the railing would get her there, but scrambling on top of the sinking ship would only delay the inevitable.

Time, she thought. It would buy her time.

Emma swam along the sunken ship, kicking toward the spokes of the paddle wheel that would allow her to scramble over to the exposed railing. She heard a cheer and glanced up to see Rashad watching her from atop the inverted vessel. He clapped his hands and then shot them into the air like she'd just scored a touchdown, urging her on. Emma felt lighter, a flicker of hope growing inside her. The horror of watching Marianna die would stay with her. She doubted she would ever forget the feel of the girl's hand slipping from her own. But she wanted to live, needed to hug her mother and father, needed to laugh with Kelsey again. She was going to live.

When Rashad screamed her name, at first she thought he was cheering her on again. Then she recognized the fear in his voice, the panic, and she glanced over her shoulder to see the enormous fin slice the surface back toward the sunken end of the wreck. The shark that had killed Marianna might still be inside the ship, but this one seemed even bigger. Its back shed water as it picked up speed, and she could picture its black eyes even if she could not see them. Staring at her, filled with numb hunger.

Emma swam. She thought again of laughing with

Kelsey, of all the times she had teased her little sister, of all the walks they'd taken and times they'd watched TV in their parents' bed, nested together with the familiar scents of their mother and father. As she swam, her body thrumming with the thunderous drum of her heart, it was a shock for her to realize it would be Kelsey she missed the most, not her mom or dad. As much as she had teased Kelsey, Emma had wanted to be a good big sister, wanted to give out all of the advice their mother had never given her.

Part of her broke, deep inside. She bottled up a scream that wanted to rip free, to paralyze her. Instead, she swam harder.

Her hand banged against the paddle wheel. Emma wrapped both hands around a thick spoke and dragged herself out of the water. She scrambled into the architecture of the paddle wheel and lay against the hull. After a moment, she got her feet on top of the spoke, then climbed along the metal, moving higher above the waves. Her feet were six inches above the water. Twelve. Twenty.

She reached the deck railing and began to slide along it, shuffling on the hull, face and belly against the rusted, pitted metal. Over her head, she heard Rashad shouting, and she glanced north and saw the shark's fin vanish, blue-white surf roiling in its wake. For a moment she felt relief.

"Emma, climb!" Rashad shouted. "You've got to get higher! Climb!"

She glanced up, saw the desperation in his eyes as he edged toward her on the curving hull, and she understood. The hull hadn't been smooth for a century, so she might drag herself up along it, but the slope remained too steep. She shuffled closer to the bow, moving along the upside-down railing, and started to drag herself up.

Rashad shouted a warning.

Emma threw herself sideways just as the shark burst from the water and struck the underside of the railing with a crunch of metal. Above her, Rashad lost his footing. He toppled backward, thumped his head on the hull, and began to slide. Swearing, he turned and scrabbled against the hull, his feet trying to find purchase even as the shark splashed down into the water and vanished again.

Rashad hit the railing with one foot. The other slipped through and he tumbled sideways to land on the railing, dangling over the waves like bait. Emma scrambled to get a better position, knowing all the while that the shark would come back. She could feel the seconds ticking by in her head.

"Let's go!" she said. "Please!"

She grabbed Rashad's arm, helped him extricate himself from the railing, and then the two of them were crawling like spiders up the pitted, rusted hull. Rashad nearly skidded down again but managed to keep going. Emma skinned her knees and scraped her hands, but she didn't care.

Something bumped the wreck. The shark, down below, gliding its bulk against the railing where it went underwater. Her pulse raced, but she kept her grip.

They reached the top together. Rashad slumped

down, whispering profanity and prayers. The wreck continued to drift and to sink. Emma and Rashad were safe for the moment, but that wouldn't last for very long. She sat up, drew her knees beneath her, and turned to look at the beach, knowing that even fifty feet might be too far for her to swim with the sharks down there. And it wasn't fifty feet—it was closer to two hundred and fifty.

There were people on the beach.

"Rashad," she said quietly, scrambling to her feet. She nearly slipped, but widened her stance and began to wave her arms and shout for help. Her mom was there, and Mrs. Hautala. Emma wondered if they could hear her, if they could see her.

"Oh shit," Rashad said. "Maybe we're not going to die."

He stayed on his knees, nervous now about falling off again, but he waved his arms and shouted.

Emma didn't look back out to sea. She knew the sharks were still there, and still hungry.

Corinne began to scream her daughter's name. She waved her arms back and forth just like Emma was doing, her whole body trembling. It felt like a nightmare, like the breathless terror of being trapped in an impossible dream, unable to wake. But she knew this wasn't a dream, knew that she had to act. If Emma fell . . .

No. Corinne rushed into the water, every muscle striving to reach her daughter.

"I'm here!" she shouted, cupping her hands around her mouth. "We'll get you! We'll come get you!"

She plunged into the water up to her waist, all else forgotten. Corinne had been worried about Rick and Kelsey, but she could not help them right now. Deputy Hayes had put out a call, and someone would be looking for their sightseeing boat. Kelsey was with her father, out of reach, but Corinne had Emma right here—a hundred yards away—and the power to get her to safety.

She took another step, prepared to dive in, and then Jenn Hautala grabbed her around the waist and spun her back toward shore.

Corinne turned on her, anger flaring. "What the fuck are you—"

Jenn stumbled toward the sand, picking up her knees as she ran. She grabbed Corinne with one hand, shoved her with the other, and though Corinne protested, Jenn maneuvered her back into the shallow surf. Jenn tripped, swore, and went sprawling on her hands and knees as a foaming wave rippled around her.

"What is wrong with you?" Corinne asked, hearing the brittle panic in her own voice.

Jenn rose, dusting off her knees. "What is wrong with *you*, woman? Take a look!" She pointed at the water.

Corinne turned to see two sharks cruising in opposite directions, crossing paths in the undulating waters that separated the sinking, drifting wreck from the beach. For the first time she noticed that Emma had stopped flagging them for help and instead seemed to be pushing her hands out, as if to keep her mother on the shore.

The wind shifted and she caught a snippet of Emma's voice. "—boat! Get a boat, Mom!"

Deputy Hayes came up beside the two women. "She's right, Mrs. Scully. Even if you had the luck to make it out to them, you'd never all make it back safely."

Corinne couldn't breathe. Her girl was there, right in front of her, a hundred yards of frothing ocean away, and she couldn't help. The boat seemed to have sunk much further in the past few minutes.

"Fine," Corinne said, turning to Deputy Hayes. "Call someone. Get a boat out here. But do it fast or it won't matter anymore."

She watched the sharks swimming. Much farther out, she thought she could distinguish the shape of another one. Corinne prayed this one would be a dolphin, but she feared everything was a predator now. Her memory flashed to the moment when she'd panicked, thinking a dolphin was a shark. Everyone had teased her, and even she had laughed, knowing how ridiculous she had looked. That memory didn't seem funny anymore.

"Hurry," she said again, watching her daughter, so close across the water, and yet impossibly far.

She heard Deputy Hayes on the radio, her voice urgent, but between the hurricane and closing the beaches, the whole area was in crisis. There were miles upon miles of beaches to patrol. Many people were in need of help. But only one was her child.

* * *

Rick felt the world stop the moment Kelsey made the jump.

He froze, hating himself for being wounded, for not being able to do this for her. Her arms pinwheeled as she took air, leaping from the deck of the sightseeing boat. Her legs pedaled at nothing, as if she rode an invisible bicycle. Her leap carried her farther than he'd imagined, but she plunged into the water nearly twenty feet from shore.

Too far, he thought. His voice caught in his throat. He wanted to scream her name, tell her to swim, to hurry, to oh-my-god-get-out-of-the-water. The pain in his side, where Captain Len's knife had gone in, flared up as if he'd been stabbed anew, but Rick dragged himself closer to the railing, got up on his feet.

Matti clutched his arm.

Jesse shouted for Kelsey to swim, to hurry, and she shouted back at him without turning around, sassy as ever. She didn't like being told what to do, his girl. But Matti had grabbed Rick's arm for a reason, and he saw it now—the first of the sharks carving its way through the water with breathtaking speed.

Paola's little boy, Emilio, cheered for her, but Rick lifted a shaking hand up to cover his own mouth, trapping the words inside. They had all agreed to this plan, all agreed Kelsey would go first, just in case the sharks could anticipate it after the first person had made it to the island. The others would have an easier time of it. They could even throw Emilio, hurl him ashore, but Kelsey was too big for that. She would have to go first.

And she had never been a great swimmer.

Rick covered his mouth, eyes wide, as he watched his daughter's pitiful attempt to swim that distance. He should have gotten her more lessons, made her a stronger swimmer. He should have done so many things.

Jesse and Paola and little Emilio yelled for her, their voices frantic now. Even the little boy could see what it meant, the shark's speed and Kelsey's slowness. Matti did not shout. He stood tall, put his arm around Rick, and waited. He was a good friend.

Ten feet from shore, Kelsey stood up.

Thigh deep.

She'd kept swimming when the water was shallow enough for her to touch the bottom.

Matti shouted, "Run, Kelsey! Get out of the—"

But he didn't need to finish. Rick's girl may not have been a strong swimmer, but she had always been fast on her feet. She bolted for the sand even as the shark skidded into the shallows behind her, so close that it slid on its belly in an attempt to take her. Kelsey splashed out of the water and turned. With a fiery rage etched on her face, and blood dripping from the cut along her jawline, she flashed her middle finger at the shark as it skidded back into deeper water.

Jesse and Matti and Emilio cheered. Paola clapped her hands.

Rick grinned, despite the pain and the blood seeping from his side, and when he tried to call out his pride to his daughter, he sobbed instead. Just once. His girl was safe. Corinne and Emma would never have forgiven him if anything had happened to Kelsey. He would never have forgiven himself.

Matti and Jesse had torn up a hooded sweatshirt they'd found on the boat and tied it around Rick's waist, padding the knife wounds as much as possible. The bleeding had not stopped, but it had slowed. Pain radiated from there and seemed to burrow down to his bones, throbbing in his skull and his teeth and the bottoms of his feet, nowhere near the wound itself. His whole body seemed to be sounding the alarm with a chorus of pain. He wished he could tell it to shut the hell up, that he was well aware how badly he needed help. But his body wasn't listening. His body was freaking the fuck out.

"All right, get moving," he said. "Jesse, you're next."

Matti nodded to his son. Jesse gave them a little salute and stepped to the edge of the deck. He watched the sharks, waiting patiently. Rick knew the sharks could not possibly have the brain power to figure out exactly what was going on, but still he worried they would notice Jesse standing there, that they would see the rhythm in this escape plan.

Jesse took a running start and jumped off the deck. He landed in the water about a dozen feet from shore, splashed down, and lurched forward. Kelsey threw her arms around him, and for several seconds the two embraced. Rick let out a breath he hadn't been aware of holding.

Matti turned to Paola and Emilio. "You ready, Mom?"

The little boy looked at his mother. Paola embraced him, kissed his forehead, whispered something in his ear and then turned him around and gave him a nudge. Emilio marched across the deck like a little soldier and presented himself to Matti. The boat shifted a little, rose and fell with a swell, but it remained stuck on the sand bar beneath the water.

"Ready?" Matti asked again, down on one knee this time, eye to eye with Emilio.

"Ready," the boy confirmed.

The sharks were coming. Both of them. But they had just turned toward that passage between boat and shore, and Rick figured they had enough time. Just enough. The boat lifted again and a frisson of alarm went through him. If they drifted away, without a motor, with holes in the hull, they were dead.

"Do it!" Rick said. "Hurry."

Matti called to Jesse, walked with Emilio to the edge of the deck, lifted the little boy into his arms. He hooked one arm around Emilio's chest and held onto the back of his belt with the other, took one step backward, swung the boy back, and then tossed him with as much strength as he could muster. A grunt of effort burst from Matti's lips.

Emilio cried out, flailing in the air. He wasn't going to make it.

Jesse ran back into the water as the sharks rushed in. Emilio stood up, waist deep and crying loudly. Jesse snatched him up under his arm like a football and made it easily to shore.

The boat rose on a swell and began to skid along the bottom and for a moment Rick felt it float free of the sandbar. He felt the flutter of fear in his chest and glanced at Matti, who nodded to say that he'd noticed as well.

Paola stood on the edge of the deck. She hesitated, waiting as the sharks circled. This time they did not swim quite so far away, as if they had recognized their error. The moment she saw them turning, fins slicing away from the island as if synchronized and then beginning to reverse direction, she clasped her hands together in a moment of prayer, kissed her fingertips, and held her hand up toward the heavens. She took three steps back, then ran and jumped.

She hit the water almost as far from shore as Kelsey had. Jesse rushed in to help her, but Paola didn't need his help. Rick marveled at how quickly she scrambled to close the distance between herself and the shore, and she stumbled out onto the sand when the sharks were still more than twenty feet away.

The next wave lifted the boat completely off the sandbar. Despite the holes in its hull that kept it from floating, the strength of the tide rocked the boat forward and then slid it sideways and backward, dragging it out. As the wave subsided, they came to rest again, but were now another dozen feet farther from North Captiva.

Matti went down on one knee beside Rick. "Come on, brother. Let's move."

Rick put an arm around him and together, the two men stood. The motion sent a wave of fresh pain radiating through Rick's side and he felt a renewed trickle of blood. He blinked, trying to clear the black spots that swam in his eyes, and he knew he had nearly passed out.

"Matti . . ." he said, sagging against his friend.

"Don't start," Matti said. "You can make this."

Rick hissed air in through his teeth and fought the pain long enough to grab Matti's face with both hands. He forced Matti to look him in the eye.

"I'm not going to—"

"Fuck you," Matti said. "You time it right, you'll be fine."

"You're wasting time. You know that's not true." Rick gave him a gentle shove toward the edge of the deck, enough to cause himself more pain. He grimaced as he stared at his friend. "Boat's gonna sink now. You help Kelsey, okay? When you get back, tell Emma and Corinne I knew I'd been an asshole, and I wish I'd had time to make it up to them."

"Rick—"

"Tell them!"

The others shouted from the shore. Kelsey screamed for her father. Jesse shouted for Matti to hurry, that they were getting too far away.

"We're *both* going," Matti said, grabbing a fistful of Rick's shirt and dragging him, staggering, toward the edge of the deck. "If the sharks are too fast, I'll abandon you, but you've got to at least give yourself a chance. You owe your girls that much."

Rick felt sick. He wasn't sure if that twist of nausea came from guilt or pain, but he fought it off. Matti was right. He didn't want his little girl to watch him die, but he didn't want her to watch him give up, either.

"Kelsey!" he shouted. "Don't look!"

Even from offshore he could make out the defiant expression on her face, but then Jesse put a hand on her shoulder and she nodded and turned away, wiping at tears in her eyes.

"We jump together," Matti said.

Rick wanted to refuse. Matti had always been a good man and this determination not to leave him behind was typical, but also deeply stupid. On the beach, with the tide coming in, Kelsey cried out for him to jump, to swim.

"Now, Daddy!" she called. "The sharks are swimming away!"

He leaned his weight on Matti, unable to look at Kelsey. It had been so long since she had called him "Daddy." His love for her fractured his heart. He owed it to Matti to refuse his help, owed it to Jesse and Jenn, because all that Matti's heroics would accomplish would be for the two of them to die together.

"Come on, man. Wake the fuck up!" Matti snapped.

Rick nodded. Steeled himself. Let the pain from his side wash over him, ignored the smell of his own blood. "Go."

Together, they stumbled the three paces to the edge of the deck. Matti had an arm around his waist, as if he were Superman and he thought he could fly Rick to shore. Rick forced his body to forget its trauma, to forget the knife wounds. He roared in pain as he launched himself from the deck. He clutched at his wound as they hit the water. The salt stung his wound as he pushed his head above water and gasped in agony.

His blood clouded around him.

Matti grabbed his hand and tugged, trying to get him moving. "Swim!'

Rick tried. With one arm, he clawed at the water. He kicked his legs, and he made some progress, but it was slow. Far too slow.

Off to his right, he could see the nearest shark prowling the shore. Its fin slashed across the water, picking up speed, and then it sank beneath the surface. Rick heard shouting. He kept trying to paddle. Matti grabbed him around the waist and flailed, trying to get the two of them to shore.

On the sand, Kelsey stood hugging little Emilio.

His little girl seemed so far away.

CHAPTER 16

⁓

Jenn had watched Emma Scully grow up. She hadn't been around during the girl's infancy—she and Matti hadn't known the Scullys that long—but it had been years. Long enough to create family bonds where no blood relation existed. Jenn felt about Emma the way she would about a niece. Her son and the Scully girls could barely recall life without one another in it. No matter what kind of distance had grown between Corinne and Rick, and as a result between the Hautalas and the Scullys, that shared history remained.

She couldn't just stand and wait. Couldn't just stand and watch while the tide dragged that old Civil War hulk out to sea, sinking Emma along with it.

Up the beach, Corinne paced in the shallows. She barked at Deputy Hayes, emotions brittle, demanding to know when a boat would show up to rescue her daughter and that college kid, Rashad, who was on the verge of sinking with her. While Deputy Hayes made promises that were undermined by the fear in her eyes, the ship vanished farther into the water. Only a twenty-foot arc of its metal spine still showed above water. They were out of time. The police might be sending a boat out, but unless it showed up in that very moment, Emma and Rashad were going to end up in the water.

The sharks had tightened their circle. They still swam around the wreck, but now it seemed calculated and more ominous than ever.

Corinne shouted and then she shoved Deputy Hayes away from her. The deputy raised her voice, and actually put her hand on the butt of her gun. That was the moment Jenn realized how insane the situation had become. They had very little time to waste, and pacing frantically on the beach wasn't going to help anyone.

She watched the sharks make another pass, scanned the water for boats, and then she decided.

Jenn turned and ran south along the beach, scanning the sand as she went. Corinne shouted after her, wanting to know what she was doing, but Jenn didn't slow down. She couldn't afford to have Corinne talk her out of this. She ran twenty yards. Forty yards. Fifty yards, and then she saw an enormous clamshell, cracked in half and at least a quarter-inch thick.

She stooped, snatched up the broken shell, and then waded into the water. With Corinne still calling after her, Jenn cut a diagonal path through the shallows, moving even farther away from Corinne and Deputy Hayes. As she did, the deputy began to join in, demanding to know what she was up to. Jenn ignored them until they started walking toward her.

"No!" she shouted, turning toward the other women, holding up a hand to make sure they came no closer. "Just wait a minute! I'm going to distract them."

"Don't be stupid!" Deputy Hayes called.

"We're not just going to wait for them to die!" Jenn called back.

Corinne looked confused, and Jenn understood that. Corinne's life had given her the good fortune to never know what it felt like to go to extremes. She'd never really had to. But Jenn knew what that felt like, and she was prepared to take those extreme measures when necessary. Like now.

"Get ready, Corinne!" she called.

In that moment the wind seemed to die, and Jenn could feel the sun full on her face, the heat baking into her skin. She let out a long breath, then inhaled sharply as she used the broken shell to slash her left arm. She tried to keep silent, but in the last moments of that cut she let out a cry of pain that startled a pair of gulls who'd been hunting bugs on the sand a few yards away. The birds took flight as Jenn stalked deeper into the water, continuing to shift away from Corinne.

"Oh my God. What are you doing?" Deputy Hayes said, jogging along the beach toward her.

Jenn ignored her. She turned to look at Corinne as she knelt down in the water. The Gulf was always warm, sometimes even hot, but she shivered with an unexpected chill as her blood seeped into the water around her.

The first of the two sharks curved away from the sinking wreck and began swimming toward her. *Come on, come on, come on*, Jenn thought, breathing through the pain and hoping it hadn't been for nothing.

"You're out of your mind!" Deputy Hayes said, standing on the shore.

But Jenn saw the second shark begin to follow the first, and she pressed her eyes closed, telling herself not to be afraid. That the beach wasn't far away, and she could make it in time—as long as she wasn't stupid. As long as she didn't wait too long.

Both fins sped toward her.

"Go!" she shouted. "Corinne, do it!"

"This won't work!" Deputy Hayes said. "Those kids are going to—"

"Shut the hell up!" Jenn snapped. "Help us, dammit!"

The deputy flinched as if she'd been struck, but then Jenn didn't have the attention to give her. She had to focus on the sharks. The two predators had split off, the fins gaining distance from each other even as they closed the distance on her, like lions pacing an antelope, wondering which way it would run but certain to kill it in the end.

Corinne plunged into the water. "Emma! Jump right now!" She waved her arms. "Both of you, do it now! It's the only way!"

Jenn watched the figures of Emma and Rashad, out on top of that sinking wreck, and silently urged them to have the courage to save themselves. Corinne was right—this would be their only chance.

* * *

At this distance, Emma couldn't see what Mrs. Hautala had done, but somehow she'd drawn the sharks away. They were headed right for her, which meant that for a matter of a few minutes she and Rashad were no longer waiting for the old wreck to finish sinking. The sharks had eaten whatever they were going to eat of Marianna, and now they wanted something more. These weren't like any sharks she'd ever heard of. They seemed more interested in killing than in eating, as if their only instinct was to destroy.

They were not going away.

If she was still out on the water when the wreck finished sinking, she would die.

"Emma!" her mother screamed as she waded toward the wreck. "Go now! Now!"

She would have expected to hear fear in her mother's voice anguish and hesitation. Instead, what she heard was ice and steel. As Emma watched, her mother dove forward and began to swim out to meet her.

Emma braced herself to jump.

Rashad grabbed her arm. "Don't be stupid!"

"Look around you. This is our shot."

"No, we can—"

Emma shook her arm loose. She took one step then leaped out over the water—or she would have if not for Rashad. He tried to grab hold of her, to stop her from jumping, and he caught her by the shoulder just enough that Emma fell back, struck the rusty hull, and bounced the last twenty feet into the undulating waves.

As she fell, she heard Rashad yelp and caught a glance of him tumbling after her before she plunged into the water.

The instant she surfaced, Emma was swimming. Terror filled her, so deeply she felt it in her veins. In her bones. Her heart pounded rapid fire, but she rode that rhythm as she swam. She knew some people might have been paralyzed by the fear that burned inside her now, but for Emma it was fuel. Her terror blinded her to anything but the need to reach her mother.

Behind her, Rashad called her name. She could hear him swimming too. Splashing. She hoped that he would make it, but she couldn't slow down now. He had saved her earlier, but there was nothing she could do now to return the favor. Not when her feet couldn't even touch the ground.

She could only swim.

Jesse saw how fast the sharks were coming, but he jumped into the water anyway. Captain Len's sightseeing boat shifted farther away, dragging on the bottom, but the boat didn't matter anymore. All he cared about was his father.

Anger boiled inside him. Anger at Captain Len, but also rage at Mr. Scully. It had been his idea to come out here. He'd fucked up and gotten himself stabbed. Jesse hated himself for thinking it. He knew Mr. Scully had just been trying to save Kelsey, and he had saved Jesse, too. But now Jesse saw the desperate worry in his father's eyes, saw the effort as he half-supported and half-propelled Rick Scully toward the sand.

But, God, the sharks were so fast. It didn't even look right, watching them—like it was something unnatural, not meant for his eyes to interpret.

On the sand of North Captiva, against the backdrop of those bare, skeletal trees, Kelsey tried to follow Jesse into the water, but Paola held her back. The woman hugged Kelsey and little Emilio against her, and Jesse was grateful. He wouldn't be able to help his father if either of those kids fell into the water. His dad would insist he help someone less capable. Now, of course, that someone was Matti Hautala himself.

"Dad!" Jesse called.

Matti halfway dragged Rick toward Jesse. The tide rushed in, the current ripping along the shore. The shifting of the sinking boat created the unsettling illusion that the water rose even faster, but Jesse didn't need anything else to amp up his heart rate. He wiped sea spray and salt from his eyes, tasting the salt on his lips, and grabbed hold of Rick as his father practically shoved the man into his arms.

"Hurry!" his father barked.

Jesse didn't need to be told. The sharks raced toward them as if someone had fired a starter pistol. Their fins sheared through the water with unnatural speed. Jesse felt Mr. Scully's weight on him, felt the way his father helped propel the other man forward, and bent to put his own strength into it. The shore could only have been twenty feet away. Probably less. But alarm bells sounded in Jesse's mind, because he had always been good at the kind of math that allowed him to gauge things like speed, spatial relationships, and how animals responded to one another. These sharks weren't stalking them or trying to cordon them off—they were simply on the attack—but they were huge and ruthless, and they were moving too fast.

Way too fast.

Jesse felt warmth in the water and thought at first that his father or Mr. Scully had pissed in the Gulf, but then he caught the scent of blood and realized it came from Rick Scully's wound. The sharks were coming for Rick, and as he drove himself harder, digging his feet into the sandy bottom and tried to get the man to shore, he felt the temptation to leave his father's friend behind. Mr. Scully had always been kind to him—

But I don't want to die!

The thought spiked through him, a primal instinct, but Jesse's love for his father took over. He wouldn't leave his dad alone with Rick. Not even with the sharks closing in.

Rick collapsed in the water. Darkness pooled at the edges of his vision and the sound of the surf receded. His daughter's shouts from the shore dimmed to a murmur. He could feel Matti and Jesse at his sides, felt himself give way so that he hung from them like a puppet, lifeless and empty. Matti said something, the words muffled, and dragged Rick up to keep him from drowning.

"Dad!" Jesse cried. "They're coming! They're—"

"Get ashore!" Matti shouted.

In the back of his mind, where his thoughts were still somewhat coherent, Rick thought about bravery. He wanted to tell Matti and Jesse to leave him behind, knowing the sharks were there, just beyond reach. He could feel them closing in as if their teeth were inches from tearing at his flesh, and perhaps they were. They all needed to get to safe place, to work together, but staying behind to help Rick might kill both Hautalas, father and son. He ought to have the courage to shake loose from their grip, to let them go on without the burden he'd become. But he simply didn't have that kind of courage, and he never had.

"Jesse, go!" Matti commanded. "Get to shore, dammit!"

Rick pistoned himself up so he could stand tall in the water, and then he saw the sharks coming in. Too close. Jesse had been breathing hard, face flushed, rushing for the sand, but now he must have seen the way his elders were looking beyond him and he turned.

The kid froze.

Rick felt the moment it happened. The nearest shark seemed to lunge, twisting toward them, crossing twenty yards in an eyeblink. Matti dumped Rick onto Jesse, pushing all of his weight on the boy, and he shouted as he dove into the water between Jesse and the shark.

So close to the beach. To the sand, and safety. So close to where Kelsey, Paola, and Emilio stood on the sand, crying out for them.

"Dad!" Jesse roared, trying to untangle himself

from Rick's arms, from the weight and responsibility his father had just foisted on him.

A wave struck Rick and Jesse from behind, and Rick had no choice but to hold on tight and let the water push them toward shore. Ten feet away now. The water turned instantly shallow, but Jesse strained against Rick's grip, screaming and trying to go back for his father.

Matti faced the shark as if he could dodge in one direction or the other. He stood with shoulders hunched, a human shield between his son and those small black eyes, those rows of gruesome teeth. Rick had no illusion that Matti faced the shark for him—this was the act of a father, the kind of man he had always wished to be. On shore, the others screamed. In the water, Jesse turned and tried to hurl himself back toward his father, but Rick could not allow that. Though pain raged through him like fever, and though blood loss sapped him of strength and stole away his connection to his own limbs, Rick put his shoulder down and mustered the last of his will, plowing into Jesse.

Matti laid hands on the shark, grabbed hold and tried to turn its snout away. The killer whipped its head right and left, plunged in and drove Matti off his feet. One hand dragged at the shark's left eye, puncturing it, clawing it out, but the other hand tried to grab at the monster's jaws and vanished inside those teeth.

As the shark drove him under, only twenty feet from shore, Matti began to scream.

So did his son.

The water frothed red and white as the shark thrashed. It twisted and rolled, determined that its prey would not escape. Rick saw the moment that Matti stopped moving, his limbs going limp. By then, his one visible arm seemed much too far away from his legs, as if the middle of him had been shredded.

Jesse screamed at him. Rick practically carried him, firefighter-style, and deposited the young man onto the sand. Paola held her crying toddler as she knelt to comfort Jesse. Kelsey rushed to Rick, even as he collapsed, blood still seeping from his knife wounds.

All of them were grieving. All of them were broken. Shattered, and in shock. But they were alive. They were safe.

Rick might be dying, but he and Matti had done this much at least. They'd kept the children safe.

That's what fathers do, he thought as regret seeped into his heart. He hoped to live to be a better father, but if this was his last act, it would have to be good enough.

CHAPTER 17

Jenn stayed in the water as long as she could. She squeezed her arm, forcing out more blood and letting it dapple the water. Each drop became its own small cloud for an instant before the sea claimed it, diluted it, turned it invisible. But Jenn knew her blood would not vanish from the sharks' senses. The killers had caught the scent in the water, and they were coming for her.

Corinne had waded in up to her shoulders. Emma swam toward her, the two calling out to each other, and now Corinne began to swim as well. The college kid, Rashad, swam awkwardly, painfully, after Emma, but the third shark remained out there in the deep, and it sped after him, fin vanishing under the surface.

The other two sharks sliced toward Jenn, rushing at the shore as if they had no fear of beaching themselves on the sand. She backed up several paces, so that the waves crashed around her hips, but she knew she was still in too deep. Sharks like these could skim into the shallows in spite of their size, and they had already proven how aggressive they were.

"Get out of the water, Mrs. Hautala!" Deputy Hayes called.

Jenn glanced toward her. The woman had her gun out, but it hung by her side. What the hell was she intending to do with that? The sharks weren't drug dealers or something; they weren't going to respond to threats.

"Come on!" the deputy said, stepping into the water, shoes and all. A wave splashed around her knees, soaking through her trousers. "Don't be stupid."

Stupid, Jenn thought. They were trying to save the lives of children.

She felt a tightening in her chest. Her blood kept dripping as she backed several steps closer to shore, and then several more. She no longer squeezed her arm, as if that would cut off the summons she had bled into the water, but she knew better.

She tried not to think about her own son, or her husband, trusting that wherever they were, they were safe.

Corinne and Emma swam toward each other but they had not quite met when Jenn knew she had no choice. She turned and ran for shore, lifting her knees high as she stomped over the waves and onto the sand, much to Deputy Hayes's obvious relief.

She had bought them as much time as she could.

But as the two sharks swam through the water where

she'd spilled her blood, Jenn felt the awful certainty that it would not be enough.

As Emma reached her mother, she heard a helicopter flying overhead. Hope flared inside her—were they here to help? Could someone shoot sharks from the air the way they did wolves in Alaska, or would the water make that impossible? She felt stupid because she didn't know, and then the helicopter started to veer away, heading back across the narrow island, and she felt angry instead.

"Oh my God," her mother said. "Emma!"

Her mom touched her face, tried to hug her there in the water, just for a moment.

"Go, Mom," Emma grunted, heart pounding. "We gotta swim."

It was as if her mother had lost her mind for a second or two, the relief of being together making her forget the danger they were in. But now her eyes narrowed with a fierce determination Emma had seen in her mother before. It was one of the reasons Emma loved her. Her mother put a hand on her back and gave her a shove to get them both moving, and then they were swimming.

"Mom," Emma huffed as she swam. Water sprayed her face, and she squinted against the salt. "Mrs. Hautala."

"I see," her mother said, breathing just as hard.

On the shore, Jenn Hautala waved her arms back and forth and then pointed into the water, where two shark fins had turned away from the beach and were swimming in a lazy, serpentine pattern back out toward the shipwreck.

As Emma swam, she watched the fins begin to turn in her direction.

"Oh no," she said. "Mom—"

"Swim, honey. Just swim!"

Emma bent her head forward. She kicked her feet and turned in the water, stretching into a sidestroke. Her muscles ached and her arms were so tired, but the thing that gnawed at her was the knowledge that she was going to die. Maybe there in the water, but otherwise up on the beach, bleeding out as her mother screamed and Mrs. Hautala called 911. No way would she make it to the sand in time. Her mother was a much stronger swimmer and Emma had already been swimming, already been terrified. Every cell in her body seemed to grow wearier by the moment, weighed down with lead.

On the beach, Deputy Hayes and Mrs. Hautala shouted for them to hurry, and Emma hated them both in that moment. What did they think, that Emma and her mom were not swimming as fast as they could? Not trying to outrace the sharks?

The sharks.

Emma turned back over, took a breath, and submerged. Hand over hand, she swam as fast and as far as she could with her whole head underwater. The sharks were there, slashing diagonally across the water now, closing fast. The flutter in her heart became a silent scream.

Then the scream had a voice.

Just ahead, Emma's mother turned to glance backward, contorted in the water. Emma did the same, but even as she turned she knew what sight would present itself. The moment she had reached her mother, all of her thoughts had been for her, and she'd forgotten all about Rashad.

Emma glanced back.

She thought of Lot's wife, from that Bible story. God had told her not to look back when fleeing the destruction of the sinful city of Sodom, but she had been unable to resist. The moment she'd glanced back, she had been turned to a pillar of salt. A statue. Emma felt just as paralyzed now as she watched Rashad tread water, smashing at the sea with his hands, frantically trying to keep the third shark away from him. Blood frothed on the rippling crests of the waves around him, and Emma knew he'd been bitten.

"Swim!" she shouted at him.

Rashad turned to look at her with wide, hopeless eyes filled with grief she would remember her entire life. Behind him, the shark's fin broke the water like a blade stabbing at the sky, and then the monster struck him from below and dragged him down beneath the waves.

Emma kept swimming.

"Honey—" her mother began.

"I know!" she rasped.

Her feet touched bottom. She glanced at the other two sharks, but one of them had peeled off to swim toward whatever remained of Rashad, the blood in the water too much of a lure. That left one continued to head toward them, picking up speed now, its path knife-blade straight, not the meandering, predatory stalking they had indulged in before.

Emma and her mother swam. From the corner of her eye, Emma saw the fin coming closer. The beach waited for them only twenty feet away, and Emma thought the cruelest part of her death would be how close she came to making it to the sand. The sun glared down on her, and she wanted to surrender.

But her mother slowed down, holding her side and breathing sharply through her teeth.

"Mom?"

"Just go!" Corinne Scully replied. "Don't worry about me. Swim!"

Emma swam. But they weren't going to make it. The shark moved so swiftly. Emma fancied she could actually hear the fin cutting through the water. She turned away now, unwilling to watch her death come for her.

The water came up to her ribs. She stood and pushed through the waves, running in slow motion. But it felt as if the Gulf wanted to give her up, drag her back, sacrifice her to the rows of teeth in that shark's mouth.

Her mother grabbed her arm and yanked her close, lifted her and hurled her out of the way. As Emma hit the water, she saw the shark closing in on her mom. She sputtered, staggered, found herself only knee deep now and less than fifteen feet from shore. Her mother tried to follow, that same look of determination on her face, but then the shark struck.

"Mom!" Emma shouted, terror stabbing into her heart.

Twisting away, fighting the pull of those jaws, Corinne screamed in pain as she somehow yanked free.

The air cracked. A gunshot echoed across the water. Emma looked over to see Deputy Hayes thigh deep in the water, aiming her gun with both hands. The deputy fired again and again. Bullets punched through the shark's thick hide, its own blood seeping out, and the beast turned out to sea, swimming away.

Emma plunged back toward her mom. Jenn reached Corinne only moments after Emma, and together the two of them half-dragged her from the surf. Her left leg had been torn up, blood spilling along her calf and ankle.

"Lay her down," Deputy Hayes said. "We've got to hurry or she'll bleed to death."

Only moments before, Emma had feared this very same thing happening to her. Now she stood back and watched as the two women lay her mother down on the sand.

In the waves, two sharks continued circling, as if waiting for them to dare enter the water again. The shipwreck continued to vanish beneath the Gulf, perhaps a dozen feet of its stern all that remained above water.

Of the shark Deputy Hayes had shot, there was no sign.

As Emma watched her mother bleed, saw her face contort with pain, she felt too empty and weary to cry.

She knew she would never go into the ocean again.

CHAPTER 18

When Kevin heard the helicopter coming back, he gripped Tyler's hand and practically yanked him to his feet. They were on the west side of Buck Key, tucked in the thick tangles of mangrove trees, but the sun shone brightly on the water that separated them from Captiva. Kevin had been staring at the houses across Roosevelt Channel with a longing he had never felt before—not because he needed some million-dollar island getaway but because he just wanted to be on dry land. Safe with other people.

Sharks had been swimming in the channel ever since he and Tyler had made their way over here. Before they had come, he had done a bit of research on Captiva and had read nothing about sharks, but there they were, aggressive and plentiful. He had spotted at least three at one point, but there was no telling how many were out there.

Hot and exhausted, arms and legs scratched to hell from the mangroves, Kevin turned to Tyler and managed to smile. "We're getting out of here."

Tyler touched his face. "Sounds good to me."

Kevin grabbed a thick mangrove that tilted toward the water. He hung out over the channel and began to wave his free hand in the air, waving the bright peach-colored T-shirt Tyler had been wearing. Tyler began to shout, holding onto a tree as he raised his hand to try to flag the chopper pilot.

"They can't hear you," Kevin told him.

"Screaming makes me feel better."

Kevin laughed, and then they were both screaming. The helicopter flew low over the water, perhaps eighty feet up. The two of them shouted and waved. Kevin nearly lost his grip and fell in, but he managed to catch himself just in time, heart pounding.

The helicopter roared past and kept going, and all of his excitement drained away. He hung his head and lowered his peach banner.

"Look!" Tyler called.

Sweeping upward, the helicopter swung back around.

"They've seen us!" Kevin said.

"I'm not so sure." Tyler pointed out at the water, where a shark swam down the center of Roosevelt Channel as if on patrol.

The helicopter dropped lower and seemed to hover above the shark, beginning to track its movements. Kevin raised the flag again and waved it, shouting, even though he knew there was no way the pilot or passengers on the helicopter could hear them.

Suddenly a boat came blasting along the channel at a speed far exceeding those posted, not caring about the wake or the danger to manatees in the area. It took Kevin a moment to make out the green writing on the side—Fish and Wildlife Commission: State Law Enforcement.

"What are they going to do? Tag it?" Tyler asked.

But when the boat slid up alongside the shark, matching its speed, and he saw two men with rifles move to the railing and take aim, Kevin knew they weren't there to study the creature.

In spite of everything they'd suffered, when the men opened fire, he felt a sadness he could never have explained.

As the helicopter lifted and buzzed away, and the echoes of gunfire fading away, Kevin and Tyler began to wave and shout again. The people on the boat spotted them, and moments later, it roared toward their location in the mangroves.

"Thank God," Tyler said, lacing his fingers in Kevin's. "It's over."

"For us," Kevin replied.

But as relieved as he was, he knew there were other sharks in the area, and as he thought about the screams of the kayakers they had been unable to save, he wondered how many sharks there were . . . and if there were others who would not be making it back to shore today.

* * *

Sheriff Reyes couldn't help it—he closed his eyes and turned away. They had already killed two sharks beneath the Sanibel Causeway. Reports had come in that at least three others had been eliminated by State Fish and Wildlife officers. Now the hunters had used their deck-mounted harpoon gun to destroy a sixth, which meant they were only a fifth of the way through with their problem.

Reyes wanted to vomit.

"I hope you're happy," a voice said from behind him.

He took a deep, cleansing breath and looked out at the Gulf. The boat rode a swell, but as much as he hated being on the water, he had his sea legs by now. Sheriff Reyes turned to face the woman behind him. "Tali. You've got something to say?"

Her assistant, Philip, had gone below half an hour earlier, looking for a bucket to catch his vomit. Dr. Tali Rocco had stayed on deck. Reyes had watched her depression deepen, watched her flinch as the hunters had killed the first two sharks and hauled their remains on board long enough to carve out the things that didn't belong in their brains—the things the military had paid the Institute to implant.

"You could have waited," Tali said, her lips pressed into a thin, angry line. "That's all I'm saying. We could have found a way to dial their aggression back down."

Reyes felt his stomach roiling. He was tempted to go down below and get his own bucket. "Yeah? What about *my* aggression? You have a way to dial *that* down, too?"

Tali flinched. "Look, Sheriff—"

"No, *Doctor*," he snarled. "People are dead. Human beings. We're not even sure how many yet, but the reports I'm getting break my heart. Your fucking sharks killed more people than the hurricane did. Worse yet, they only did what they were designed to do, programmed to do, by you sick assholes."

Tali paled, staring at him. She looked like she wanted to fight back, but couldn't seem to find the words.

"What do you want us to do?" Reyes asked. "How many people should your monsters be able to kill before we stop them?"

Tali hesitated a moment before she nodded once and turned away. He knew the day had been difficult for her, but he could summon no sympathy at all.

In his pocket, his cell phone buzzed.

"Reyes," he answered.

"Sheriff, it's Wilkins. That cell phone you asked us to track? Pretty sure we've got its last known location on Cayo Costa."

Reyes thanked him and ended the call. He glanced at Tali, then beyond her at the shark hunters, and decided they could keep an eye out for fins in the water on their way to Cayo Costa. It wouldn't take long to check out, and at least for a few minutes, they wouldn't be killing anything.

Maybe they'd get lucky and save some lives instead.

*   *   *

Jenn knelt in the sand on Corinne's left, while Emma knelt on her right. Blood had soaked into the sand and the towel around Corinne's leg, but the pain on her face had faded. She had slipped in and out of consciousness, but it was the blood loss that worried Jenn the most.

"Mrs. Hautala," Emma said. "Do you think—"

She couldn't finish asking her question. Her face contorted with worry as she glanced out at the water. A boat had appeared, off to the south, and it seemed to be headed their way. Deputy Hayes had arranged for an emergency evacuation, a boat that would take them to Lee Memorial Hospital on the mainland, and Jenn understood that it was urgent. She couldn't send Emma alone with her mother in this condition, but the desire to stay right here and wait for Matti and Jesse to come back made her frantic inside.

"She'll be okay, Emma," Jenn said. She had no idea if this was the truth, but she couldn't think of any version of the truth that would comfort the girl. "I'm going to stay with you both. We'll get her to the hospital and they'll take care of her."

Emma nodded, but Jenn could see the girl's hands trembling. Of course she trembled. She had seen people die horribly today, and now her mother was bleeding into the sand. No matter what else happened, she would be seeing the blood and violence of this day on the nightmare screen inside her head for the rest of her life. They both would, and Jenn hadn't even seen much of it up close. It occurred to her what a strong, courageous person Emma had become, and she felt a sudden surge of pride in the girl.

Then she thought of Jesse, and her own fear spiked higher. Where was her son? Where was her husband? Emma's father and little sister were still missing as well.

Jenn turned to look at Deputy Hayes, who stood a stone's throw up the sand, talking to the spring-break girl Simone, whose friend had been killed in a shark attack earlier in the day. Hayes put a comforting hand on Simone's shoulder. Three of the college girl's friends had died today, and she was definitely going to need all the emotional support she could find. Jenn felt badly for her, but her sympathy withered in the shadow of her own fears.

"Deputy," she called. "I'm going with them. I'll leave you my number. Please call me as soon as you get word about the sightseeing boat. We need to know everyone's okay."

"I'll call as soon as I know anything," Deputy Hayes replied. "You have my word."

Jenn turned to watch the boat glide up onto the sand fifty feet away. EMTs jumped out, splashed in the rippling water that foamed on the shore, and then raced toward them. Exhaling, Jenn stepped away from Corinne, then went around and shifted Emma backward to give the EMTs access to her mother.

"It's going to be okay," Jenn told Emma, taking her hand.

The girl squeezed her hand tightly. "How do you know?"

Jenn glanced at Deputy Hayes and the hollow-eyed Simone, and decided not to answer. The truth, of course, was that she didn't know. She was an adult, a mother, and telling a fourteen-year-old girl that things were going to be okay was pure instinct.

"Mrs. Hautala," Emma persisted. "How can you think it's going to be okay?"

"I just do," she lied.

Together, she and Emma watched the EMTs prep Corinne for transport, put her on a stretcher, and load her onto the boat. As Jenn climbed into the boat with Emma, and they set off across the waves toward the mainland, she began to tell herself things were going to be okay, just as she had told Emma.

It wouldn't be very long before Deputy Hayes called to tell her just how wrong she had been. For Jenn Hautala, things were not going to be okay at all.

Not ever.

Rick wanted to black out. Jesse had surrendered his T-shirt, torn it into strips, and then he and Paola used it to bind the stab wound in Rick's chest, but they could do nothing about the blood he had already lost. His head pounded as the sun beat down on them. The skeletal trees on North Captiva provided little shade, so Jesse and Kelsey sat close together, their bodies partly shielding Rick from the sun. The slash on her jawline had mostly stopped bleeding, but the cut looked wicked and would no doubt require stitches.

Kelsey had a hundred questions, wanted to hear that

she was safe a dozen different ways, and needed reassurance that her mother and sister were also safe. Rick knew she must be afraid for them all, particularly after what she had just endured, and witnessed. She had watched sharks kill Jesse's father, a man she'd known her whole life. A man who had always been so kind to her. But Rick had a feeling her questions were more for his sake than her own. She had to have seen how pale and he weak he was. Rick felt on the verge of slipping away into unconsciousness. His eyelids were heavy and he struggled to keep them open, and she would have seen that, too.

"Daddy!"

His eyes snapped open. "Yeah, honey. I'm still here." He did his best to smile.

"Told you," Jesse said quietly, holding nine-year-old Kelsey's hand in his. "He's okay."

"He's *not* okay," Kelsey admonished him.

Rick forced his eyes to focus on Jesse. He saw the emotions warring on the young man's face. His father had died to save him, and to save Rick. Grief must have been tearing him up inside, and it manifested in the way his shoulders sagged and in the pain that shone in his eyes. But Jesse still managed to give Kelsey a reassuring smile, to bump playfully against her.

"You calling me a liar?" he asked.

"No?" she said uncertainly. "I just—"

"I'm not okay," Rick said weakly. "But I will be. Listen to Jesse, sweet girl. He's in charge right now."

Kelsey made a grumpy face and Rick felt his worries ease. If she could be that irritated with him, then for the

moment her fears for him had abated. Now all he had to
do was manage not to bleed to death before help came.
If he died now, she would never forgive him.

"There!" a little voice shouted. "A boat!"

Rick glanced over. Little Emilio had been sitting
with his mother, Paola, about twenty feet up the beach.
Rick and Paola had spoken some, but they were all in
shock and found they had little to say to one another.
Paola had lost her husband, Ernie, and Emilio had lost
his father. The two had been speaking in quiet Spanish, and sometimes in English, as the woman tried to
find a way to explain to her son that, yes, his father had
been killed by a shark. No, Daddy wouldn't be coming home. Yes, it had been real, and the sharks were
still out there. The mother and toddler had taken turns
crying, and Rick had to fight not to cry as well. He was
too weak for tears, and he didn't want to scare Kelsey
or shatter the brave front that Jesse had constructed.

"A boat!" Kelsey echoed.

With a grunt of pain, Rick struggled to sit up. Jesse
and Kelsey helped him, and then he could see the large
craft sailing toward them. It took him some time to
make out the words on the side and to decipher the
logo of the Sanibel Island Maritime Research Institute.

The boat began to slow, veering off course, turning
slightly north.

"What are they doing?" Jesse asked, his voice angry and brittle. His father had died and Rick figured
he must have known, consciously or subconsciously,
that he would have to grow up quickly now.

"Hunting," Paola said, pointing toward the boat.

It took a few seconds for Rick to identify the apparatus on the back of the boat. His eyes fluttered and darkness threatened to envelop him. Jesse put a hand on his shoulder to steady him.

"You still with us?" Jesse asked.

Kelsey whipped her head around to stare at her father, examining him intently.

"I'm not going anywhere," Rick said, managing a weak smile to reassure her. He thought he glimpsed the real grief hiding inside Jesse in that moment, but the young man covered it up quickly.

"They're going after the sharks," Paola said.

"It's like a gun," little Emilio said.

The little boy was right. The apparatus mounted on the boat was some kind of harpoon gun. The boat plowed through the waves, then idled slowly, waiting for the nearest shark to come after them. When it did, the man controlling the harpoon gun fired it into the water, and the result raised a small, victorious cheer from several people on the boat.

Kelsey shuddered and turned to press her face against her father's shoulder. When she glanced up at him, there were tears in her eyes.

"Hey, honey . . . no," he said. "We're going to be okay now. It's over."

"I know."

He figured the fear and shock had just built up inside her and now that she could let it go, the relief had overwhelmed her.

But then she went on. "It's just sad."

"Sad how?"

Kelsey shot a guilty, apologetic look at Jesse. "I mean . . . I know the sharks were horrible. What they did . . . but it's sad those people are killing them. They're just animals, right? Weren't they just doing what sharks do?"

Rick shifted and managed to get an arm around her. Pain jolted him, radiating from his wound, but he didn't know what else to do for her. Rick had not been the best father—he knew that—but he also knew that even the world's greatest father could not have erased the damage that had been done. It would take years. Perhaps a lifetime. He would give her all of the years he had left.

Beside them, Jesse cleared his throat. His gaze seemed hollow, but he sat up straight, putting on a brave face, perhaps thinking his father would have wanted that.

"This isn't natural," he said. "These sharks . . . they've been twisted somehow. Somebody *did* this." His eyes narrowed and his expression turned darker. "And whoever it was, I hope to God someone makes them pay."

Out on the waves, the research ship turned toward shore. Little Emilio broke away from his mother and raced down to the water, jumping up and down and waving his arms excitedly. Paola ran after him and scooped him up, staring in terror at the sea—but of the other sharks, for the moment, there was no sign.

When Corinne Scully woke from surgery, she found her family sitting around her. Her eyes opened slowly, her head heavy and her mouth dry. Pain throbbed in her leg, but dull and distant, as if the remnant of a dream.

Rick sat sprawled in a chair beside her hospital bed, pale and in a hospital gown himself, a hanging IV bag pumping fluid into his arm. Kelsey had a bandage on her face, along the left side of her jaw, but her eyes lit up when she noticed her mother was awake.

"Mom!" she cried happily, rushing from the windowsill where she'd been perched. She hugged her mother hard, but she didn't cry. Corinne hugged her back, and didn't want to let go.

Over Kelsey's shoulder, she saw Emma leaning against the wall. She'd had her cell phone in her hand, but now she let it dangle at her side, staring at her mother. After a moment, she stuffed her phone into her back pocket and came over to put a hand on her dad's shoulder.

"You're alive," Emma observed.

Corinne almost laughed. "He took a chunk out of me, though," she replied.

Rick reached out and took her hand. "You're still with us. And Emma's alive because of you."

"My hero," Emma said, with a slight smile, and none of the sarcasm she usually employed. She meant it, and Corinne fought to keep from crying.

Corinne squeezed Rick's hand and looked around at her family. They were changed—all of them. Hardened by this, sharpened by it, perhaps a little more awake and aware of the dangers of the world. And to its gifts, as well.